MOST LIKELY TO SCORE

LAUREN BLAKELY

COPYRIGHT

ALSO BY LAUREN BLAKELY

Big Rock Series

Big Rock

Mister O

Well Hung

Full Package

Joy Ride

Hard Wood

One Love Series dual-POV Standalones

The Sexy One

The Only One

The Hot One

Standalones

The Knocked Up Plan

Most Valuable Playboy

Stud Finder

The V Card

Most Likely to Score

Wanderlust (February 2018)

Come As You Are (April 2018)

Part-Time Lover (June 2018)

The Real Deal (Summer 2018)

Far Too Tempting

21 Stolen Kisses

Playing With Her Heart

Out of Bounds

The Caught Up in Love Series

Caught Up In Us

Pretending He's Mine

Trophy Husband

Stars in Their Eyes

The No Regrets Series

The Thrill of It

The Start of Us

Every Second With You

The Seductive Nights Series

First Night (Julia and Clay, prequel novella)

Night After Night (Julia and Clay, book one)

After This Night (Julia and Clay, book two)

One More Night (Julia and Clay, book three)

A Wildly Seductive Night (Julia and Clay novella, book 3.5)

The Joy Delivered Duet

Nights With Him (A standalone novel about Michelle and Jack)

Forbidden Nights (A standalone novel about Nate and Casey)

The Sinful Nights Series

Sweet Sinful Nights

Sinful Desire

Sinful Longing

Sinful Love

The Fighting Fire Series

Burn For Me (Smith and Jamie)

Melt for Him (Megan and Becker)

Consumed By You (Travis and Cara)

The Jewel Series

A two-book sexy contemporary romance series

The Sapphire Affair

The Sapphire Heist

ABOUT MOST LIKELY TO SCORE

It should have been a simple play...

She needed a football player to step up and be the star for a charity calendar. I needed a sharp and savvy publicist to manage a brand-new sponsorship deal. I scratched her back. She scratched mine. And oh hell, did Jillian ever drag her nails down my back on one hell of a hot night. Okay fine, it was several hot nights on the road.

Now we're back in town and it's time to set the play clock back to when we were simply player and publicist. Given the way the last few years have gone, I can't risk this deal, so it's hands off for us once again. Trouble is, I want more than than just another night with her.

What's a guy to do when he's always been most likely to score, but the woman he's falling for is just out of bounds?

* * *

I don't date players. And I definitely don't sleep with

players. And I absolutely don't fall for a certain player when I get to know him and learn he's more than just sexy — he's clever, funny and has a heart as big as his . .. well, you get my drift.

But my job is at stake, and I can't afford to lose that as well as my heart. The problem is, I think I've already lost that game.

What's a girl to do when the clock is running out, but the man she's falling for is off limits?

PROLOGUE

Jones

I can lay claim to some pretty impressive stats, and for the last few years as a star receiver for a winning NFL team I have, but my favorite one to share is this—ten and three-quarter inches.

Pretty big, huh?

You don't get into the double digits too often.

That's nearly as long as a football.

And that makes me a one-of-a-kind guy.

C'mon.

I'm talking about my hands.

And yes, other parts are close to a foot long, too.

But they don't call me The Hands for nothing. These hands have won championships. These hands have caught circus catches in the biggest games. These hands are a beautiful target for game-winning passes. I know exactly what to do with these hands.

Especially when it comes to enjoying the soft, sweet

flesh of a woman. A touch here, a touch there, and I can have her melting beneath me. They're a multi-purpose asset, and these hands—and other parts—have come out to score quite often after hours. There's no better way to enjoy a career as a pro baller, as far as I'm concerned.

Except when it comes time to clean up my act.

Turn over a new leaf. Start fresh. Remake myself into a good, upstanding citizen and kick those party-boy ways to the curb. Fine, I can do that. I can absolutely do that.

And hell, do I ever need to after some of the shit I've had to deal with in the last few years.

But a little help would be nice, and there's only one person I can turn to. One luscious, delicious, fantastic person. None other than the woman I've been lusting after for years.

Damn shame we're going to be spending so much time in close quarters in the next few weeks, especially since everything needs to remain hands-off.

That is, until it doesn't . . .

1

JONES

I'm buck naked.

I often am.

I'm not an exhibitionist. I simply find I don't have a need for clothes most of the time, unless I'm on the field or at a public appearance. *Obviously.*

Pretty sure I was one of those naked kids. You know the type. Runs around in the sprinkler in his backyard in the buff. Streaks down the hallway with nothing on. Oh wait, that was me in college, too, and I did that stunt on multiple occasions. So often in fact, I was nicknamed Flash. I was fast. Still am. Like a motherfucking silver bullet.

Right now, I'm all in with the birthday suit attire, the costume for the annual *Sporting World* body issue.

Okay, perhaps I'm exaggerating. I do have one thing on—my Adam's fig leaf comes in the form of my hands holding a strategically-placed football to cover the goods.

The pigskin is doing its part to make this photo printable in the magazine, though all the shots of star athletes in this issue are in the nude. A tennis player will lob a ball, the racket covering her breasts and her lunge obscuring other not-safe-for-work parts. A swimmer will glide through crystal waters, the angle ensuring it's not a triple-X centerfold shot.

The photographer with the ponytail and lip piercing snaps pictures of me and asks for a smile.

I oblige.

"Love it," Christine says emphatically, her lips and that metal hoop in the bottom one the only parts of her face visible since the lens covers the rest. "How about a little tough-guy look now?"

Because tough guys hold footballs in front of their junk.

"This is my best badass pose," I say, narrowing my eyes and staring at the camera like I'd stare at the secondary of the Miami Mavericks.

"Oh yes, more of that, right, Jillian?" Christine shouts to the other person here in the studio with us.

That person is Jillian, and she hasn't looked my way since I strolled in here and dropped my drawers. Damn shame.

From her spot leaning against the far wall, the team publicist answers in a crisp, professional tone I know well. "Exactly. We love his tough-guy face."

She doesn't even look up from her phone.

I keep working it for Christine, doing my best to make sure my blue eyes will melt whoever is looking at the picture when the magazine hits newsstands and Internet browsers in another few weeks.

It's an evergreen kind of issue, since the body edition is one of the most popular. Gee, I wonder why. I've no doubt this shot of me with a football for my skivvies will quickly surpass the previous most-searched-for image of yours truly—the game-winning catch I made in the end zone in the Super Bowl two years ago.

But, to be fair, there's another shot of me that's searched for maybe a tiny bit more. I like to pretend that shot doesn't exist.

"The camera loves you," Christine croons as the snap, snap, snap of the lens keeps the rhythm.

"The feeling is entirely mutual," I say, pursing my lips in an over-the-top kiss.

Christine laughs. "You are my favorite ham in all of sports, Jones. That'll be a perfect outtake for our website."

"That's a brilliant idea," Jillian chimes in. "Make sure to send me a copy for social, please."

"Absolutely," Christine answers.

I sneak a peek at the dark-haired woman by the wall, that silky curtain of sleekness framing her face as she smiles a bright, buoyant, outgoing grin at the photographer then drops her head back down.

Damn.

Jillian Moore is one tough nut to crack.

I'm nearly naked in front of her, and she hasn't once looked my way.

As the woman behind the lens shoots another photo with my favorite ball covering my favorite balls, Jillian doesn't even spare another glance.

I'm going to need a whole new playbook to get this woman's attention.

2

JILLIAN

I won't look down.

I repeat my mantra over and over, till it's branded on my brain.

This might very well be my biggest challenge, and I mastered the skill of *eyes up* many years ago.

But now? As I stand in the corner of the photo studio, I'm being tested to my limits.

I'm dying here. Simply dying.

The temptation to ogle Jones is overwhelming, and if there was ever a time to write myself a permission slip to stare, now would be it. An excuse, if you will. For a second or two. That's all.

The man is posing, for crying out loud. He's the center of attention. The lights shine on his statue-of-David physique. Michelangelo would chomp at the bit to sculpt him—carved abs with definition so fine you could scrub your sheets on his washboard, arms that could lift a woman easily and carry her up a flight of stairs before he took her, powerful thighs that suggest unparalleled stamina, and an ass that defies gravity.

I know because I've looked at his photos on many occasions. In the office. Out of the office. On my phone. On the computer.

In every freaking magazine the guy's been in.

It's my job to be aware of the press the players generate.

But it's not my job to check out his photos after hours; however, I partake of that little hobby regularly. He gives my search bar quite a workout.

Still, I won't let myself stare at him in person, not in his current state of undress. My tongue would imitate a cartoon character's and slam to the floor.

If I gawk at him, I'll start crossing lines.

Lines I've mastered as a publicist for an NFL team.

It's something my mentor taught me when I began as an intern at the Renegades seven years ago, straight out of college. Lily Eckles escorted me through the locker room my first day on the job and said, "The best piece of advice I can give you is this: don't ever look down."

I'd furrowed my brow, trying to understand what she meant. Was it some wise, old adage, perhaps an inspirational saying about reaching for the stars?

When she opened the door to the locker room, the true meaning hit me.

Everywhere, there were dicks.

It was a parade of appendages and swinging parts, sticks and balls as far as the eye could see.

The truth of pro ballers is simple—they let it all hang out all the time, and they love it.

So much so that the running joke among the female reporters who cover the team is that with the amount of swagger going on in the locker room when ladies are present, the TV channels should all be renamed the C&B networks.

But when you work with men who train their bodies for hours a day, and then use those same physiques to win championships, you can't be a woman who ogles them in the locker room.

Can you say tacky, trashy, and gauche?

It's not easy, but after all these years with the Renegades, I've learned how to handle the locker room games.

The guys will drop pens.

The guys will drop bandages.

The guys will drop trou.

Astonishingly enough, there's never a need to pick up a pen, a bandage, or a players' pair of pants for them, but they'll ask. Oh yes, will they test anyone with a pair of breasts.

Many women fail.

I've witnessed this initiation of every female reporter who's set foot in the locker room on my watch. Last year, a new gal from an online outlet let her big eyes stray across the entire offensive line. Not only did she get an eyeful of skin and meat, each of the three-hundred-pound-plus linemen did a little dance and shimmy for her. Her face turned beet red, and the next time she appeared in the locker room, all the guys went full synchronized monty, singing, "Take it all off."

She laughed and tried her best to interview them.

But their answers were straight out of the bullshit handbook and became even more ridiculous the more she giggled as they talked. She never earned another assignment to cover the team. They didn't take her seriously after she checked them out.

I love my job, I want to be respected, and I absolutely want to be taken seriously.

That's why I won't even risk looking at Jones's ridiculous body, not now from my spot against the wall in the studio, and not even when the photographer, who I know well from having worked on tons of *Sporting World* spreads with her, lowers her camera and calls me over. "Come see these shots, Jillian. Pretty sure they're the definition of cover-worthy."

That piques my interest. There are never any guarantees which athlete will make it from the pages all the way to the cover, and with a dozen elite stars from all sorts of sports tapped for the shoot, the odds are slim. But the chance to have one of my guys on the cover would be quite a coup for the team. For me, too, since I pitched him for the issue. Not only does he have the body, he has the personality to shine through.

I join her and peer at the back of her Nikon as she toggles through shot after shot of the sexiest man I've ever seen. My mouth goes dry. A pulse of heat races down my body as I ogle him in the viewfinder. Fine, I'm not unbiased, but I dare anyone to disagree that he's cover-worthy.

"Are any decent? Or do you think we need to shoot the whole round again on account of me being so unphotogenic?" Jones calls out, that deep, rumbly voice tingling over my skin.

"That's true. You really do take awful pictures," I say drily, since he knows he takes nothing of the sort.

"That's what I figured. They're all hideous, no doubt."

I glance at Christine. "You can find a way to Photoshop these and make him look decent, right? Maybe halfway normal?" I ask, a desperate plea in my voice.

Christine laughs. "I'll certainly do my best, but I can't promise anything. I'm not a miracle worker." She winks in his direction, making sure he knows we're kidding.

"That's a shame. Why don't I check them out with you?" Jones suggests in a serious tone, going along with the ruse.

My pulse quickens to rocket speed when I hear him drop the football to the floor with a *thunk*.

Dear Lord, he's naked right now. One hundred percent naked.

Eyes up, eyes up, eyes up.

"I'll just grab my towel," he says, and I breathe a massive sigh of relief. He won't be standing next to me in his naked glory after all. God bless towels so very much.

I glance up from the viewfinder and keep my gaze on Christine, whispering, "These shots are to die for."

Christine gives a knowing smile. "No doubt. I might need some for my personal stash," she says under her breath.

I nudge her. "Naughty girl."

"One of the perks of the job."

Jones strides over to us, and I'm so glad he has that towel around his waist. As he moves next to me to check out the pictures, his bare arm a mere millimeter away making me catch my breath, he shifts something to his shoulders.

I gasp when I realize what he draped on them.

His towel.

His freaking towel is on his shoulders.

Jones Beckett, object of my dirty dreams, is in my personal zone, without a stitch of clothing on.

Christine appears unfazed. I want to know her trick.

I draw a quick, quiet breath, calling on all my reserves as the three of us crowd the camera, admiring this man's ability to pose. "You're the ultimate ham," I tell him, keeping the mood as light as I can.

May he never know he's killing me with his nearness.

"Oink, oink," Jones snorts.

Christine laughs. "I'm sure she means pig with great affection."

"I accept her compliment one hundred percent. Pigs are fine creatures," he says. I glance up briefly from the small screen, and a bolt of heat runs from my chest down my body as his gaze meets mine. His blue eyes are the color of a lake under the summer sky. His jaw is strong and square. His hair is dark and cut short.

For the briefest of seconds, I'm so damn tempted to let my eyes wander down his pecs to his belly, then lower still. I'm only human. I can't help it. I want to see what was hidden behind the football. But I'll be either disappointed or ecstatic, and since I'll never be able to conduct a thorough investigation of any of his parts, it's best to do what I've practiced for many years. I lift my chin, look away, and review the photos.

Flipping through every gorgeous shot.

"I'm going to go back up this card now," Christine says when we're through and excuses herself to huddle with her laptop in another section of the studio.

It's just Jones and me, some lights, and some equipment. A black cloth hangs on the back wall. All noises echo. I flash him a professional smile and swallow past the dryness in my throat, fixing on my professional demeanor like it's a well-tailored skirt. "Great work today. I'm so glad you could make time to do this issue." As one of our marquee players, the man is in demand, so I need to make sure he knows how grateful I am.

"No need to thank me. It was *all* my pleasure." His eyes darken as he stares at me with something like heat in them, a fire that makes no sense to me. "I hope it was yours, too."

I blink. "I'm sorry. Excuse me?" I've no idea why he's acting this way. Why he's dipping his words in the innuendo fondue more than usual.

He shrugs happily, tugging the towel off his neck. "Just saying, I hope it's not too *hard* for you to have to be here."

"It's not too hard at all," I say, taking my time with each word, so I don't overstep, or read something into nothing. He sounds like he's flirting, but that's his MO. The man has been known to toy with me on many occasions. He's a fun, lovable wiseass, and I need to do my best to always remember that about him—*this* is a game.

"It's not?" He raises an eyebrow, then his gaze drifts downward. "Hmm. I thought it was."

With a deadpan tone, I say, "Nothing hard about being with you. In fact, I'd say it's a veritable barrel of monkeys."

He laughs, running that towel over his head, even though his hair isn't wet. "You know what they say about barrels of monkeys."

"No, what do they say, Jones?"

"They get into monkey business." He turns, tosses the towel to the floor, and strolls away.

Mayday, Mayday. The plane's going down. I'm about to get a full serving of perfect booty in my ocular zone. I snap my gaze to my cell phone. Dear God in heaven, thank you for making phones. Thank you for giving us devices that are useful for distraction at moments like this. As I scroll through my messages as if they're the height of fascinating, I try to figure out what he's doing with his towel games.

Is he baiting me in a brand-new way?

The wheels turn in my brain then pick up speed. Yes. That has to be it.

He's playing reindeer games with me, using a towel and his naked body as the game pieces.

Which makes sense. He's a baller, and these guys are competitive in every single pursuit. But little does he know this valedictorian, summa cum laude girl has 206 competitive bones in her body, too.

I won't bend down. I won't look down, either.

I stare straight at the back of his head and call his name. He swivels around, a question mark in his eyes.

I point to the floor. "Jones. You need to pick up your towel."

"Can you—?"

I shake my head. "Not a football's chance in hell. And please, don't ever insult my intelligence again." I smile. "I've been with the team since the guys invented the drop-the-towel game."

He squares his shoulders, heaves a breath, and walks right up to me, as if he's challenging me to stare at his naked physique.

My chin has never been higher. I might as well be watching the ceiling. All I can see is his face.

When he reaches me, he whispers in a husky, dirty tone, "How's the air up there?"

I smirk. "It's clean. Pure as the driven snow. Now, be a good boy and pick up your towel."

Then I turn around, and I swear all the breath nearly rushes out of me with relief. I need to get the hell out of the photo studio.

I've had a crush on this man since he joined the team. I might be able to act like a robot thanks to extensive training, but I'm only human. A female human, and my blood is heated to Mercury levels right now.

Must. Cool. Off.

I head to the door in desperate search of a bucket of ice water to stick my whole head in, when my brain snags on something I forgot.

I curse under my breath then square my shoulders, calling out to him, "Jones, I need a picture of you for the team's Facebook page. As part of the body issue promos."

I swear I can feel his satisfied Cheshire cat grin forming behind me.

"You want me in the full monty, too?"

"Put the towel on, jaybird. I'm not posting a nude photo, and I'm not scooping *Sporting World* and showing you holding a ball. Just a simple shot of you here at the photo studio. So put the towel on, and smile for the fans who love you."

"If you insist."

I count to ten, since Lord knows he'll drag out the time it takes to sling a towel around his waist. Then, five more seconds for good measure.

I turn around, and he's decent. I raise my phone, and

he preens for the camera, doing walk-like-an-Egyptian poses.

He's such a clown, I can't help but crack up. "You're a certified goofball," I say, laughing.

"Just trying to entertain the crowd."

"Your crowd of one."

"And that one deserves a great show," he says, then flashes me a grin. The brightest, most winning smile I've seen.

When I post it to our feed later, I know hearts will melt and panties will fly off tonight.

But not mine.

They definitely won't be mine.

3

JONES

I have other hobbies besides needling Jillian with nudity. For instance, I enjoy embroidery, I really dig knitting, and I love collecting stamps.

Just kidding.

I have nothing against those hobbies, but the things I'd enjoy most in the off-season are all the activities I can't do. Mountain biking? No way. Paintball. Hell no. That could lead to one hell of an NFI—non-football injury—and I know some serious nimrods who have earned complete and absolute dipshit status from firing off pellets of paint and pulling Achilles tendons in the process.

And how about the idiots who ride ATVs over dirt hills, only to crash, crack a fibula, and end up on the injured reserve? No, thank you.

Knock on wood, I've lived a mostly injury-free life for the last five years in pro ball, and I intend to keep it that way. I've only missed two games, and both were due to minor muscle strains.

Durable is my middle name.

That's why, since today I'm not playing the one sport that's allowed—golf—I'm parked next to my big brother in my spacious kitchen, my dog, Cletus, in my lap. The camera is rolling, and there are two glasses of beer on the island counter in front of us.

Yeah, we drink and spit for our hobby. Not Cletus, though. Water all the way for the little guy.

Trevor raises a glass of brew and adopts an adventurer's tone. "I found this delicious brew while trekking through Nepal."

"Is that so?" I arch a skeptical brow as he waxes on, spinning an apocryphal tale of climbing through the mountains to come across an enclave of Sherpas crafting brews.

I scratch my chin. "And you brought it all the way across the world to me? Wow. You must really love me."

"Only the finest for my little brother."

"Aren't you so damn sweet?" I raise the glass, take a sip, let it swirl around on my tongue, and then spit it in the bucket we nicknamed Pliny for his favorite beer. But this isn't just a spit for show. This beer is nasty.

"That tastes like ass," I declare, crinkling my nose. Cletus raises his chin, giving me a curious stare with big brown eyes that are two sizes too large for his tiny head. He's a little mutt—a little Chihuahua, a little Min Pin, a little dachshund, a little trouble.

Trevor rolls his eyes. "Why do you say that? Have you actually tasted ass?"

I crack up. "Can you even say ass on your show?"

"It's the In-ter-net. We can say anything." He taps the glass. "So, why would you say this marvelous beer tastes like a donkey's heinie?"

"Did I say donkey?"

"Naturally, I assumed you meant a jackass's ass. My bad."

"Look," I say, laying out my beer assessment like we do every week for his show. Our banter is off-the-cuff, of-the-moment. "It stinks like a sunflower, and it tastes as if it's been sitting all day in the heat of the swamp. I believe that officially makes it swamp-ass swill."

Trevor nods as if he's reluctantly accepting my answer. "Fair enough. But wait. I have more." He gestures like some sort of magician as he reaches below the counter for another brew or two. "What other beauties have I brought today for sampling?"

Yeah, he's a little over the top. It's part of his shtick. The oldest of the four of us, Trevor is a former brewmaster who now hosts a popular online video series about tasting beer. He's a bona fide beer expert, and besides being a pro baller, that's about the coolest job you can have. He has a more serious video show, too, a taste-testing one, that's beloved by beer experts and beer lovers alike. This is the one we do for fun, where we goof off. Both shows make bank, though, since he's a genius when it comes to business. He knows all the ins and outs of turning his passion into a money-maker, thanks to a degree in finance.

After we test a few more beers, spitting them all out in the bucket, Trevor flashes a smile at the camera. "That's all in today's edition of *Two Bros Who Like Brew*. I'd like to thank our regular color commentator, my one and only little brother. Jones, as always, your opinions are born of immense depth and great knowledge of the field of beer. Truly, your insight astounds me."

I point at him as Cletus yawns in my lap. "As does yours when it comes to football. Like the time you told me how I should run almost out of bounds then back in to catch a forty-five-yard pass from Cooper Armstrong while avoiding defensive coverage." I shake my head in amusement at that ridiculous bit of Monday-morning quarterbacking from him.

"Ouch. He questions my knowledge of the game, folks. You witnessed it firsthand."

We say goodbye, then he signs off and hits the stop button on his digital camera.

"More than one million views of the last episode. Damn, I am so funny." He blows on his fingers, too hot to handle. Cletus yaps at him. "Even your dog agrees with me."

"I'm pretty sure that was a bark of disagreement. Right, little dude?" I look at Cletus, who tilts his head to the side, clearly a yes. "All right, you're a good boy."

I set him down, reach for a tiny biscuit, and ask him to spin. My brown and white ten-pound dog executes three perfect circles, so I give him the treat. Cletus has won awards in dog agility trials because he's so fucking awesome he blows all the competition away. His jumps are magnificent, and his pole-weaving is a thing of beauty. Natch, I taught him everything he knows.

He rushes off with his treat, squirreling it away in one of his many dog beds. He has a couple in every room, but I swear he's not spoiled.

I stand to my full height. Trevor looks up at me, shaking his head. "Seriously. Are you ever going to find your real dad?"

It's a running joke.

I'm seven inches taller than Trevor. One of the tallest receivers in the NFL at six feet, five inches, I don't fit into my family. No one else comes even close to six-foot, not our other brother, David, and not our dad. My sister, Sandy, is a foot shorter, and our mom is the shortest of all, a little less than five four.

I laugh. "What can I say? I'm a freak of nature."

"Freak is right." Trevor rubs his hands together then adopts a more serious expression. "Thanks again for doing my show with me."

I smack his shoulder. "You know I love it. You don't have to thank me."

"I know, but I appreciate your time. You're in demand."

I scoff. "You're family. There's no pressure on my time from you. I'm just glad you're back in town," I say, since he used to be based in New York.

"Me, too. Also, you are in demand. Speaking of, are you ready for tomorrow? Time to roll up our sleeves and plan your next steps with the new agent."

I groan and scrub a hand over my jaw. "I hate that word. Agent basically means thief."

Trevor pats my shoulder and nods sympathetically. "Yeah, but Ford is one of the good ones. He's not going to screw you out of your money."

I scoff. "They all do, don't they?"

"Not all of them." He tips his forehead to the door. "I'll swing by in the morning, and we'll talk to him on the course."

I might have made some questionable choices. I might have partied too hard and too long. But I never screwed anyone who didn't want it.

Can't say the same for my old agent.

4

JILLIAN

I'm not lacking in confidence. But this crush? C'mon. I'm a smart girl. I know better.

Guys like Jones don't date girls like me.

And by girls like me, I don't just mean Asian girls. Though I do.

But mostly, I mean girls with serious jobs. I'm the director of publicity for the team. That's not what Jones is looking for in his arm candy of choice.

Jones Beckett has dated go-go dancers, cheerleaders, and models, as well as a soccer star and an actress best known for baring all. He doesn't date girls with office jobs who aspire to have a VP after their name. He dates girls who are vice presidents of hot racks, executives in charge of the lap dance, and heads of the department of perfect tits and ass.

He's been photographed with one beautiful babe after another.

But every now and then, the ladies photograph him. Like the morning after the team's Super Bowl win two years ago. That's when a buxom blonde named Chelsea tweeted a selfie with Jones sleeping in her bed. Her face in the frame with our snoozing star receiver, she captioned the pic so cleverly with her newly acquired knowledge: "*It's true what they say about a size of a man's hands.*"

Yep. Our player had become more famous for swiping right than for his game-winning touchdown pass.

I wouldn't call it a PR disaster, because what single pro baller doesn't want to celebrate his Super Bowl win in that kind of biblical fashion? But it became a feeding frenzy for the media outlets, hounding us for details on Chelsea. Who was this woman who had Jones Beckett in her bed?

SHE WAS A WOMAN ON TINDER.

That's it. That's all.

The cat was out of the bag. Jones used Tinder. Whoop-de-doo. That was how he became the poster boy for the hookup app for a few months. That is reason #1089 why I don't take my unrequited crush on him seriously. For starters, I'm one in a long line of women who have a crush on him.

Second, Jones isn't just a player. He's a *playa*.

That's why a crush is a crush is only a crush.

Besides, even if I were to let myself entertain it more —which I won't—all I have to do is remind myself that none of the girls he's dated look like me. They look like they are from California, Texas, Mississippi.

Blonde. Blue-eyed. All-American.

I'm from here, but my blood comes from China. My very American, very Californian parents adopted me from the city of Wuhan in the province of Hubei when I was nine months old. So, while I'm 100 percent Cali girl, I also have eyes a little narrower, lashes a lot straighter, and hair that can't be any color but black.

In any case, I'm better off devoting my dating energy on guys more like me—men with jobs in buildings rather than ballparks. Truth be told, though, it's been a year since I dated anyone seriously. My job is my focus. I love it madly, and that's why I don't mind showing up at the office at seven thirty on most mornings, like I do several days after the shoot.

That gives me quiet time to get a head start on the day. At my desk, I pop in my earbuds, and turn on my favorite playlist, starting with Bishop's "Be My Love." I dive into my emails, including one from my friend Jess in Los Angeles, who I've mentored. She's coming to town soon and would love to get together. I write back in all caps and with exclamation points then tackle my messages from reporters. With training camp starting in a few weeks, questions are pouring in. Which rookies will get playing time? Will we re-sign our star running back, Harlan Taylor? How has our quarterback, Cooper Armstrong, been looking in the off-season? That last question comes from Sierra Franklin, one of the local TV reporters who also hosted the bachelor charity auction I organized last year. Funny thing about that auction—she met her fiancé that same evening. He worked at the hotel where the auction was held, and they hit it off and are getting married in September.

I write back.

Cooper looks amazing, but not as amazing as I know you'll

be in your wedding dress. You're going to be a beautiful bride!
Can't wait for your big day!

I clean out the rest of my inbox, and I'm powering through my morning round of press clippings when my boss, Lily, calls me into her office. Leaving my earbuds and phone behind, I head down the hall, knock on her door, and push it open the rest of the way.

She's a whirling dervish, radiating fire and excitement. I adore Lily. Her drive and tenacity are unparalleled. She stands at her desk, bracelets jangling on her wrists, wild red hair thick with springy curls, her green shirtsleeves billowing as she stabs the computer monitor.

"Look," she shouts, poking the screen again. "Look at this."

I step closer, train my gaze to the screen, then pump a fist. "Yes."

She sashays over to me on her four-inch platform heels, doing a victory dance and offering her hand to high-five. I smack back.

She grabs my shoulders for emphasis. "*Cover.* He's the freaking cover. *Sporting World* just sent me a sneak preview. The issue runs in a few days, and you did it."

Did I? Or did Jones, with his insanely photogenic style? I simply attended the shoot.

I give credit where it's due. "It's all Jones. He truly knows how to work it."

She waves a hand. "These men. They might have God-given talent, but don't let them take all the credit. You pitched the right guy."

I shrug happily. "Fine. We rock," I say with a

proud smile, then I look at the winning shot. An amusing scowl graces his face, and an intense glare marks his blue eyes, making him appear tough as nails, untouchable even, like he is on the field most of the time. He's pulled footballs out of the air that should have been incomplete passes. He's saved potential interceptions on countless occasions. And he's fought off the scariest defensive coverage, scrambling, doubling back, and finding the holes so he could catch and cradle the ball.

He's fearless, focused, and fast as hell on his feet.

Lily drops into her cushy leather chair, sighing happily as she twirls in the seat. "I feel like I could celebrate with a full-fat latte."

I laugh as I grab a seat. "Now you're really going crazy." Lily is the queen of skinny lattes.

"This is such a popular issue, and I also love that *finally* Jones Beckett is in the spotlight for something other than the size of his prick."

My jaw itches to drop at her bluntness. But in PR, you learn to keep a smile on your face nearly all the time. I show no reaction, even though she's totally right.

"Remember Chelsea?" she asks, as if I could forget.

I smile sarcastically. "Good old Chelsea, queen of the naughty selfie."

Lily laughs, dragging her hand through her copper curls. "And how about Annika Van der Holden?" she asks, referring to one of the models he was seen with, as she continues taking a stroll down Jones's Most Notorious Press Moments Lane. "Do you remember that shot?"

Inside, I cringe as the memory of Jones, holding a bottle of champagne and planting a kiss on the twig's cheek, flashes before me. I mean, the very lovely model. Who wore a vagina-length dress in the photo.

"I do remember it. I wanted to buy her a new dress, maybe put a coat on her shoulders."

Lily smacks her desk. "You and me both. And then there was the shot of him, his asshole agent, Chuck Margulies, and some random topless woman sticking their heads out of the sunroof in a limo. Although, in the topless woman's case, it was more than her head sticking out the sunroof." She points to the screen, her bracelets jingling a pretty tune. "But this? This is what we want."

Our marching orders for the last few years have been to maintain a pristine image for the team. We've had a good run. Our starting quarterback is engaged to the girl he's loved his whole life, and they're both huge charity supporters. Our kicker is involved in literacy efforts in the city. While Jones is a generous supporter of charity like most of the guys, his wild-child status, not to mention getting caught in the crossfire in the fiasco with his agent, has tainted his coverage. Maybe the body issue can help rehab that image.

Which brings me to something I need and want from my boss.

My pet project, so to speak.

Our players work on many charitable endeavors, but I'm also allowed to shepherd a project each year. I've organized an annual bachelor auction that's been a huge hit, but with the quarterback now off the market, I might need to shift to a new effort.

I have one.

I clear my throat. "There's something I'd like to work on, Lily. It intersects with what we've been talking about. We haven't done this before, but I've been researching, and I think it could be an amazing charity project."

"Do tell."

When I share the details, her eyes light up. She stabs her desk with a manicured finger. "Yes. Do that. But I think it should be with one guy. One who would benefit most from this."

I tense. "And who would that be?"

She smiles, nodding to the screen.

Equal parts excitement and nerves flare through me. Working that closely with Jones can't possibly be good for my libido. I'll have to double down, triple down on my stony-faced stoicism in the presence of his hotness, and that won't be easy.

But working that closely with him might be very good for my job, so I'll have to find a way. "I'll put together a proposal for him."

I rise and make my way to the door, when Lily calls out, "By the way, the VP of publicity post is opening up in the fall."

I blink and square my shoulders.

"I'd love to see you land the job," she adds with a knowing smile when I turn around.

My heart zips through the sky. There's nothing I want more than to keep moving up, and the chance to rise from director of publicity to VP is tremendous. "It's open? You think I can nab it?" My question comes out as a squeak. I can't wait to tell my dad. He's going to be so excited.

She smiles broadly. "A project like this can go a long way toward making a case with the GM for why it should be you."

I nod enthusiastically as a million ideas for magazine pitches, photo ops, and fundraisers flash through my brain. "I'll reach out to Jones right away."

Screw my libido. He might be the path to a promotion.

5

JONES

The ball arcs majestically, curving through the blue sky then landing with a soft *thunk* on the green, five feet away from the flag for the eighth hole. I pump a fist and head to the little white orb that tortures me most days on the links. My dirty little secret? I suck at golf. But I love it. Just fucking love it.

"You get this hole-in-two, and I'm landing you a job on the PGA tour," Ford says.

I roll my eyes. "If you can land me a job playing golf, then you should find a gig for one of your golf pros running pass routes."

"And maybe you can nab me a job as the closer for the San Francisco Giants," Trevor chimes in.

Ford brandishes his golf club at my brother like a magic wand. "Abracadabra. You now have a hundred-mile-per-hour wicked curveball." He turns and shoots me a serious stare. "For the record, all my magic tricks are legal. Everything is one hundred percent above board in my business."

"As it better be." I head to the ball, lining up the shot.

My previous agent, and the money manager he worked with, are in prison now for embezzlement. Turned out my agent wasn't actually investing the money from my contract like I hired him to do. Nope. The bastard furnished false financial statements to make it only look like my money was turning into more money.

In reality, he gambled it. Then gambled some more. Then used more to pay those gambling debts. The manager helped him cover it all up.

Poof. Millions of dollars up in smoke.

That's a bitter pill to swallow.

I was wary of signing with any agent again, but my buddy Cooper convinced me, since he's worked with Ford his whole career. I need someone who is above board, without question. But we're still learning how to work together, and I'm not sure I trust him, or anyone, for that matter, who isn't related to me.

"All I want is to know that the money I earn goes to me and to my family. That's all I need," I tell him, since I'm well aware of what it's like to not have it. When I was growing up, my dad worked as a truck driver and my mom was a nurse. With four kids to feed and a house that was mortgaged to the hilt, money was stretched thin in those years, but they made it all work somehow and still made sure the four of us went to college, thanks to loan after loan after loan.

Fortunately, I nabbed a scholarship, so my school was paid for. After graduation, when I was drafted in the fourth round, I didn't earn the highest signing bonus or the fattest contract, but it was more than enough to pay off the loans for my brothers and my sister.

And my parents' mortgage.

And then to buy a new home for them.

That's just what you do. When you get that kind of jack at age twenty-three and your parents worked their asses off your whole life, you buy them a new home.

Despite what happened with my agent, none of the Becketts are suffering. We're all doing just fine, thank you very much. But still, I don't like that a whole heap of my hard-earned dough was siphoned off.

I want to protect what I earn so my family is taken care of, and so I'm taken care of when I can no longer play. One wrong step, one illegal hit, and you can be toast.

You need to sock your money away while it's coming in, because the gravy train can end on any given Sunday.

Ford swings his club like a pendulum. The man is a torrent of energy; stillness is anathema to him. "I hear you loud and clear. You know that's what I'm already doing on your behalf. But I want to turn things around for you. I'm talking to some brands. It's high time we start getting you some marquee sponsorships to match your star power."

That was another thing that had vanished. Deals my agent lined up for me went belly-up. I was radioactive, right along with Chuck and his money manager. "That's all well and good, but Margulies promised that, too, and no one wanted to do business with me after working with him. You really think you can pull off sponsorship deals?"

Ford stops mid-swing then drops his club. "Yes. That

is my job, and I take it seriously. And you aren't with Margulies anymore. You're with me."

"I need you to be clear with me on what they want and don't want. Margulies set me up with an energy drink company two years ago, and he said they didn't care what I did. There were no clauses or whatnot. Then boom—a picture of Annika and me leaving a club shows up"—I mime slicing my throat—"and it wasn't even the shot where she had the bottle of champagne in her hand."

"Exactly," Trevor adds, leaning on his club. "It was a guilt by association thing, and they dropped him, and that's why we need you to be upfront about this. You need to set the expectations."

"I will," Ford says. "You have my word."

"And I need to know everything," Trevor says to Ford. "That's why I'm here. That's why I'm involved this time around. It's my job to look out for my brother and make sure he doesn't run into the same shady shit as before. I'm going to vet everything. Be his eyes and ears."

Ford spreads his hands to show there's nothing up his sleeves. "Whatever you need. I want this to be an open book. No back-room deals, no shenanigans, no secrets." Ford looks to me. "You need me to go through Trevor, we'll do that."

I glance at my brother. He gives me a meaningful look that says *I've got your back*.

"Let me deliver this hole-in-two, and then you can tell me about these deals." I tap the ball and *bam*—it rolls beautifully into the hole.

Lucky me.

After we finish up the round, we amble off the

course, heading for our cars. Ford tugs off his golf glove at the edge of the parking lot. "Listen, I have a new company I'm talking to. A quick-serve food chain that makes all organic food. Tofu and kale and all that good-for-you green shit you probably love."

I grin. "Of course I eat organic. How the hell do you think I'm as durable as I am? No corn chips or fried crap for me." I flex a bicep.

"But beer counts?" Ford says with a wink.

I laugh. "Beer always counts. It's like a tax exemption. Same for chocolate chip cookies."

"Excellent. Glad to see you have your priorities straight. I'm all for making the most of those, too." Ford tosses the glove into his bag. "In any case, this deal could be good for you. I'm going to keep talking and see what they're looking for, but listen, it'll help your cause if we don't see any more shots of you and half-dressed women hanging out the sunroofs of limos."

"I think half-dressed is an understatement." I heave a sigh. "Also, that was a long time ago."

Ford points at me. "And elephants have long memories. If you can keep that party-boy image of yours in the rearview mirror, we can get some sweet deals. Make you a golden boy. America's sweetheart. Earn back some of the money that was stolen. Be patient, and I'll make sure you're taken care of," he says, clapping my back then shaking Trevor's hand. "Now, I need to go and do my job, and I will keep you both apprised."

Ford takes off, and as I slide into my sleek black Mercedes, my phone buzzes in my pocket. I grab it, and a very pretty face appears on the screen. Long, silky black hair, milk-chocolate eyes, pretty lips like a bow. I snapped the picture of Jillian at an event last year when she was standing at a table in the corner, nursing a club soda and looking pensive.

"Jones, did you just take a picture of me?" she'd said, when she noticed me holding up my phone.

"Yes, it's a free country."

"Let me see it." She made grabby hands.

"See. You look all serious," I'd said as I showed her.

"I look mad." She parked a hand on her hip. "Take another where I look happy."

I shook my head. "Nope. This angry face will make me answer the phone when you call because I'll think you're pissed at me."

"And that entices you to pick up?"

"Hell, yeah. There's nothing as motivating as a woman ready to tan your hide. Just ask my mom. *Jones Edward Andrew Beckett, get inside.*"

"Should I use your full name, then, any time you're in trouble?"

"Please do," I'd said, then I winked and walked away.

But I'd answer Jillian's call no matter what picture I had for her contact. Trevor gets into the passenger seat as I bring the phone to my ear. "Good afternoon, Jillian, and yes, if you continue to insist over and over, I will take you out to dinner tonight at the fanciest restaurant in San Francisco, and you can make a pitch for why you want me to be your boy toy." I heave a sigh. "But I must warn you, it'll have to be a good pitch."

Trevor shakes his head, clearly amused, while Jillian laughs on the phone. "Whew. I'm relieved. I already have the new Gabriel's restaurant reserved."

"Please make sure it's a private table in the back."

"As if I'd book anything else for you."

"All right, then. Lay it on me."

Her voice turns more serious. "Actually, I do have an offer I want to run past you. That's why I'm calling."

My ears prick. "An offer? Fine, if you won't be my bride, I'm still willing to service your needs every night."

"You're relentless, you know?"

"I do believe that's how ESPN described how I chase down the ball. *Jones Beckett is relentless downfield, watching his quarterback like a hawk circling prey, ready to swoop out of any formation and use those panther-like paws to catch nearly any throw.* That was a nice article. But do panthers catch footballs?"

"I don't know, but I do believe they have large paws. Speaking of animals, that's why I called. I know you like dogs because I've seen your beer show with your brother and Cletus, but do you like cats, too?"

"Making a pussycat purr is my favorite thing to do."

She chuckles. "Good. I have a proposition for you."

"The answer is yes. I'll come over to your house, and you can introduce me to your half dozen exotic cats."

"Do I look like a crazy cat lady?"

I shrug. "I prefer not to pigeonhole cat lovers. You might very well be a crazy cat lady in the guise of a sharp, brilliant publicist."

She ignores the last comment.

"Can you meet me tonight at eight?" She gives me a location. Huh. She was serious when she said Gabriel's. That place is sweet. "And I have a private table reserved. I don't want diners taking pictures of you."

I'm tempted to make a joke, to tell her she can snap any kind of photo of me she wants, but given my track record and her serious tone, I decide to leave that one untouched.

"I'll be there."

I hang up and meet my brother's gaze. His brow is scrunched, and his lips are curved up in a grin.

"What?"

He drums his hands on the dashboard. "On a scale of one to ten, how obvious do you think it is that you're hot for her?"

I flub my lips and turn on the engine. "Please. I just like to have a good time. Nothing more to it."

He hums, sounding doubtful.

"What?"

"Just keep it that way, okay? The *nothing more to it* way."

"You are such a big brother sometimes."

"Dude, she's the team's publicist."

I shoot him a look. "I'm well aware of her job, and we get along fine."

"I'm glad, and all I'm saying is I'd like to make sure we don't see shots of you and her topless in limos."

I narrow my eyes, bristling at the comment. "You don't know Jillian. That would never happen. She's not like that."

"Then it's harmless flirting. I can live with that."

"Good to know, *Dad*."

I drop him off, return home, and get ready to meet Jillian.

Since naked doesn't do the trick for her, plus restaurants usually don't admit birthday-suited patrons, I show up at Gabriel's freshly showered, shaved, and wearing jeans and a crisp black button-down, the cuffs rolled up, since she once said that a well-dressed athlete is hard to resist.

Fine, she might have been talking about the fact that she wanted us all to wear tailored suits for a charity auction last year, but I'm taking it as a personal piece of fashion advice.

The hostess greets me with a smile then leads me through the restaurant to a private table in the back. Jillian's not here yet, but five seconds later, I turn around to see her entering the room, and all I can think is she looks good every single time I see her, and tonight I want to peel off that black dress.

The red high heels, though?

She can leave those on.

6

JILLIAN

With exposed red-brick walls, flickering candles on the tables, and framed photographs of a couple tangoing on the streets of Buenos Aires, the restaurant has a romantic feel.

Perhaps I should have met him at the office.

Or at a playground.

Or a hair salon.

My dad's house, even.

Anyplace at all besides the private room at a trendy French-Brazilian establishment that's earning all the raves.

Deservedly so.

The scallops are to die for. They've been melting on my tongue. Jones spears a piece of the grilled potatoes, since he insisted we share two appetizers. That's not romantic at all. That's totally what business associates do. That's what I tell myself, at least.

"Try this," he says, offering me the food on the end of his fork.

My eyes widen. My heart thumps stupidly fast. Am I

supposed to eat off the end of his fork? That's kind of intensely couple-like.

Why did I pick this perfect place? The mood is too seductive, and he looks like a dream. That black shirt and the way it fits him should be criminal. It stretches across his pecs and hugs his biceps. The cuffs are rolled up, revealing his muscular, ropy forearms.

His hair is freshly combed, like he took a shower right before he arrived. My breath catches at the thought of Jones in the shower, soaping up that big, sexy body, running his hands across that chest, along his arms, down his legs. I wonder if he touches himself in the shower. Oh God, there's a five-alarm fire raging in my body now as I picture finding him in his shower as he pleasures himself, and it is literally the hottest Tumblr feed my brain has ever edited.

I press my thighs together and think of bunnies and baby chicks.

"It's tasty," he says, waggling the fork at me.

I bet he's tasty.

Then I realize he's not offering the food to me romantically. He's toying with me again. This is probably a brand-new game. Just like how he tried to get my goat on the phone earlier today. That thought cools me down a few degrees.

I smile and take the fork, since I don't like being fed. I eat the grilled potato, and it makes my mouth sing. "Oh my God, that's amazing."

"Well, I did pick a great place," he says, shooting me a grin.

I laugh, feeling better now that we're back to familiar ground. I know the rules to this game. The teasing game. The toying game. "Oh, sure. You truly have amazing taste in restaurants, Jones."

He squares his shoulders and puffs out his chest, as if I've just shot him straight up with a hearty dose of pride with my compliment.

"I'm so glad you approve of my choice," he winks, knowing full well it was my pick. He raises his beer and offers a toast. "To the person who truly has great taste in where to eat." His eyes lock on mine, and for the briefest of seconds, there's no teasing in them. Just that flash of heat I swore I saw at the photo shoot. He holds my gaze for a moment longer than I'd expect. Then another. And it both unnerves me and turns me on to a vastly inappropriate degree. He won't look away from me. His blue eyes are melting me. My body hums, and my bones vibrate.

Must. Find. Strength. To. Break. Hold.

"That poster is so great," I say, tapping my glass of iced tea to his as I glance at the picture of a couple tangoing.

He follows my eyes. "Yeah, they look totally hot for each other."

Okay. That was not the best deflection strategy. I bring the glass to my lips and nearly drink the whole thing down, praying it reduces the red-hot temperature in me.

"That must be some delicious iced tea," he says drily.

One more chug. One more gulp. Done. I set it down with a smile. "Delish," I declare.

I don't drink when I'm out for work. I don't drink at all with players. People make foolish decisions when they drink. I can only imagine letting my guard down with him. I can imagine the words that would fall stupidly out of my mouth after a few glasses.

Take me home tonight. Put your hands on me. All over me.

I growl at my inner voice, a reminder to never say those words out loud. Or in my head, either, frankly.

"Are you ready for my proposal?" I ask in my most professional tone, as I brush several strands of my hair away from my face, my fingertips dusting my stainless-steel earrings.

Setting down his glass, he angles closer, studying me. My ears, I think. "Are those . . .?" He points at my earlobe. "Cherries?"

I smile, raising a hand to touch the jewelry as if I need to remind myself. "Yes. They're my favorite."

"Favorite fruit?"

"Yes, but also favorite symbol. They symbolize luck in Chinese culture."

"Oh yeah?" A lopsided grin forms on his face. "I'm fascinated with superstitions and symbols. Is that because of cherry trees or cherry blossoms? I thought the cherry blossom was more a Japanese thing?"

I smile, loving his enthusiasm for the topic. "The cherry blossom is, but red is a very special color for the Chinese people, and since cherries are red, they've become a sign of luck and good fortune. Even though I wasn't really raised in a Chinese household, I've picked up a few little things that I like from the culture. Besides just rice," I say, with a little laugh, "which I do love."

He cracks up. "That's awesome. And do you wear the earrings for good luck, then? Are they your good luck charm?"

"I suppose they are. My parents gave them to me when I started my job with the Renegades."

"They totally work. You're a rock star."

I raise an eyebrow playfully. "And maybe I also just like cherries."

His blue eyes twinkle. "And I like good luck. I'll take as much good fortune as I can possibly get on the field," he says, rapping his knuckles on the wooden table, reminding me that Jones has always been one of the more superstitious athletes. Last year, he asked me to cut his teammate Harlan's hair, saying the guys needed to start up a new ritual because an old superstition had been broken.

"You hardly need good fortune," I tell him.

"But I'll take it. Also"—he leans closer and cups his hand over the side of his mouth—"I love cherries, too."

My lips part, and my skin heats. It's nearly impossible to talk about cherries without sounding sexual, and it's inevitable that Jones would sound that way to me. *Cherries.* The word seems to hang between us like it means something else.

I snap myself out of it. It means he's a player.

And I'm not his type, so I won't let myself linger on the dirty ways he says sexy-sounding fruit. I swallow, trying to center myself. "Proposal time."

He waggles his fingers at his chest. "Give me all the deets. Just lay it on me."

I clear my throat, launch into my pitch, and tell him what I have in mind.

He nods excitedly, raising both arms in victory. "You had me at puppies."

"I did?"

"There's literally nothing more to say."

"You'll do it?" I ask, my voice rising in excitement. I'm not asking him to build houses in the 110-degree sun, but I didn't expect a yes in seconds when I pitched him on my idea for a charity calendar benefiting local animal rescues. Twelve months of photos of Jones, posing with adorable animals.

"You're surprised?"

"Yes, but I'm also thrilled. I just didn't know if you needed to talk to anyone first."

"Nope. I don't need to consult Ford or Trevor or anyone. I want to do this."

"Seriously?" My smile widens.

He laughs, leans forward, and pats my hand. "You say that like it's a surprise I'd do something nice. I did your bachelor auction last year, and the year before."

I flash back to the auction last season. I was tense, wound up before it started. I wanted it to be an amazing event. Jones found me backstage and reassured me that everything would be great. For a moment, I linger on that sweet memory of his voice, his kind words. That didn't feel like toying with me at all. It felt real.

"You were great at the auction. It meant a lot to me," I say softly.

He squeezes my hand, and I tense, then give in to the momentary sensation of his big hand covering mine, reassuring me once more.

"And I'm all in with this, too." He lets go of my hand, and I wish he'd touch me again, even though I can't let my mind go there.

"This is a one hundred percent volunteer project," I say, making sure he's clear on the terms. When I mentioned the project to Jess, a talented photographer, she offered to waive her fee and work for a day since one of the shoots coincides with her trip here. "You'd be donating your time freely."

"Puppies, Jillian. Puppies."

I smile. "There will be kittens, too."

"Meow," he says, brandishing his hands as claws. His huge hands. My mind flickers briefly to how those hands would look wrapped around my waist. They're so big, they'd cover me, hold me, dig into my hips. A ribbon of heat unfurls in my body, and I can feel my cheeks flush.

"You okay? You just thinking about me and all the pussycats?" he asks with a wink.

God, I'm thinking about him making me purr, and it's filthy. It's wanton. The way my body reacts to him is dangerous.

I need to keep my head in the game. "I am. I have some great shots planned. We'll do them all in the Bay Area to support local rescues. It shouldn't take up too much time. Probably a week or ten days, and it would end shortly before training camp begins."

"Sounds perfect. I only have one stipulation."

My heart sags. There's always a catch. "Sure. What is it?"

"We need to take one of the pictures at the Miami Humane Society."

"That's in Florida," I say, after a beat.

"It is?" he asks in mock surprise.

"Jones," I chide.

"I had no idea where it was located. Are you sure it's in Florida?"

"Ha ha."

"Where is Florida? Is that all the way on the other side of the country?"

I sigh playfully and then hold up my hands in surrender. "Why do you want to—?" Then I remember. "Cletus is a hurricane dog."

Last year, Jones helped one of the local rescues that had taken in animals evacuated from shelters during the big hurricane. He'd donated time then adopted a dog.

"His name would have been Irma if he'd been a girl. I'm glad he's a boy, though, and it would mean a lot to me if we could support the shelter where he's from."

"From one adoptee to another, I completely understand."

He smiles, that same winning grin he flashed in the studio.

Of course, this also means I'll be traveling with Jones. Across the country. Alone.

And I'm not sure my libido will be able to take it.

* * *

The top floor of Nordstrom in Union Square is packed. The sleek black chairs are filled with sharp-dressed women in pretty blouses, trendy skirts, and hip slacks. Some men are here, too, their form-fitting button-downs and designer jeans making it clear they're visiting to buy for racks in their stores.

My friend Katie grabs two seats reserved for her in the second row from the front. She's a buyer for a chain of upscale boutiques, and she snags invites to all the private shows put on for those inside the industry. Since I have a long-standing love affair with clothes, I'm the lucky duck who accompanies her from time to time.

"I'm dying to see the new Angel Sanjay line," Katie

whispers as she tucks her blond curls behind her ears. "He has the best work clothes that make you look hot, but not slutty."

"I find it's always a plus to go to work looking like something other than a ho," I say, tucking my purse under the chair. "Plus, we're going shopping after this, right?"

Katie rolls her green eyes. "Duh. Obviously."

"I'm dying to get a new outfit. Because . . . new outfit."

She waves away that nonsense. "There is never a need to justify the purchase of a new outfit."

I hold up a hand to high-five. "You speak the truth."

As we wait for the designer to show off her new fashions, I tell Katie I'm heading to Stinson Beach tomorrow for the first day of shooting with Jones for the calendar. "But I think I'll wear jeans and a nice blouse," I say, musing on the outfit choices for an outdoor photo op.

Katie laughs. "How do you think that's going to help your crush? When the guy you're hot for cuddles a puppy on the beach—I mean, that's so not going to make your ovaries explode."

I roll my eyes, just to prove how immune my ovaries and I are to Jones. "It's going to be fine. If I've managed this long, I can manage even longer."

Katie arches both eyebrows. "And then when you fly across the country with him. That ought to be a piece of cake."

I snap my fingers. "Easy as one, two, three. I've only traveled with him at least eight times a year for the last few years—more if you include all the playoff games the team went to."

"On a jumbo jet. With fifty-three other players, not to mention coaches, staff, and personnel," Katie adds, shaking her head in amusement, a smirk on her freckled face.

"It's going to be fine. Yes, I've lusted after him for years, and yet, amazingly, not once have I thrown myself at him. I think I can handle this," I say crisply. "Plus, I didn't even think about Jones when I dated Kevin last year."

"Kevin," she says, her voice dripping with disdain. "Kevin Stone, aka, VP of Dickhead Decisions. Is he still with the wench? I didn't see her at the fundraiser we went to."

I shrug. "I don't keep tabs on him personally." Breaking up with Kevin when I found out he'd been cheating on me was, obviously, a no-brainer. Cutting him out of my life has been a teeny bit harder since he's the sports anchor at one of the San Francisco TV stations. It's impossible to avoid him when we run in the same circles, but even though I find him highly irritating as a man, I've mastered keeping our professional interactions focused solely on the team. Most recently I spotted the pair at a summer carnival fundraiser that all the local teams sponsored along with his station. All things being equal, I'd rather not run into him and his new woman, but they both waved to me and tried to make small talk like they were utterly charmed we'd met. I swear the guy is missing a key strand of DNA if he thinks I want to chitchat with the two of them. I said hello in my best professional tone then joined our quarterback and his fiancée at the Skee-Ball game.

I didn't let it gnaw at me. I wasn't in love with him,

so I refused to let an asshole like that claim squatter's rights on any of my mental real estate.

Katie pats my leg. "I love your laser focus, Jillian. I love the way you don't linger on men who are total shits. God knows, I've needed a year's worth of yoga classes to let go of some of the bastards of this world. And I teach the damn classes."

Katie's like a superhero—fashionista by day, yogini by night. It's rather impressive the way she balances it all. But then again, I suppose that's what yoga is all about. Or so she tells me. I prefer faster forms of exercise.

I toss my black hair off my shoulder. "It's an art. I learned it from my dad." My father worked in the news business his entire career. He had to learn to compartmentalize, to shrug things off, to keep moving forward. I picked up that skill from him, and am I ever glad I did.

"You could teach classes in it."

"I've already devised a full syllabus," I say, peering ahead to the runway to try to catch a glimpse of any backstage action. It's still quiet behind the wings.

"But let's not 'art' the topic of Jones," she says in a low voice, sketching air quotes.

I scrunch my brow. "What do you mean?"

"You know what I mean."

The designer jumps onto the stage, and all eyes turn to the beanpole man with golden skin and hair cut at several angles. Angel Sanjay says a few words about his vision for this collection—giving voice to the natural feminine desire to look pretty while still looking professional—saving me from the friendly inquisition from Katie. As he exits the stage, pop music plays overhead, and a high-cheekboned brunette sashays down the runway, modeling a classy black pencil skirt and a blouse with a geometric print. The neckline is sexy but still appropriate for work.

As the model turns the other way and the next one slinks down the runway in a pretty pink sheath dress I'm sure I need to possess, Katie leans close and says, "You want to know what I really think?"

"Obviously. I asked you."

As the music pulses, she whispers, "I want you to know that I absolutely applaud your spirit and your commitment to resisting jumping Jones Beckett. In fact, I'm thinking of giving you a trophy."

"Thanks. It'll look great on my mantel, even though it's completely unnecessary." I wave my hand as I hunt for analogies. "Jones and I are like east and west . . . hot pepper and ice cream . . . a bikini for a ski weekend."

She arches a brow. "Some people like pepper on their ice cream."

I crinkle my nose. "The point is, we're not going to happen. I'm not his type, and that's fine. I *like* my type. I don't need to be *his* type to be happy."

Katie gives a quiet slow clap, and I take a tiny bow in my chair. Then she leans closer. "But you do know some girls wear bikinis when skiing?"

I point to my chest. "Not this girl. I wear ski gear when I race down the hills of Tahoe and leave everyone in the snowdrifts," I say with a smirk, since skiing is my jam. "Also, he can't ski. It's not allowed. So that just proves my point even more."

Katie tsks quietly. "I don't buy it. I think Jones Beckett wants to ski down your mountain."

"I love you, girl. Truly, I do. But there is no reason for me to believe the attraction is mutual."

"There is every reason. You're a total babe, with hair I covet, a body to die for, and a face that would launch a thousand ships. You don't realize that because you're so focused on work you don't think of yourself that way."

"And yet Kevin still found it necessary to stick his dick elsewhere."

"Because he's a dick," Katie says loudly, so loudly that the woman next to her shoots her an admonishing stare.

Katie clasps her hand to her mouth in an *oops* gesture. Then she cups her hand over my ear. "Just think about it. I saw the way he looked at you at the fundraiser a few weeks ago, when you and I were playing Whac-A-Mole . . ." She stops, adopts a saucy tone, and says, "Like he'd been playing whack a mole to thoughts of you."

I give her my best I-can't-even-believe-you-said-that face. Ever. "I won't even pretend that's, one, dirty, or two, accurate."

"Think about it."

No way. There's no way I'm going to think about it.

Katie's a friend. She's supposed to think I rock.

I won't ever confuse that for Jones wanting to jump my bones.

Even though I kind of can't wait to go to Stinson Beach with him tomorrow.

7

JONES

I peer through the oven window, trying to get a better view. "C'mon, little pie. Bake your ass off."

Harlan rolls his eyes. "You do know it doesn't bake any faster if you watch it?"

"But if I talk to it? Encourage it? That'll help, right?"

Harlan scratches his chin. "By all means. Chatter away."

I stare at the crust rising in Harlan's stove. "You can do it. Bake harder. Bubble over."

"What do you say we play a round of poker while we wait? You know the saying—pies like privacy," Harlan says, slapping the candy cane potholder on the counter of his kitchen, smack dab in the middle of the rest of his collection of Christmas-themed potholders. His sister's a baker, his mom's a baker, his grandma's a baker, and so he learned how to make the finest pies in the South while growing up surrounded by all those baking women.

Now, the women in his family give him potholders every year for his, you guessed it, Christmas birthday.

"Fine, but you know I'll kick your ass since you can't bluff for shit," I tell him.

He jerks his head back, narrowing his eyes. "Those are fighting words. I can bluff just like I can handle a play action fake better than your sorry ass."

"No shit. That's your job. Mine is just to carry all those beautiful passes into the end zone . . . and *score*," I say with a grin. That's the benefit of being a wide receiver when the team's quarterback is one of the best passers in the game. I get lots of action on the field. "Cooper can't resist throwing to me."

"I'm sorry. Were you saying you wanted this pie, or you wanted me to gobble it up all by myself?" Harlan cocks his head to the side, staring at me with brown eyes.

I hold my hands up in surrender. "I'm saying I'm going to make sure Coop hands off to you more often."

"That's what I thought, pie boy."

We park ourselves on the stools in the kitchen in his Pacific Heights home, less than half a mile from my house. He's our star running back, and it's both my job and my pleasure to give him as much shit as possible, since he does the same for me.

After a few hands where the lead changes each time, I bluff with a ten of clubs, beating his pair of twos. I mime pulling a huge pile of coins toward me, but we don't play for dough. I'll collect the prize in another way. "I'm going to enjoy the ever-loving hell out of you carrying the rookies' pads on day one of training camp."

He flips me the bird as he heads for the oven. "Did you want this pie to give to your girlfriend or not?"

I roll my eyes. "You're seriously holding the pie hostage *again*? The pie was not part of the bet, and you know I'm legally required to give you shit every time you lose at poker."

"Fine, and far be it from me to take this fine cherry pie away from you, since we both know it's pretty much your one chance to get Jillian to give you the time of day. No woman can resist a Taylor-made pie."

"I'm not trying to get a chance with her," I say, since she's displayed zero interest in me that way. Though that hasn't ever stopped me from trying to wear her down with a little flirting, a little teasing. But the pie isn't a way for me to charm the panties off her. The pie is simply a pie—a token of my appreciation for all her support, and for giving me the chance to be the star of the calendar. "Nah, she's helping me out with the calendar, so I just want to do something nice for her."

"If you didn't want to sleep with her, would you do something nice for her?"

"I don't think with my dick."

He clasps a hand to his belly and guffaws. "That's a good one." He wiggles his hands. "C'mon, tell me another."

"Fine, fine. You got me there. Obviously, I think with my dick. But I'm not a dick. I like the woman. I want to do something nice for her because she's a cool chick."

He puffs up his chest. "You've come to the right wingman, then. The Taylor family pies are way better than merely *nice*. I do believe they've been known to induce major swooning in womankind."

He opens the oven and, evidently pleased with what he sees, he slides out the tray, grabs the pie, and sets it on a cooling rack. We head downstairs to his state-of-the-art home gym, work our asses off for thirty minutes, and then I grab the pie and head for the door.

"Good luck, man. You're going to need it," he says.

"Don't I know it."

I'm hoping this pie is the start of something.

* * *

When I get bummed about the money stolen by my ex-agent, I like to take a good, long look at my home—three stories, hardwood floors, modern fixtures. It's all mine, and I own every square inch of it. I don't like that I was hoodwinked, but in the scheme of things, I still have so much, and I also have what matters most. A place to lay my head and leave my hat. Or helmet, really.

That's all I need. My family is healthy and happy, so I can't complain, just move forward. Besides, it could be worse. I wasn't the only one screwed. One of my teammates, Garrett Snow, was robbed of nearly everything. A second-year starter, most of his rookie bonus went up in smoke. Poor guy—he wound up injured in his second season, too, out with a torn ACL. I haven't seen him in a while, so once I'm home, I fire off a quick email to the guy, checking in to see how he's doing.

One hour later, with the pie in a small shopping bag, I lock the door to my home a block off Fillmore. I walk down the steps to the sidewalk on a summer afternoon that feels like winter, since that's how San Francisco behaves at this time of year. The fog layer hangs heavy in the city today, the dampness seeping into my bones. I grew up in Sacramento, and it is devil's horns hot there, so I gladly embrace the city by the bay and all that I have here—cool air, a home, and a steady job.

Okay, fine. Two out of three ain't bad. There's

nothing steady about a gig playing pro ball, but I wouldn't change a damn thing. I'm happiest when I'm chasing a target and carrying that football to the end zone.

That's the closest thing to heaven as far as I'm concerned—crossing the white chalk by the goalposts and putting six points on the board. Fucking bliss. Beautiful, heart-pumping bliss.

I wait at the curb for about thirty seconds, then a black town car pulls up. I lift my thumb in the air like I want to hitch a ride.

The window slides down in the back, and Jillian pokes her head out, a pair of big red sunglasses on her face. She pushes them up into her hair. "Hey there. Want a ride? I have candy, and I lost my puppy. Will you help me find it?" she says in a singsong voice.

"Oh yes. Do you have Skittles, please?"

She tosses her head back and laughs. "Tropical Island flavor."

I let my tongue fall out, like a dog, then I grab the handle, yanking open the door. My throat goes dry when I see her seated on the cool black leather.

Holy sexiness.

I can't even joke about hitchhiking and stranger danger or anything at all in the universe, because she stuns me. She wears jeans, pink sandals, and a silky soft blouse that falls perfectly against her breasts, revealing a hint of flesh. A slim silver chain with a heart locket hangs on her neck. That lucky pendant gets to touch her skin.

"You look . . ." I search for the right word. Hot? Luscious? Pretty? Good enough to lick from head to toe? So sexy I want to strip you down to nothing and get acquainted with every square inch of your body? I stave off a throaty groan of appreciation, swallowing it harshly. But I don't entirely want to hide how I feel, either. I want her to know what I see when I look at her.

And compliments are part of the strategy to get her to see me in a new light. "You look beautiful."

Her face is blank at first, as if she's not sure what to make of me. Confusion flickers across her pretty brown eyes, the color of melting chocolate. Then, a spark of something flickers. Maybe happiness? Appreciation? She's so hard to read.

"Thank you. You always look sharp."

I'll need to work harder to earn anything other than a professional compliment from this woman. I slide into the car, set the bag on the leather seat, and gesture to my getup. "You like my *sharp* bathing suit?" I point to my trunks, then flip-flops, then the T-shirt I'll take off at the beach for the shoot.

She raises her nose, as if she's sniffing. Maybe she's ferreted out the scent of a delicious cherry pie. But she doesn't mention it. "It's perfect. Exactly what I wanted you to wear."

I peer at her outfit. "You have a bikini on under that?"

"No way." She shivers for effect as the car pulls away and threads into light morning traffic on the way to the bridge.

"You're not going to swim while I shoot?"

"It's sixty-nine degrees at Stinson."

I snicker. "You said sixty-nine."

She laughs. "That joke never grows old."

"And I don't intend to ever retire it from my joke repertoire."

She bends her head and hunts through a few canvas bags by her side, as well as one of her endless number of purses. Fishing around, she finds what she's looking for. "First, this." She hands me a magazine.

My smile spreads when I flip it over. "Damn. Nice work."

"It's all you," she says, gesturing to the shot of me on *Sporting World*. "The whole spread is amazing, but Lily and I are quite partial to the cover."

Pride spreads through me. Landing the cover of *Sporting World* is no small shakes. "This is going on my wall of glory."

"That sounds like exactly where it belongs. And," she says, reaching into the purse once more, "I have a gift for you."

I blink, surprised and a little excited. "You do?"

"I was thinking about our conversation at dinner, and I thought you might enjoy some pomelos, since they're a sign of luck. So I picked some up for you at the market."

"I'm going to sound like the biggest dolt, but what's a pomelo?"

She hands me a red mesh bag filled with three grapefruit-size fruit. "They're like oranges, but more mellow and with a less citrusy flavor." She nibbles on the corner of her lips. "I know you're a health nut, so I figured fruit was a good thank you gift. Is it okay?"

Any gift from her is a great gift. I smile. "I love it. I will eat the entire bag. Probably tonight."

She smiles widely, her white teeth gleaming. "They symbolize prosperity, so with the season starting I figured you can't really get enough of that."

I pat one of the fruit. "I will take all the good fortune

I can possibly get. Question, though." I tilt my head, quizzically. "I've always wondered about kumquats? What do they symbolize?"

Her expression turns serious. "They're a symbol for the fruit with the naughtiest-sounding name in the universe."

I smack the seat for emphasis. "There's literally no way to say that name and have it not sound like a filthy sex act."

"Yes, that may be why I tried to avoid eating it with my family while growing up. It's a hugely awkward word to say in front of your parents."

I rip a small hole in the bag with my index finger and yank out a pomelo. I hold it high above my head like it's Simba and I'm in *The Lion King*. "And with this fruit, I will have a kickass year." I set the pomelo next to me on the seat. "Speaking of fruit and gifts," I say as the car winds its way out of the city, heading toward the Golden Gate Bridge. "Seems great minds think alike."

I dip my hand into the shopping bag and give her the small cherry pie. "Open it," I tell her, nodding to the tinfoil.

She brings it to her nose. "Oh my God, it smells delicious. I thought I smelled baked goods when you got into the car, but then I figured you were endorsing some amazing new pie cologne."

I laugh and drag a hand through my hair. "If there is ever a pie cologne, count me in."

"Yeah, me, too. Because I thought you smelled good enough to eat." Then her mouth falls open, and her eyes widen in seeming shock. She shakes her head, as if she's course correcting. "I meant . . . you smelled . . . The car smelled . . . gah."

She drops her head to her free hand, and I can't stop laughing. I also can't resist patting her back. "It's okay, Jillian. I am absolutely good enough to eat." When she raises her face, her cheeks are flaming red. I point at them. "And look, the color of your cheeks is good luck."

"I can't believe I said that. Forgive me."

"There's nothing to forgive." Especially since I'm hoping her awkwardness is an omen that my luck with her might be changing. I nod at the pie. "Open it."

She peels back the aluminum foil and stares at the treat with wide, hungry eyes.

"I baked a cherry pie for you. As a way of saying thanks for thinking of me for the calendar."

She raises her face. "You bake?"

I shrug. "I'm learning. Harlan's the baking master, and I like to stay busy during the off season, so this summer I worked on agility training with Cletus and I learned to bake a few things from Harlan. He won't share the recipes, though, so this one I just helped with. But it's fresh out of the oven, since I went over there this morning."

"To make it for me?" She puts her hand on her chest, her eyes wide and vulnerable.

"You said you love cherries . . ."

"Oh my God," she murmurs, lowering her eyes.

"Wait. You're not gluten-free, are you?"

She snaps up her gaze. "No way."

I hand her a fork from the bag. "Want a bite?"

"Will you share it with me?"

"I don't usually indulge in sweets. Training regimen and all."

"More for me, then," she says with a glint in her eyes.

"But maybe I'll allow myself one small bite."

She digs into the pie, takes a bite, and murmurs her appreciation. Her eyes sparkle. "Jones," she whispers, like we have a secret, "this is amazing."

She's complimenting the pie, but I'll take it. Oh yes, will I ever take it. "I'm glad you like it."

"Here," she says, forking a chunk of pastry and filling.

I open my mouth, waiting for her. She freezes, then does that thing again where she nibbles on the corner of her lips, before she extends the fork to my mouth. Keeping my eyes on her, I close my lips on the pie, savoring the crust and the sweet, juicy flavor of the cherries.

I don't break eye contact. I watch her the whole time, mostly because she can't seem to stop looking at me. She never looks at me for this long. She never looks at me like she can't stop.

I like her eyes on me.

I like it so fucking much.

When I'm done, she takes the fork away, and her hand seems to fall languidly at her side.

"Yes, I do love cherries," I say. "So very much."

8

JILLIAN

Katie was wrong.

My ovaries are so fine.

They can handle this photo shoot, no problem.

Really, what's so hard to take about a six-foot-five, two-hundred-fifty-eight-pound guy with toned, strong muscles everywhere on his frame hugging a mixed-breed Australian shepherd puppy?

And for the record, I only know his height and weight because I've memorized those stats for every single player on the team. They're handy when reporters ask, and they do.

But I've added a few more details for this guy. Beautiful veins in his forearms. A lopsided grin. A happy trail skating down his fine ab—

Screech.

I slam on the brakes. I shouldn't be admiring his body, even though now would be a good time to do so since he's wearing those casually sexy swim trunks.

On the beach.

With the sun beating down on said muscles.

With waves cresting in the background.

Maybe he needs me to oil up his arms, his pecs, his back.

Nope, Katie, nothing is tough about this at all.

Unless ovaries exploding inside me is a rough experience, because . . . oh my stars.

The puppy named Lulu is licking his face now.

Jones cracks up, belly laughs radiating through him as the white, black, and brown six-month-old puppy with crystal blue eyes bestows a popsicle-worthy kiss across his lips.

That lucky puppy.

That dog has all my good fortune.

"Please feel free to hire me for all team photos you ever need in the history of team photos," my friend Jess says as she stops for a moment to check the back of her camera.

"You know I do my best," I say with a smile, since she honed her eye shooting celebrity pictures in Los Angeles, and she's a wiz behind the lens.

As she takes more photos for the calendar, I grab a few shots for social media. Like with the body issue, I don't want to scoop the calendar. But, as part of my publicity plan, I want to dole out teasers of what fans will be getting when they flip open January, February, March, and so on.

"Lulu, you are too cute for words," Jones coos to the pup, and my heart can't take it. I turn on the video camera and record this unscripted moment, moving closer but staying out of the photographer's shot. My sandals are in my bag by the picnic table, and my bare feet sink into the sand.

The pup rewards Jones's sweet nothings with

another long lick across his lips. The Marin County Humane Society rep, a kind woman with curly black hair, bounces on her toes, clearly proud of her animal choice for the shoot.

Lulu laps her tongue across Jones's mouth, and he can barely take it. His laugher booms, loud and buoyant over the squawking of seagulls. He flops onto the sand, the puppy scrambling up his chest, making sure the man can't escape from her kisses.

It is literally the cutest thing I've ever seen in my life.

Jess is all over it, knowing this is the golden ticket, better than any posed shot. The pro athlete is exactly where we never want to see him during game-time. Flat on his back. But right now, it's perfect, with Jones in the sand, his tanned skin on display, his muscles rippling as he holds the dog, his smile as wide as the sea behind him.

I thought I needed to take fifty cold showers to get over that look he gave me when eating the bite of pie, but I won't need any to get over this moment.

Because it's not sexual.

It's not lusty.

It's wholly endearing, as he makes a six-month-old puppy named Lulu fall for him.

That dog might be my soul sister.

A few minutes later, as Jess packs up her gear, Jones says to the dog, "What am I going to do with you? You give me those puppy-dog eyes, and I don't stand a chance."

"Are you tempted to adopt her?" I ask as I walk over to him and Delia, the woman from the animal rescue.

He heaves a sigh. "If I could, I would. I've already

had to convince my brother to be Cletus's babysitter during the season."

I nod, understanding the dilemma of a traveling man. An idea strikes me, though. "Would you want to post a photo of her on the team feed and say she's looking for a home? We can tag the humane society."

A smile lights Delia's face. "We would be so very grateful."

"Let's do it," Jones says.

He scoops the dog higher in his arms, pressing his face to her snout. I snap a shot of man and beast. I don't know which one is cuter.

* * *

"Have you always been a dog whisperer?"

"My animal magnetism is pretty impressive, isn't it?"

I laugh, as we walk the puppy down a deserted stretch of beach. Jones asked Delia if he could take Lulu for a stroll. No surprise, Delia said yes, and I gave Jess a quick goodbye hug before she left. "That's one word for it. But tell the truth," I narrow my eyes and ask him in a faux accusatory voice, "did you slather Alpo all over your lips?"

"You caught me, but it was beef jerky. I gnawed through a whole stick while you weren't looking, just to excite Lulu."

When she hears her name, the pup spins in a circle in the sand, then scampers to the end of the leash. Jones walks a little faster, as per Lulu's wishes, and I keep pace, too. "Seriously, what's with your animal charms?"

"So you admit I'm charming?" he asks with mischief in his eyes.

Charming as in the ultimate flirt, yes. "Lulu seems to think so," I concede drily.

"But what about you? If you admit I'm charming, I'll tell you."

I pretend to punch his arm. "You're relentless. And fine, you're incredibly charming to canines. What's that all about?"

Jones pumps a fist. "I knew you'd admit the truth." We wander along the shoreline, the waves crashing lightly against the sand. "We didn't have dogs when I was growing up, and I wanted one so much. I asked my parents all the time if we could get a puppy. I had this whole campaign planned for Christmas when I was eleven. It was free adoption day at the Sacramento shelter, and so on." He turns to me, his gaze locking with mine. "But we never got one."

The sadness in his blue irises hooks into me, and tugs on my heart. "Were your parents allergic?"

He shakes his head. "Nope. Honestly, we didn't have the money. My parents were strapped for cash my entire childhood. They said they wanted to get a dog for the four of us, but they couldn't afford another mouth to feed, and that was that. I always told myself that I'd adopt a dog once I was drafted, but then I didn't want to bring home one that I couldn't take care of, being on the road so much. It wasn't until Trevor moved to the city that I knew I could finally get a pet. Plus, obviously, I was helpless to resist Cletus. Once I met him while I was helping out at the shelter, I had to take him home." He holds his arms out wide. "He gave me no choice."

"Cletus is the very picture of irresistibility. I can see why you were powerless against his charms."

"He gave me a puppy dog face, and that was that."

Jones bats his eyes, imitating Cletus it seems, then tips his chin at me. "What about you? Did you want a dog?"

My feet sink into the sand as we traverse the beach and memories of my childhood wishes return. "I wanted everything when I was a kid. I was an only child, so I was convinced I needed a four-legged friend since I didn't have a brother or sister. I'd have taken anything. Dog, cat, hamster, bunny. I even tried to get a hedgehog once."

"A hedgehog? Those are pretty damn cute."

"I know. But I had no luck, either. My mom was allergic to everything, so we never had any pets. The ironic thing is my dad finally got a dog a few years ago after my mom died."

Jones stops in his tracks, reaching for my arm. "I didn't realize your mom had passed."

Sometimes, I think I know him well. I work with him, share his stats and performance with the media, and I sit down with reporters when they interview him. But that's superficial. There's so much we haven't talked about. So many conversations we haven't had. "She had a heart attack four years ago," I say, doing my best to keep my tone even and ignoring the lump in my throat that forms inevitably when I talk about her.

"I'm really sorry."

"Me, too," I say softly. "She wasn't that young, though. Not that that makes it easier necessarily. But she was sixty-five. She was over forty when she adopted me. My parents were both a little older. They didn't have any luck trying to have a child the old-fashioned way. Ergo, I'm their kid."

He wraps an arm around my shoulder and gives me

a squeeze. "I'm sorry you lost your mom, Jillian. I would be devastated."

"I was, but my dad was the one who took it the hardest. I was worried about him for the longest time. I still worry about him, but he's doing so much better." I reflect on the shifts I've seen in him recently. He laughs more, smiles more, and spends time with friends. He's healing. "I think that's why the dog helps so much. It gives him something to focus on, someone to love. And I try to visit him as often as I can."

"That's what you should do," he says, squeezing my shoulder once more.

My eyes drift to his fingers, spread over my shoulder. For a moment, I flash back to dinner, to my dirty fantasies of his hands.

I never expected the first time he'd have them on me for so long, it would be like this, borne of some kind of comfort.

Or that I would like it this much.

Especially since he doesn't take his hand off me for the rest of the walk.

9

JONES

"Dude, how much weight did you put on in the off-season?"

The smart aleck comment comes courtesy of Cooper Armstrong as we round the far end of the practice field at our training facility two days later.

"You're slower than a Pop Warner lineman today," our kicker Rick goads, climbing on the insult train.

From behind my shades, I raise my eyes to their backs. The two of them are several feet ahead of me. Harlan's running in front of them.

Huh.

Truth is, I may have been running slower than usual because my mind drifted back to yesterday and the second photo shoot Jillian set up. The shot she planned was golden, as in . . . everything. The dog was a golden retriever mix, and the photog snapped a sweet image at the edge of Sausalito with the Golden Gate Bridge rising majestically. The pooch put his paw on my leg as we sat on a rock, the gorgeous blue waters of the bay behind us.

Afterward, Jillian and I grabbed lunch at a place on the water and chatted about our top fantasy baseball picks as a Giants game played on the flat-screen in the background. Turns out the chick has a wickedly good eye for fantasy sports, and her baseball team is leading in her league. "Confession: I get very ornery if I lose," she'd admitted.

"Confession: I get pretty damn annoyed if I lose the Super Bowl."

She'd laughed. "Yeah, that does seem to be a bit of a bigger deal."

It's funny how I've had my eye on her for the last few years, but I'm only recently learning all these fascinating details about her, from her family to her fantasy addiction.

But now I'm dragging at laps since my mind is on the woman, and that won't do.

I pick up the pace. "The only weight I put on in the off-season is all this muscle." I peel off my T-shirt and throw it straight at Rick. He dodges it, naturally, and I run past Rick and Cooper, flexing my biceps.

As I speed up, I turn around, running backward so I can fully enjoy flipping the double bird to my teammates. "And I will see you fuckers downfield. If you ever wondered who was the fastest on this team, you're about to be schooled."

Spinning around, I take off. Sunglasses on, I sprint the final lap as if I'm racing to catch a football, sweeping past Harlan, too. And he's a fast bastard. But I'm faster.

That's the point of these feet, this heart, this body that I try to keep finely-tuned every day. You don't get a job as a wide receiver for one of the best NFL teams in the country if you can't move your feet like Hermes.

I earned a 4.3 in the forty-yard dash at the combine. That's the fastest on the team.

When I reach the goalpost, I slap it, then rest my elbow against it and adopt an oh-so-casual *Road Runner waiting for Wile E. Coyote* pose until the guys catch up with me.

Cooper holds up his hand to high-five. "That's what I want to see every goddamn Sunday on the field."

"And that's what you get."

"I know it. I love it."

Rick is the last one, joining us at an easy pace. "Nobody cares how fast I run. I save all my energy for my golden foot."

"And it is golden indeed," Cooper says, and we head for the first row in the stands, where I left a water bottle and a little good luck treat for my guys.

After I down half the bottle, since we've been working out for two hours this morning, I reach into a red mesh bag—a bag of pomelos. I bought a few more after I worked my way through the gift Jillian gave me. No lie. Jillian was right. Pomelos are delicious and now I have a new favorite fruit.

"Gentlemen, this may become our new good luck ritual for the season. Turns out this fruit is mighty tasty, and a harbinger of all good things to come."

Harlan grabs one, rips at the thick rind, and asks in his familiar southern drawl. "Does this mean the cherry pie worked?"

I shoot him a quizzical look. "What does one have to do with the other?"

Harlan chuckles. "Oh, right. You thought I wouldn't notice that you're suddenly eating pomelos. I am well aware that Jillian has these on her desk. I do pay attention to what goes on around us."

Rick slaps the seat in front of him. "That's fantastic. Jillian is giving you special gifts now. What other presents are you giving each other?" Rick wiggles his eyebrows.

I slice a hand through the air, cutting off this direction of conversation since I don't want them thinking Jillian is doing favors of any sort for me. One, she's not, and two, there's her professional rep among the guys to think of. I need to scramble to protect her privacy. Just like I'd do on the field if a cornerback sneaked up on me, I hunt for a way to escape the secondary. "It was a thank you gift for doing the calendar, guys. That's all. Even if I wanted something more, there's nothing happening, and I respect her choices."

Cooper claps me on the back. "Good man, and there are plenty of other fish in the sea. But what I want to know is this." He stops to scratch his chin as I wait for him to say more. "How the hell is your big ego handling the rejection?"

Harlan smiles faintly in faux sympathy. "It must be a brand-new feeling. Do we need to take you to therapy to process all this?"

I shake my head, amused and impressed at their bottomless appetite for giving me shit. "Yes, please schedule me an appointment right after yours."

Harlan laughs, chewing on a slice of fruit. "I do have a long-standing appointment with a shrink, since it takes time each week to process how awesome I am." He finishes the slice. "I'm as awesome as this fruit. Holy shit. This is good."

And we're back to safer ground. Grabbing another

pomelo from the bag, I hold it over my head. "Not only do pomelos bring good fortune, but they're full of antioxidants that are so very healthy for you," I say, adopting a TV-commercial-style tone.

"You can say that again." My agent's voice booms.

I snap my gaze to see Ford striding over to us as I peel one. "How'd you get in?"

"Magic," he says, snapping his fingers. "Or maybe the equipment manager told me all my favorite clients were here, and look at all of you. But especially you," he says, pointing at me. "You're already sounding like a spokesman."

Cooper claps my back and speaks to Ford. "See? I told you we could clean up our wild child."

"That's why I'm here," Ford says, grabbing his shades and removing them with the kind of panache you only see from the coolest dudes on film. Still, I won't let his slickness sway me. I've been burned, and I want to see what the man has to offer. He points two fingers at me. "Can you say Paleo Pet?"

"Uh. Yeah. *Paleo Pet.*"

He thrusts a fist in the air. "I love it. And I have a delivery of Paleo Pet Food for Small Breeds coming to your house this afternoon to see if your man Cletus likes it."

I knit my brow. "Someone is sending me dog food? I know my last agent was a thief, but I do have enough dough to buy food for a ten-pound Chihuahua mix."

Cooper slaps his thigh, laughing at me. "Dude, I think someone's trying to tell you Paleo Pet is courting you and Cletus."

And the switch goes on. The light flashes bright. "A dog food company?" I scratch my head. "I guess I didn't make the connection because you said you were chasing down an organic quick-serve restaurant."

"And that's still in play," Ford says, rubbing his palms together. "Don't you worry—I have lots of irons in the fire for you. But this one got hot real quick, and Paleo Pet is one of the fastest-growing pet food companies. Big budget, big plans, and now Paleo Pet has big eyes on you, and if your little guy likes his chow, and if you feel good about it—well then, we might have ourselves a sweet new deal."

I blink, processing the unexpected news as I pull off a section of fruit. "What do you mean they've had their eyes on me?"

"They came running to me like a dog with a tennis ball, wanting to play fetch as soon as they saw your pics the last few days. You're like a politician kissing babies and then endorsing diapers. Apparently, when your feed is full of you kissing dogs and trying to find homes for rescue pups, the dog food makers of the world all want to romance you." Ford parks his hands on his hips. "Plus, why didn't you tell me you won an all-county dog agility competition this summer? I had to track that shit down on my own."

Harlan's eyes bug out. "No way. That is rich. You didn't tell us that, either. Do you and Cletus do synchronized handstands in a ring or something?"

I roll my eyes. "No, asshole. He jumps and weaves through poles and climbs ladders like the badass dog he is. I taught him all that this summer, like the badass trainer I am."

"You have a secret skill, and you kept it from us." Harlan runs a hand through his long hair. "I cannot wait to have a field day with this."

I hold up a finger. "If you have a field day with this, then I will steal all your clothes from your locker and leave you with nothing but a little pie-baking apron to wear after a game."

Harlan seems to consider that. "I would gladly wear an apron and nothing else. I'm not ashamed of my body or my baking skills."

"And we are now legally required to prank Harlan with an apron," Rick declares, drumming his hands on the stand in front of us.

"And yes, Cletus won the blue ribbon because he is smart and I am awesome. Case closed. I don't brag about it because I just do it for fun. For a break from the game and all that stuff. I'm not trying to make a name as a dog agility dude or whatever."

Cooper holds up his fist for knocking. "And I thought the time you leapt ten feet in the air and nabbed a ball that was en route for interception was quite possibly one of your finest moments. But this might top it."

Ford clears his throat. "Gentlemen, I know I've interrupted a critical moment as the four of you debate important issues while warding off scurvy, but I need to speak to this man."

"Take him away," Cooper shouts.

Ford waves for me to join him. "We have business to discuss. And go get your T-shirt. It's not the equipment manager's job to pick it up."

I nod, oddly enjoying Ford's directive. I like that the guy cares about little things, like not leaving clothes on the field.

I trot to the shirt, grab it, and tug it on, then say goodbye to the guys as I leave the field with Ford. He gives me the down-low on the potential deal. I nod, taking it all in.

"Call me later and let me know if you're in. I have an idea I need to work on in the meantime to make this deal go swimmingly."

I raise an eyebrow. "What's the idea?"

"Don't you worry about it. Let me take care of the details."

* * *

Cletus parks his little butt on the tiled floor, waiting as patiently as a dog possibly can. It's one of those sits where he's on edge but doing his best to be a good boy.

I scoop some of the Paleo Pet food that's supposedly made from ingredients Cletus would have captured in the wild ten thousand years ago if, you know, a ten-pound lap dog was capable of stalking deer or elk.

"All right, buddy. Give me your best *Top Chef* verdict." I rattle the silver bowl and set it on his blue place mat with a cartoon bone illustration on it.

He chows down, finishing off his dish in less than forty seconds then giving me some serious puppy-dog eyes as he wags his tail.

I scratch his chin. "You might as well just say *may I have some more, please*, the way you wolfed that down in mere seconds."

Let me be frank. Cletus doesn't disdain a lot of food, being a dog and all. But he seems to dig this chow, so that works for me.

I hold up my palm, and he lifts his paw in response. "High five." Cocking his head to the side, he puts his tiny paw against mine, and I get such a kick out of the size disparity that I snap a shot and post it online, tagging it #helpinghands.

I take him to the small backyard that's a rarity in the city, and he runs through a few of his favorite obstacles on the mini course I set up. "Good boy," I tell him as he races up a ramp then down the other side. Afterward, I leash him and we head through the hilly streets of our hood to burn off the rest of his energy.

Along the way, I check my email. A note from Trevor about when he wants to shoot his show again. An email from my mom saying she can't wait to see me when I visit for dinner soon. I spot a reply from Garrett Snow, the left tackle who tore his ACL.

Recovery is taking longer than they all thought. But that's just the way the cookie crumbles. Or the knee, I should say! Let's grab a beer sometime? I'm in town.

I heave a sigh as I write back with a *Yes, let's make a plan, and I'm sorry to hear.*

My mind trips back to the game last season when he was hit hard on a pass rush, landing wrong on his left knee. Trouble was, his injury was exacerbated in the worst way possible. I saw it in replays—I was the one who caught that pass. He was the one who went down in a pile, a reminder that the game is here today and gone tomorrow.

That's why I need to make the most of my opportunities. I dial Ford. "I have a verdict."

"I can't wait. Give it to me."

"The food is Cletus-approved, so I guess that means I have a Paleo dog."

Ford hoots. "Excellent. That also means we have a sponsorship deal."

"Yes. We have a deal. I'm in," I say, since the terms he shared earlier were good.

"Fantastic. I'll send the papers today, and you and Trevor can review and e-sign them."

"We'll do it."

"Now listen, I told you I had an idea for the deal. Are you ready?"

I nod. "I'm ready. Hit me."

"You know how Paleo Pet loved that shot of you on social the other day?"

"Yep. That's what got their attention, and that was Jillian's idea."

"It's like you can read my mind."

"What do you mean?" I ask as we stop at a light on Fillmore and wait for it to change. A woman with light blue hair walks past me and then snaps her head in my direction, perhaps recognizing me.

She raises her phone, and it's clear she's taking a shot. I smile for the candid camera, Cletus waiting at my side.

"What I mean is this: social media is everything these days. They found you on social, you're doling out bits and pieces of the calendar on social. Your image is on social. And image is so key these days to sponsorships deals. Brands are cautious as hell. They've been burned by things athletes say and do. And since we want to keep you on the straight and narrow, I asked a certain someone to help out."

A strange feeling of dread courses through me when

the light changes. I head into the crosswalk. "Who's the someone?" I ask carefully, hoping he doesn't say a name that starts with *J*.

"Jillian." He says it as if he's Santa, delivering me a great and wonderful gift.

My feet feel leaden. My shoulders sag. "And her job is what exactly?"

"She said she'd help you with your social media. Make sure we keep you on the right path. The thing is, now that you're getting on the sponsorship gravy train, we really can't have you riding the gravy train of women. I know that's one of the best parts of being a pro athlete, and I'm not asking you to keep your dick in your pants. I'm just asking you to keep it off social media. Can you do that for me? Be good, behave, keep up a wholesome image? Jillian knows PR, and she's more than happy to help."

As I walk past a row of pastel-colored Victorian homes, I nod, a little heavily. His directive doesn't bother me, per se, so I'm not entirely sure why I'm bummed. But I am. "I'll be a good boy."

Though it feels a little bit like I'm a dog who doesn't come when called, and the only way to keep me in check is with a leash. Hell, maybe I am. Maybe I've been too bad, too naughty. Maybe I've been caught on the kitchen counter, eating the people food one too many times. There's a part of me that's a little irked, a bit irritated at what my reputation has come to. I never set out to be a party boy. Hell, I don't even think I'm some sort of poster child for the wild NFL lifestyle. I've definitely reined it in over the last year or so. But I understand that perception sometimes dictates reality. A few bad pictures, a couple of inappropriate shots—along with a bad seed of an agent—and I'm tarnished.

Ford is simply trying to untarnish me.

I suppose it can't hurt to do what he says.

I suppose that also means it would look bad if I kept flirting with the woman who's supposed to be helping me look like a good boy. Put aside the fact that she's displayed zero interest in me—even if she were to suddenly, out of nowhere, be awed by my charming-as-a-Chihuahua-meets-a-golden-retriever self, would that be the brightest idea to let something happen?

She's going to be the behind-the-scenes director for my new image. If I'm trying to be the face of a brand for the first time in more than a year, I need to make sure I'm conducting all my business aboveboard.

Which means I probably shouldn't try to make Jillian my bedroom business.

That's why I'm bummed, since this new world order means no more cherry pies for Jillian. Time to turn down the flirting dial with her.

But the next day when Jillian rings the bell, I'm not so sure I want to be a good boy. The way she looks in that pink dress makes me want to be very bad.

10

JILLIAN

Standing on his porch, Jones looks me over from head to toe with those intense blue eyes, and my stomach flips like a traitorous creature.

I set a hand on my belly, as if that will calm me down. But it's ineffective, and I have to wonder if the guy does this on purpose—gives women those I'm-undressing-you eyes. Whether he *knows* the effect he has on us and he uses it for fun.

Then, I want to smack my forehead, because of course he does.

That's why I'm doing the calendar with him. That's why his agent asked me to help him out. Because he *has* an extraordinary effect on women, he's a notorious flirt, and he's too well-known for his antics. We need to make him known for other things.

Like how he rescued that dog.

Like how he loves his family.

Like how he looks out for his friends.

He raises an arm, resting his hand against the frame of his front door. "So," he says, taking his time with the word, like he plans to play with it as a cat does an insect, "are you officially my PR person now?"

A nervous laugh bursts from my throat. "I thought I'd always been your PR contact for the team."

He runs his hand through his hair, flashing a lopsided grin then a wink. "Sorry. I meant are you my *personal* PR person now?"

That word zips through me like an electric charge. A light gust of wind blows my hair across my cheeks, and I tuck the strands behind my ear, grateful for the temporary distraction courtesy of San Francisco's windy morning. I shiver lightly from the chill. "Yes, that seems to be the case, and I'm happy to do it."

He cocks his head to the side. "Are you like my babysitter?"

My jaw drops. "What? No. No. No. That's ridiculous. I'm not a babysitter."

He arches a brow. "A nanny?"

I smirk. "Jones, I would hope you've outgrown the need for a nanny."

"That's up for debate, it seems. But maybe you're my governess?"

I roll my eyes and gesture to the car at the curb. "I'm not your nanny, I'm not your babysitter, and I'm definitely not your governess. I'm here to help you create the best image possible. I can market, publicize, and help you manage putting the best foot forward," I say, my tone earnest, my meaning important. "I believe in what I do. I know you're a great guy, and I want the world to see what I've seen in the last couple days."

"Yeah?"

"That's why I said yes when Ford asked for my help. I'm not interested in being anyone's au pair. I am very interested, though, in showing this city what good things our team does on and off the field. Including you." I take a breath and try to read him. To understand what's beneath the teasing. I think I know what it is. He wants a choice. "But if you don't want me to help out, I'll step back and we can stick to just the calendar. I told Ford I'd do this for your new deal, because I want to be the one to help you if you need it, and it's the kind of help I can give. Since you signed the contract yesterday, and the folks at Paleo Pet are local, they want to stop by the shoot later today. Take some pictures, chat, and so on. I'm happy to be there by your side the whole time, making sure you're comfortable with everything, and you're represented in the best way possible. But if those aren't your wishes, and if it isn't what you need, then I'll be hands-off." I hold up my palms as if I'm backing away.

In a heartbeat, he grabs my wrists. Possessively. A thrill rushes through me, like a drumbeat pulsing in my veins. I look away from him briefly. I can't make eye contact when he does this, when he touches me. If I do, he'll know. He'll realize I'm just like all the other women who fling panties at him, who chase him down in bars, who line up at the players' entrance to become his football floozy for the night. I won't ever be someone's football floozy, and I can't let him see for a second that I want some of the same things those other women want from him. *Him.*

"Don't be hands-off," he says, his voice soft. He runs a thumb over my wrist. "You have very nice hands."

I roll my eyes because it's the only way I can hide that my stomach is flipping and flopping from that one gentle slide of his thumb on my skin.

"And you have nice eyes that you roll at me as if I can't tell you're rolling them."

I turn my gaze back to him with a smirk that I quickly wipe away. "Do you want me to help you with your image? If you don't, say the word, and I'll respect it."

With his hands around my wrists, he stares into my eyes, and it's unnerving. He doesn't blink. He doesn't look away. This must be how he is on the field, watching like a hawk, staring, studying, developing a plan in a split second. The man has such intensity behind those blue eyes.

They're darker than usual, then they seem to glitter. Turn playful, even. "Nah. I'm just feeling you out."

Feel me up instead.

I shut my eyes momentarily, willing away the thought. This is how the man reels them in. He's charming and funny and sweet, and so good-looking it hurts my chest sometimes. It's dangerous how handsome he is and how much that affects me. I can't let the way my body reacts to him sway me. We're coworkers, and I have a job to do.

I open my eyes, square my chest, and smile my best PR grin. "I'll make sure it's fun. I promise."

"Anything with you is fun." Then his tone turns more serious, more earnest. "And listen, Jillian . . ."

"Yes?"

"I really appreciate you wanting to work with me on this. I'm a lucky bastard to have someone like you helping me."

I wink. "Wait till you get my bill."

He flinches as if surprised by this news. "Yeah? So it's a lot?"

Given how many times he toys with me—hello, towel ploy—I can't resist a little payback. "Oh, Ford didn't tell you how much I cost?"

"No, he didn't mention it."

I purse my lips as if he's going to be shocked at the number. "You want to know? You think you can handle it?"

Parking his hands on his hips, he says, "I think I can handle it." But I detect a few nerves still under his bravado, and they amuse me to no end.

I draw a deep breath as if this will be tough for him to stomach. Then, I borrow a page from his playbook, lean in a little closer, and whisper, "It's free."

He's silent at first, then a smirk spreads across his face, and he shakes his head, amused. He slow claps. "Well played, Jillian. Well played, indeed."

I toss my hair over my shoulder. "By the way, that was for the *Sporting World* shoot when you thought I would pick up your towel and stare at your ass."

He pretends to peer at his butt. "It's a nice ass."

"Why don't we get that ass in the car and get out of town for the day?"

"Let's do it," he says, and touches my shoulder. "But I did mean it. Thank you."

I smile, a huge, genuine grin. "You're welcome."

As he shuts the door to his home and locks it, my phone beeps. "My father is calling," I tell Jones, then say, "Hi, Dad," into the phone.

"Hey, sweet pea."

"What's going on? I'm heading up your way right now," I say as I walk down the steps.

"You are?"

"Yes, I have a photo shoot with one of the players in

St. Helena later this afternoon, and then another one in the morning in Yountville, so I'll be staying in wine country."

"And you aren't going to come by and visit? I'm devastated."

"I just saw you last week for lunch. Sheesh, you're demanding."

"Can I help it if I like seeing my little girl?"

"Dad," I chide as I reach the town car. "I'm not your little girl."

Jones smirks and grabs the handle, opening the back door. *Thank you*, I mouth.

"You are, sweet pea, and always will be," my dad says, as I settle into the black leather seat. "And for that, I suppose I'll forgive you for not seeing me today."

Buckling my seat belt, I laugh. "I'll come up next weekend again. And when the season starts soon, you're coming to all the home games."

"Damn straight I am. I'm a Renegades fan for life."

"That's the only kind of football fan to be," I say, and Jones winks at me, giving a thumbs-up as he buckles into the seat next to mine. "So what are you up to today?"

"I taught class this morning, and now I'm waiting for a new desk to be delivered. Do I know how to party or what?"

"A new desk is clearly the definition of a fiesta," I say as the driver pulls away from the curb.

"When will you be in Napa? In case I feel a disturbance in the Force."

"It's about an hour and twenty minutes."

"By my estimate, that gives you a full hour to snooze in the car."

Briefly, I glance away from Jones. "Dad, I only did that in cars when I was younger."

"I bet you fall asleep now," he says, then his line goes quiet for a second. "Sweet pea, I need to go. That's the delivery company. I'll talk to you later."

After I end the call, Jones gives me an *I'm waiting* look. "What?"

He gestures for me to keep talking. "Tell me about your dad."

"You want to hear about my father?" I ask, my brow knitting in curiosity.

He crosses his arms. "Yes. Contrary to my party-boy reputation and the word on the street about the size of my hands, I have a big heart, too, and I want to know about Mr. Moore. You said he teaches?"

I can't help but smile at the way he makes light of himself at the same time he earnestly seems to want to know about me. My heart warms like someone turned on a lamp and it's glowing, brightening the room. "Yes, he's an adjunct professor at a community college in Napa, teaching digital journalism to freshmen. He loves it. I think he was antsy being retired and needed something to do with all his energy."

"That's awesome. Good for him to find an outlet like that. Do his students love him?"

"I get the impression they do. They seem pretty engaged."

"And it sounds like he's chosen wisely when it comes to sports. Did I catch on correctly that he's a Renegades fan?"

"He goes to every home game."

"I love him already. You're pretty close to him? You see and talk to him regularly?"

"Yes, I try to visit him at least every other weekend. We've always been close. He's the person I've turned to for career advice over the years. He's never led me astray."

A huge smile crosses Jones's face. "Love that. Just love it. That's how it should be, you know? Being able to lean on and depend on your parents, your brothers, your sister." He tilts his head and scratches his chin. "But I'm curious about something. What did he think you'd do on the drive up?"

I grumble, "Sleep in the car."

"You managed the ride to Stinson the other day without napping. But that was a much shorter drive."

I wave a hand and fix on a grin, giving my best perky face. "I won't fall asleep. I'm wide awake."

But in thirty minutes, I'm yawning as we pass the San Rafael exit. As we cross to Novato, my eyes flutter shut.

True to form, I wake up forty-five minutes later in wine country with my head in Jones's lap.

My head is in his lap.

I don't move. This might be a dream. I blink. The world is sideways, and Jones's hand is in my hair. He's actually running his hand across my hair. Gently. Casually. Sweetly.

It feels better than it should.

It feels so incredibly good. Like comfort I didn't know I needed. Like friendship I wasn't sure we had.

I close my eyes, and pretend to sleep until the car pulls into the lot at the winery. This is all I will ever get of him, and I want to savor these last few minutes with his hands on me.

* * *

A curious orange kitten scampers over a wine barrel then climbs to the next one above it, balancing beautifully. He's like the king of the jungle—or the king of the winery where we'll shoot today's picture for the month of March. The winery is attached to a hotel, and we'll be spending the night here.

As the humane society rep watches the furry-faced creature, my phone beeps with a text message. I slide it open to see a note from Liam McHenry, the guy who owns Paleo Pet and is overseeing the new deal. He's arriving any minute, he says. I excuse myself to wait for him out front.

When a pickup truck pulls up, and a tall, trim, and surprisingly handsome sandy-haired man steps out, I'm surprised he's Liam. But the license plate—MEOW ARF —is a big tip-off.

I'm surprised because I expected Liam to have a driver. That's what I'm accustomed to when guys from big sponsors show up. I figured he'd be sporting a tailored suit, too, rather than jeans and a crisp button-down.

His smile shows off straight white teeth. "You must be Jillian. Ford Grayson raves about you."

"Pleasure to meet you, Liam." We shake hands. "And a little bird told me Cletus raved about your dog food."

Running a hand through his hair, Liam laughs. "Man, we are thrilled about Jones. Love that guy. Love his commitment to excellence. To healthy eating. To being the best in every single game. He just delivers on the field, doesn't he?"

"You can't argue with fifteen hundred and two yards

for the season and fourteen yards on average per pass," I say, sharing Jones's stats from last year. "Not to mention his love of animals. He'll be a great face for your brand."

"I'm stoked, Jillian. When I found out about him and Cletus, I knew he was the guy I needed to take us to the next level." Liam rubs his hands together. "He's such a fan favorite already, and we really want to make sure the moms who buy our dog food love him the way we love him."

That sparks my curiosity. "Your consumers are mostly moms?"

"That's what our research has shown. They're the ones who seek out the specialty pet food, since they're usually already into organic food for their kids, and so many dogs and cats these days are just like family."

I make a mental note to remind Jones that Paleo Pet sees itself as a family-centric brand. "You need to come see Jones's co-star today, then. This little kitten will melt your heart, and we can also take a shot of just you and Jones to post on social—something to show you're now in business with him." A picture like that can help spread the word about the sponsorship and continue to present Jones in a new light. A true win-win. The calendar teaser shots, though? Those I keep for the team feed.

I gesture to the door of the winery. Liam quickly strides ahead, holding it open for me. "I'm glad we're working together, Jillian."

"Me, too," I say, not because Liam is handsome, but because he's straightforward, confident, and laid-back.

And fine, it doesn't hurt that he's easy on the eyes.

When we reach the room with the barrels, Jones

glances over then does a double take when he sees Liam with me.

As if he's surprised for some reason.

But then the look on his face turns to a scowl.

I have no idea why he'd be upset with a sponsor, but I'll have to remind him later to keep on a happy face.

11

JONES

What is this feeling in my chest?

It's like a ball of steel lodged in my sternum. I'm tight, a little tense, a bit frustrated.

It's not exactly like when we've lost a big game, but this is damn close to how I feel when I'm home in January watching the playoffs on TV rather than competing in them. In fact, this is like when I watched our rivals, the Los Angeles Devil Sharks, hoist the Vince Lombardi trophy over their heads last year when they won the Super Bowl.

"Meow." From his spot on top of the wine barrel, Smoky bats at my shoulder again with a white paw that was burned in the fires a few months ago. The little dude is now nearly recovered, thanks to the local rescue that found and saved the stray, putting him in a foster home till he's able to be adopted. I give the cutie a kiss then return him to my shoulder for another shot, as per the photographer's orders.

"Perfect! A five-pound kitten perched on a two-hundred-fifty-pound athlete," the photographer coos as he snaps a shot.

Briefly, I glance over at Jillian, waiting for her to correct the guy. She knows my stats like the back of her hand and nearly always fires off corrections. But she doesn't shout *he's two hundred fifty-eight* since she's too busy charming my new sponsor.

That's when I know what this emotion is.

Jealousy.

Raw, bitter jealousy.

What the hell? I'm not a jealous guy when it comes to women. Never have been. But then, I've never really had the opportunity. Truth be told, I've never had a problem winning a woman over, and I'm not aware of a time when I lost out to another dude. Maybe I've had a lucky streak, or maybe it's the gift of being a pro baller. Either way, that's how it's been.

I sure as hell don't like this feeling when it comes to women, and I despise it when it comes to Jillian. As Smoky clambers over my shoulders while I lean against the wine barrels, I can't stop sneaking glances at Liam and Jillian, chatting in the corner. When I tune into their conversation, they're not even talking about pet food or sports. They're talking about school because it turns out he went to Stanford, just like her.

Fuck.

My ego is a little bit crushed. Now I have to contend with a brainiac CEO who has the good fortune to be a ringer for Ryan Gosling. Clearly, I have no choice but to ham it up. I kiss the orange kitten on the nose, inducing oohs and ahhs and huge smiles from everyone here at the shoot.

Including Jillian.

Take that, brainy boy. I've got a kitten and I'm not afraid to use it. I smooch the little fellow once more as the photographer encourages me to keep it up. As we move through different poses and set-ups, heading outside to the vineyard for the final round, I might walk a little taller, I might strut a little prouder, and I might generally do my best to make sure the camera—I'm *only* doing this for the camera—is having a field day with the pussycat and me.

When the shoot ends—complete with social media pics for the new deal—the kitten stretches in my arms, shuts his eyes, and purrs.

"You're a natural charmer," Liam remarks with an easy smile.

"Smoky's the one with all the moves." As I stroke the critter's soft head, it occurs to me I could take a clue from him in how to let go.

Be chill. Be cool. Liam is my new business partner, and I can't be envious of him, especially since there's no real reason to be. After I hand off Smoky to the humane society rep, I join Liam and Jillian at the outdoor table on the patio, sliding quickly into chatting about the partnership, upcoming plans, and the next steps with the deal. The entire time, I'm the casual, laid-back guy he hired, not the jealous asshat I was in my head a few minutes ago. As we segue away from business and riff on the toughest defenses in the league, Jillian's phone rings.

She picks up and listens then says, "Well, that doesn't sound very helpful, Dad."

A pause comes next, and I eavesdrop on her conversation even while Liam asks a question about the Baltimore secondary.

"I know you're terrible at putting things together," Jillian says. "It's not something you learned at journalism school."

My ears prick with interest, though I still manage to share my thoughts with Liam on that team's new cornerback.

Jillian continues, "I'll come do it."

That gets my attention even more.

"Dad. Let me help you, or at least let me use Task-Rabbit and send someone over." A quick silence follows. "Dad. It's what they do."

I clear my throat, reach across the table to set a hand on her arm, and smile. "I'll put your dad's desk together."

Her eyes light up. "You will? Are you sure?"

I nod. "Absolutely."

Liam laughs and holds up his hands. "Better him than me. I am not handy."

I puff up my chest. "Fortunately, I am."

She tells her dad she has a better solution, and he seems to agree to it. I relax for the rest of the conversation dissecting the pass rush, because I have something Liam doesn't have.

The chance to help Jillian where she needs it most right now.

* * *

I pat the top of the desk then knock it with a fist. "Sturdy as a three-hundred-fifty-pound lineman," I say to Aaron Moore. "Wait—this desk is way sturdier."

Jillian's tall, gray-haired father smiles from behind his horn-rimmed glasses as he surveys the newly assembled oak desk in his office. "My, that's some fine work. And to think Jillian said you were just a pretty face."

"Dad!"

I peer over my shoulder to catch a glimpse of red splashed across her cheeks, as she lounges in a leather chair in the corner of his office. But there's no denial from either one of them, and I won't deny, either, that I'm digging the fact that she told her dad she thinks I'm handsome.

Her dad winks at her then turns to me. "Thanks for doing this. Think it's cool for me to tell all the guys at the wine bar tonight that the all-pro receiver put together my desk?"

I smile as I set the screwdrivers in the tool set. "I'd expect nothing less. But only if you mention my pretty face."

"Jillian? You don't mind if I mention to the other fellas that you think Jones Beckett is pretty?"

Her jaw drops. "Dad! Are you trying to hit a new record for embarrassing me? You do know I work with Jones? As in *professionally*?"

Aaron drops his voice to a stage whisper. "Don't worry. I'll tell all the other widowers that she said you were a cutie-pie."

With a shit-eating grin, I nod. "Deal."

He extends a hand. "But seriously, I can't thank you enough for helping. Ever since my Vivian passed away, I've had to tackle all this fixing stuff on my own, and I'm terrible at it."

I raise an eyebrow. "Your wife was the handy one, sir?"

He nods proudly, gesturing to their home. "She was.

She kicked my butt around the house. Knew how to fix a furnace, rewire a dryer, hang a door."

"Damn," I say with an appreciative whistle as I snap the tool set shut. "That's impressive."

"You're telling me." He points to his daughter. "She taught this little lady how to fix a broken sink and how to install a new electrical outlet."

"You don't say? Jillian, you've been holding out on me. I had no idea you were so handy. And you didn't even offer to help me with the new desk." I pout.

She tips her chin at her dad as his golden retriever mix slumbers at her feet. "He refuses to accept my help."

Her dad jumps in. "She's my daughter. I can't let her do that stuff for me," he says then winks. "Plus, I mostly wanted bragging rights with the guys when she said you'd do it."

Jillian points to me. "Besides, you seemed all too happy to fix the desk, which gave me time to answer this pile of emails from reporters wanting to know about you and Paleo Pet, so there." She takes a beat. "And I made some trades on my fantasy baseball team that'll put even more distance between my Fire-Breathing Dragons and everyone else."

I shoot her a smile, laughing at the name of her fantasy team, as I inch the desk a little closer to the wall. "I was happy to do it." I swipe one hand against the other. "There you go. Jones Beckett, Furniture Assembly Specialist, at your service."

"You're a good man. How can I thank you?" her dad asks.

I rub a hand along the back of my neck and peer into the hall. The walls are lined with photographs, classic school shots of Jillian from over the years. "I'd really love it if you could show me some pictures of Jillian. Including, but not limited to, shots where she has braces, missing teeth, and terrible haircuts, since then I'll forever have something to hold over her."

Her brown eyes widen. "Jones. You're a troublemaker!"

Her father nods enthusiastically, pushing his glasses up the bridge of his nose. "I'll show you the whole lot, but bear in mind even with missing front teeth and a haircut she gave herself when she got bubblegum stuck in her bangs, she was still the loveliest kid ever. A ray of sunshine, too. We always used to say we were so damn lucky because we were matched with the happiest kid ever. She smiled all the time. Still does."

As if on cue, she demonstrates, and it looks all-natural. It's the genuine kind that comes from deep within as she listens to her father tell stories.

"She has a great smile," I say to him, but I'm looking at her.

And she's looking back at me. For a moment, our gazes hold, and I swear something flickers between us that wasn't there before. She's lingering longer, looking deeper, keeping her eyes on me more than she has in the past.

I'll take that, even though I shouldn't want it at all.

But I can't *un*want it, not now, not even in front of her dad.

He ushers me down the hall, giving me the tour of each school photo hanging on the wall, from her first-grade shot with a bowl haircut, to her second-grade one with two missing teeth, to a seventh-grade image when she wore braces with light blue rubber bands.

In every single shot, she flashes a bright, cheerful grin. "I sometimes wonder where that smile came from. I wish I could take credit for it," Aaron says, tapping a frame.

"I bet you can, sir. You're a good father. You bring out that smile by giving her a home and loving your kid."

"That's always been easy, from the first day I met her."

He waves me along, showing me some high school shots of her skiing, winning a medal for taking first place in a race, then her graduation shot, with Jillian wearing a cap and gown. "Valedictorian," he says, pride rich in his tone.

Jillian follows behind, and when I catch her gaze, she mouths to me, *He's such a dad.*

But she's not making fun of the guy. She's simply acknowledging that he's doing what he's supposed to do —show off his kid. Near the end of the row of pictures is one last shot that looks to be from her senior year of high school. Her long black hair falls straight over her shoulders, her eyes sparkle, and there's a confidence in her smile that says she knows she's going places in life.

Her father heads to the living room, where the dog has migrated, now snoozing on the couch. "Down, Merlot. Make room for the people."

The dog obliges, sliding off the couch and resuming his nap on the floor as her dad grabs a photo album from a shelf under the coffee table. He pats the couch, and I sit next to him, with Jillian on the other side. She peers at the album then groans. "Cue the embarrassment soundtrack now, please," she says as he flips open to her baby pictures.

I laugh instantly as I check out the shots of her

dressed like a Michelin Man toddler for the winter, complete with rosy red cheeks. "In China, they tend to always think babies are cold," he explains. "They dress them warmly year-round. When we were there adopting her, it was September, and Chinese women would stop us on the street to say 'lucky baby' and 'baby is cold.'"

Jillian wraps her arms across her chest and shivers in an over-the-top fashion. "Evidently, I was freezing all the time."

Laughing, Aaron points to a photo of a baby Jillian licking a popsicle in the middle of a Chinese market. Her mom holds her, and the look on Jillian's face is pure happiness. "Yes, she was freezing with her popsicle."

He flips through the album, showing me pictures of the now twenty-eight-year-old woman when she was a tiny thing. My eyes land on one in particular—a shot of Aaron next to his wife, holding a black-haired baby. Emotion floods their expressions. I can see tears in their eyes, in the set of their mouths. "This was her gotcha day," Aaron says softly, reverently. "This was at the hotel in Wuhan. There were about eight other American families. All had traveled to China at the same time after they'd been matched with girls from the orphanage. They brought the girls into this meeting room at the hotel, called out our last names, followed by each baby's Chinese name, and then we held her for the first time. We fell deeply in love with her right away. It was instant."

As I stare at the photo of the newly minted family, all I see is that love. It's present in every single pixel. A lump rises dangerously in my throat, but I tamp it down. "This is beautiful, sir. She was a lucky girl to be matched with you and your wife, and I'm sure you feel you were just as lucky."

"I did. I still do."

I raise my gaze and meet Jillian's eyes once more. In them, I see a hint of a tear. She looks away, wiping a finger over her cheek as she purses her lips.

Aaron wraps his arm around his daughter, tugs her close, and plants a quick kiss on her cheek. She doesn't flinch, she doesn't say, *no, Dad*. She lets him, and it's one of the sweetest moments I've ever seen.

* * *

After we say goodbye, the door clicks shut behind us and we head down the stone path to the car. "Thank you so much for helping him. I can't tell you how much it means to me. He tries hard to be independent, but he really did rely on my mom for a lot of things."

"I can see that in him. He was a man very much in love."

"He was," she says, and her voice wobbles as we reach the car. She grabs the handle then stops and gives me a curious stare. "Why did you want to see pictures of me as a kid?"

Even though I'm supposed to be a good boy, even though I ought to shut up, I can't resist saying, "I'm curious about you. I like hearing stories about who you were so I can better understand who you are now."

She blinks like she can't quite believe what I've said. "You're curious?" she repeats, as if I spoke in a foreign language. She taps her chest. "About me?"

My smile broadens. "Yes. Yes, I am. In fact, I think we

should have dinner together tonight at the hotel to satiate my curiosity."

It's only dinner. I'm not suggesting we stay the night in the same room. But just so we're all clear that this meal is on the up and up, I add, "We can talk about the sponsorship and other stuff."

"I'd love to talk about the deal," she says with a smile. Then, with a wink, she adds, "And other stuff."

Of course it's on the up and up, I tell myself. Of course it's professional curiosity. I didn't ask her for any other reason. Besides, I've managed to be such a good boy so far, there's no reason why I'd stop obeying all the rules.

After all, there's a lot on the line with this sponsorship deal, and I'm determined to keep it.

No matter how curious I am about Jillian, professionally or personally.

12

JILLIAN

The dining room at the inn is stuffed with wine country visitors. Long, lingering dinners among groups and couples play out at the tables, and the bar is packed, too. But getting a table won't be a problem since I made a reservation as soon as Jones suggested dinner.

That's my job, after all. I requested a table in a corner and asked the manager to seat us quickly, if possible. Too many times I've gone out to dinner with athletes and they've been inevitably mobbed by people seeking autographs. There's nothing wrong with that, and Jones has always been generous with the fans. But that sort of attention is best on the way out of an eatery, so you have an excuse to say goodbye, rather than on the way in, when everyone stares and snaps pics during a meal.

While I'm not dining with the likes of Tom Cruise, the reality is a star athlete is a local hero, recognizable by many. Add in the team's winning record and Jones's own performance on field, and that's a recipe for lots of photos and lots of stares. Jones is the second most popular player on the team, behind the quarterback, so I have to do my best to make sure he can enjoy simple things, like a business dinner.

As we reach the hostess stand at the end of the bar, I conduct my requisite scan of the dining room, making sure Jones won't be mobbed.

I home in on a tiara at the far end of the bar. A sash. A pink shirt with the words *Maid of Dishonor* on it. My radar pings instantly,

warning me to closely watch the bachelorette party with its dozen women wearing slinky, short dresses and the maid of dishonor who's urging them all to do shots.

As the blonde in the pink shirt guzzles her tequila, her eyes stray to the man at my side. Setting down the glass, she blinks at Jones, and the scene seems to play out in slow motion. Her hungry eyes roam up and down his tall frame, then return to his face as recognition sets in.

She turns to the brunette next to her and whispers in her ear. The brunette snaps her gaze to Jones, her jaw falling open.

I touch his arm, whispering, "Beware of bridesmaids at ten o'clock," just as the hostess arrives with a cheery, professional smile on her high-cheekboned face, asking if we're the Moore party of two. "I can seat you right away."

Jones knits his brow, indicating he didn't hear me. I squeeze his arm tighter and try again to warn him. But the bachelorette party blitz has launched. The women scramble, rushing toward him as other diners jerk their heads at the commotion.

Jones is no stranger to a defense coming in his direction. Even so, there's little anyone can do to avoid this tackle.

My God, are you Jones Beckett?

We love you!

Sign my sash!

Sign my shirt!

The maid of dishonor jams her pink polka-dot-encased iPhone close to him, and says, "Can we please have a picture?" while the hostess asks the women to please give him some space.

Jones simply smiles.

Which is precisely what I want him to do, but when I see the maid of dishonor wedge herself next to him while calling over the woman in white, I can see how this will play out on Twitter.

Jones joins bachelorette party.

Jones parties with the bride.

The Hands gets his hands on the bride.

I wrap my fingers tighter around his arm, and tug him away with a hard jerk. "Excuse me, ladies. I have to take him to an interview right now. Have a wonderful wedding, and go Renegades."

Like the badass publicist I am, I guide him out of the restaurant in seconds, before anyone can get a photo of him that could be taken out of context. I march him through the lobby to the elevator, and then I stab the up button, keeping a watch for any stray bridesmaids.

He looks at me, slightly bewildered. "You're like a bodyguard."

I laugh while shaking my head. "Not in the least."

"No, you fucking are," he says, his tone full of admiration, as if he's seeing a new side of me. "I've known you to move through reporters on the field like that"—

he snaps his fingers to demonstrate—"but a wild pack of bridesmaids is riskier than running through the Dallas defense."

"And that's exactly why I dragged you away."

"Understood. But there's only one problem." His stomach rumbles. "I'm hungry."

I laugh. "I'm famished, too. But there are other restaurants in this town. I just wanted to get you away from there so we could regroup."

He raises a finger, indicating he has a question. "Scale of one to ten: what are the chances if we leave for another restaurant that they might find us on the way?"

I curve up the corner of my lips, considering. "I give it a seven." I pause, cycling through options. "Do you like room service?"

He scoffs. "Who doesn't like room service?"

Kevin, for one. My ex shuddered at the prospect of food delivered to a hotel room. "I knew this guy who hated it. He refused to order room service, no matter how tired he was when he traveled."

"Does not compute."

I roll my eyes. "He said it was a cop-out. He had this whole routine he did about how room service always takes forty-five minutes and all you get is a Cobb salad and cold french fries."

"Let me guess. This guy is an ex?"

I smile sheepishly. "An ex and a cheater, too, to be precise."

Narrowing his eyes, he mutters, "Asshole." He inches a little closer, dropping his voice to a whisper. "Don't worry. I don't suffer from that problem. Not the asshole part, not the cheating part, and not the room service part. Quite the contrary. I could write a song about it, give a speech on the wonder of room service, pen an ode to how awesome it is to be able to order a grilled cheese sandwich and tomato soup to be brought to your room. That's how much I like room service."

"Me, too."

The elevator arrives, and we step inside quickly as he offers me a hand to high-five. When I smack it, he threads his fingers through mine while the door closes. He doesn't let go. I don't think it's romantic, but I'm also not sure what this is. Maybe it's friendly? Perhaps it's some sort of solidarity gesture, since we're partners in this getaway plan and fellow aficionados of room service.

Too bad my skin tingles as he touches me. My chest heats and my lips part. My body longs for more contact. The craving for him magnifies, and I wish he'd take my wrists in his hands, lift them over my head, and crush his mouth to mine.

But that's a dream.

He lets go to press the elevator button for the fifth floor, and my hand feels strangely empty now without his, so I cover up the lonely sensation with more chatter. "Let the record reflect that room service is literally one of the greatest inventions ever. Quite possibly up there with electricity and the wheel."

See? I'm so not bothered by him dropping my hand.

I'm over it.

"Let's get it, then."

"Definitely," I say as the elevator slows at my floor. As the doors open, I wave a quick goodbye, since he's staying on the seventh floor. "See you tomorrow."

He steps out into the hallway. "*Together*, Jillian. Let's have room service *together*."

Stopping in my tracks, I blink and swallow hard. "Together?" It comes out like a croak. "I thought by room service you meant we'd go to our separate rooms."

He shakes his head, his blue eyes sparkling with playfulness. "Not when we have *other stuff* to discuss. Want to get room service in my room? Or yours?"

His eyes drift to the elevator behind him. The doors have closed, and it's heading down.

I'm not sure which room feels more dangerous. His or mine. Mine or his.

"Yours? Since it's your floor?" he suggests, and at least now I don't have to figure out the answer to a trick question.

I take a shaky breath and say yes.

We walk down the hall in silence. When I stop at room 508, I take out my card key with nervous fingers, fighting like hell to keep it steady as I wave it over the card reader.

For a brief moment, I picture other women he's taken to other hotel rooms. I wonder if he had room service with them. Talked to them. Helped their fathers assemble desks. Looked at their baby photos.

Then I ask why I'm torturing myself thinking of other women, and their dads, and their desks, and their baby photos. When I turn the knob, open the door, and step into the room, I banish them from my brain.

I can't think of anything but the huge risk I'm taking by letting him into my room.

And yet, it's a risk I want to take.

I don't mind eating alone. I meant what I said—I love room service with a deep and abiding passion.

But I'm also learning how much I like being with him. Maybe that's the bigger risk. Perhaps it's the bigger issue, too—not what other women have done in hotel rooms with him, but if they've enjoyed talking to him as much as I do.

I fervently hope the answer is no. I want that part of him all to myself.

* * *

We share most of the food, working our way through a Caesar salad, a mango and mint salad, an appetizer of salted edamame, a steak for him, and french fries for me.

"Just one," I say, waggling a fry. "You can do it."

He laughs, shaking his head. "You temptress."

"You healthy eater, you." I swipe the fry through some ketchup and brandish it like an offering. "Can you resist now?"

Rolling his eyes, he grabs the fry and pops it into his mouth, chewing then making a satisfied smack of his lips. "There. Just so you know I'm not afraid to break the rules every now and then." He holds my gaze as he says that, and I want to look away, but I can't. I just can't. I like looking at him far too much for my own good. So much *I* might break the rules if I have a chance.

He taps the table. "I'll have you know, you addicted me to a certain citrus."

"You bought more pomelos?"

He nods. "I can't get enough of them."

For some stupid reason, that makes me happy.

As we eat, we talk about the calendar and the sponsorship, but quickly the conversation moves to other matters. I ask him about his family and learn how close he is to his two brothers and his sister. He tells me he's saving money in retirement accounts for all of them, and his greatest dream is to provide for every single Beckett. I learn, too, that he bought his parents a spacious new home, and he provides for them so they no longer have to work.

"That's seriously amazing, Jones," I say.

"They're as cool as your dad. You should meet them someday." The offer sounds so earnest that I nearly believe he means it.

"That sounds nice." I can almost picture driving up to their home, bringing a huge bouquet of fall flowers, meeting his mom and dad, chatting with them, since I'd be so eager to get to know the parents of my—

I swerve the car in the other direction. The not-my-boyfriend-in-any-way-shape-or-form direction. "I bet they're so proud of you for all you've done on and off the field."

"They are, but I'm proud of them, too. Raising four kids on next to nothing wasn't easy, and that's why I work hard to take care of them now. I guess that's why some of the things that happened with my last agent were so frustrating. I'm not suffering financially. But I want to be able to do everything I possibly can for them."

I nod, completely understanding the drive to help, to support. "I get it. I feel the same way about my dad. That's why I try to see him as much as possible. Just to be there."

"The least we can do is take care of the ones who took care of us. Hell, that's part of why I'm so glad my brother moved back to San Francisco from New York. He's the sibling I'm closest to, and helping him with his beer show is my way of repaying that smart bastard for the way he helped me in high school."

"He did?"

Jones nods. "He's the creative one in the family, and since eleventh grade essays on Huck Finn are the foundation of hell, Trevor made sure I didn't burn in the fiery depths." He pauses, then winks. "I bet you loved high school essays."

I narrow my eyes. "Confession: even though I was an English major, I think essays ought to be abolished. They are the devil's work."

His hand rises for another high five. Once more I smack back, and foolishly I wait for him to link hands with mine.

But he doesn't.

Instead, he gathers the plates on the tray, carries it to the door, sets it outside, then dials room service for a pickup. He brushes one hand against the other, and my heart free-falls. This is when he leaves. This is when our evening ends.

He raises a hand. "Question."

"Answer."

"How do you feel about movies?"

"Love them. The good ones, that is."

"*Mission Impossible*? Is that a good one?"

I laugh like his question is crazy. "Duh. More like a great one."

He gestures to the big-screen TV facing the bed. "Want to watch? When we checked in, I saw it was on pay-per-view."

The free-falling heart screeches to a stop. "Yes." My answer comes out more breathlessly than I intend.

I know this is a bad idea. I know this is flirting with

danger. But if we managed to eat dinner and chat in this hotel room, we can certainly manage to watch a movie.

He eyes my bed then hops on it, stretching out his long legs and parking his hands behind his head. He looks over at me, and I'm officially frozen. He'll need to pluck me from the ground like an ice sculpture because I can't move.

Where am I supposed to watch? The floor? The table?

The answer comes when he pats the spot next to him on the mattress.

My insides go up in flames, and a million dangerous thoughts speed through my head. Do I actually lie down next to him? Do I put my body near his? Horizontal and inches apart?

I'm fully clothed. He is, too. But still . . . that's a bed.

"Do you . . .?" I start to ask, but talking is so hard in this overheated state that I can't finish the sentence —*think this is a good idea?*

He must sense my question because he rolls his eyes. "It's a lot more comfortable than sitting in those awkward chairs for a two-hour flick," he says, reaching for the TV remote on the nightstand and clicking to the menu. "C'mon."

Here goes nothing.

I lie next to him, and he turns on the movie.

I don't know what to do with my arms. I let them hang at my sides, but I bet that looks dumb. I cross them at my chest. I bet I look mad. I lace my hands together across my belly. I bet I look prim.

I want to just lounge and stretch and be cool as Tom Cruise rappels into a vault in the CIA's headquarters, but I can't focus. I can't think about a single thing that

Ethan Hunt is doing on the screen when I'm literally six inches away from the man I've crushed on, lusted after, and now fear I'm starting to like.

Truly like.

Jones watches the screen intently, and I wish this was hard for him, too. All I can think about is the six inches between us and how much I wish they were zero. Half a foot feels insurmountable. But at the same time, if I moved my hand a little bit, then maybe a little more, I would touch his leg.

Subconsciously, or perhaps not so subconsciously at all, I let my hand fall from my waist to the mattress. A little closer now.

His gaze roams to my hand, dangerously near his hip.

He turns to me. His eyes lock with mine, and my breathing stops. I want to look away, but I want to stare into his deep blue eyes. With his voice a little gravelly, he asks, "Do you like the movie?"

My heart thumps hard against my chest. I lick my lips. "It's great."

"You're not going to fall asleep, are you?"

Lifting my neck a little, I shake my head, my hair spilling against the pillow. He watches as my hair moves. I watch his face. He looks at my hand. I glance at his hand. I swear it slides a millimeter closer to mine, then another, then more.

I'm a shooting star.

I'm lit up.

My body is full of electrons and neurons, pulsing and glowing bright.

His eyes stay on mine, not on the screen, not on Ethan. "If you do, though, you can fall asleep on me."

I swallow, but I can't get past the dryness in my throat. I don't think I can get past the desire to take him up on that, to snuggle up against him like the orange kitten, to let him pet me, stroke me, touch me.

Make me purr.

"Want to?" he asks. Is he saying what I think he's saying?

"Sleep on you?" Each word has its own longitude and latitude.

He nods. "Rest your head on me."

Oh God.

Oh, my.

I can't even process this moment. My brain has gone haywire, like a pinball machine out of whack, buzzers and lights whirring in a mad cacophony.

He lifts his arm, making room for me to rest my head in the crook, right there. I want to, and I'm terrified of how much I want to.

"You already slept on me in the car," he says, low and playful.

A soft laugh bursts from my throat, and I scoot a few more inches, resting my head on his chest. My body lines up with his. Our hips touch. My breasts are near his broad, strong chest. Our legs are so close I could drape one over his.

I glance down at my body to make sure I haven't flung myself at him.

Whew.

Good. I'm still lying flat on my back.

I stay like this, not moving, because if I do, I'll moan, I'll groan, I'll murmur. I'll blurt out something dangerous like *touch me, kiss me, take me.*

Briefly, I try to focus on the screen, to zoom in on the

secret agent. What would the king of impossible missions do in this risky situation?

He'd find a way out of danger. Clearly, the only path for me is to go full possum.

With Ethan Hunt somewhere in Prague, my mind drifts, my eyes flutter closed, and I fall asleep.

* * *

Later, I wake to a dark room. To a clock flashing 3:25 in bright green. To a TV screen showing the soft blue glow of the hotel's pay-per-view menu.

And to a hand on my waist. To a big, strong body pressed to mine. To an arm slung across my stomach.

And something else.

Something hard against my butt.

Very hard. Very long.

Soft, steady breath flutters across my neck, the gentle whoosh of a sleeping man.

A man who is wrapped around me. Who's snuggling me. Who's erect.

I don't even try to fight off a grin. Inside, I'm doing a dance. No, a striptease, because Jones is hard as he touches me.

But wait. I shouldn't read anything into this. It's not about me. It's a three-thirty-in-the-morning erection. It's a dream hard-on. It's the body's natural reaction to sleep.

Only, I want to read everything into it, especially as he murmurs something unintelligible and tugs me closer, lining my body up against his. Like that, he buries his face in my hair, and I melt into a puddle of woman as he spoons me, breathing in my hair, his lips close to my neck.

I'm on fire. I'm turned on from head to toe, aroused in every molecule of my body. If he touched me where I want him most, I'd go off like a rocket. If I slid a hand in my panties, I'd finish myself off in seconds.

It never takes long for me to reach the cliff when Jones pleasures me in my fantasies. He's taken me to the edge so many times. Countless times.

I let out a soft noise, a quiet moan as I wriggle the slightest bit against him, wanting to feel his length. Wanting the reminder once more of this turned-on man, even if it's only sleep that did it to him.

But what if it was sleep plus me? I sigh, a needy, desperate wish of a sigh.

I should leave. But it's my room.

And he's sound asleep, so I can't kick him out.

I have no choice but to stay like this, tangled up with him.

I close my eyes and pretend he's mine for now. I pretend he belongs to me, and we're together, all through the night. I drift off like that, and it feels as if I'm floating on a cloud.

When I wake at seven thirty, the bed is empty.

He's gone.

13

JONES

"Jump!"

Cletus takes off on command, scurrying across my parents' yard and flying through the old tire swing hanging from a tree.

"Dude!" I raise my arms, and he leaps at me. I bend to my knees as he hops onto my thighs, slathering me with a dog kiss. "Did you see that, Mom?"

My mom laughs from her post on the porch, raising her wine glass. "I don't know who I'm more proud of—son or dog. Both have serious athletic skills."

"Dog," I answer as I put Cletus back on the grass and head to the deck. "The dog is way more talented."

"What's really impressive," my dad deadpans as he spreads barbecue sauce on a chicken breast on the grill that Sunday, "is that this kid who hated school is now teaching his dog all sorts of tricks."

"I didn't hate school, Dad."

My mom chuckles, slapping her thigh. "And he's a comedian, too, Paul."

He winks at her. "He always did make me laugh, Barbara."

Moving behind my mom, I drop a kiss to her head. "I had a B-plus average in high school, and don't you ever forget it."

My dad flips a chicken breast. "How could she? You drove me crazy, kicking and screaming every step of the way to that B-plus."

I point my thumb at the house. "I'm going inside to see if I'll be the recipient of less abuse from Trevor."

"Good luck with that," my dad says, and Cletus stays outside with my parents as I go inside, where Trevor has set up for his beer show. Since we're having lunch with them today, we're shooting here.

I slide the glass door closed and join him in the kitchen.

* * *

I spit a mouthful of pale ale in the bucket at the counter.

Shaking my head, I frown and stare longingly at the beer glass in my hand, which holds more of the tasty brew. "That pained me to expectorate."

Trevor jerks his head back and raises his eyebrows in appreciation. "Look at you. Using your SAT words."

"Thanks to you."

He drums his fingers on the countertop. "But tell me more about the suffering you endured during the ejection of this beautiful IPA."

He loves to talk in this over-the-top highfalutin manner for his show, and it cracks me up. But my job is to remain immune, a deadpan sidekick color commentator. "Allow me to explain. It pained me so greatly because this beer is absolutely delicious. It's what I want to drink while I kick back, relax, and watch something as good as, say, *Mission Impossible*."

Trevor shoots me a curious look. "I thought for sure you'd say a game. You know, like a sporting event."

Me, too. I meant to say a basketball game, or a baseball game, my leisure viewing of choice.

But my mind has been fixed on Jillian ever since the other morning when I left her room like my house was on fire. I can't get her out of my head since the night I fell asleep with her in my arms. I'd like to say I simply conked out, barely even aware of curling up next to her. But that's not true.

I didn't want to leave her. When the credits rolled and she was still sound asleep next to me, her warm body wedged against mine, I chose the path of least resistance—I closed my eyes and fell asleep, just for the chance to be near her.

Waking up with her all soft and sleepy in my arms, wanting nothing more than to tug her close, turn her to me, and kiss her breathless, was hard as hell.

Like my dick that morning.

Which might've been why I took off like I was being chased downfield by a fleet-footed safety hell-bent on trying to tackle me before I reached the end zone. I'm not sure if I've ever skedaddled out of a room faster in my life. But if I didn't leave, I might have tried more with her. More than cuddling, more than holding her in my arms.

For all I know, she might not even be aware I spent the night with her. She might have slept like a log all night long. But either way, she clearly understood the score. Hell, she acted like it was no big deal. We were both cool and casual later that morning, like nothing had happened.

And that's exactly what did happen. Nothing.

I return my focus to Trevor, and we finish out our latest episode of beer reviews. When we're done, he slides a beer bottle to me.

"To take home. For the next time you're watching *Mission Impossible*," he says, laughing. "That was a random reference."

"I guess my mind might have been on the movie, since I watched it the other night." I clear my throat. No point pretending with him. "So listen. You know Jillian?"

He looks at me, narrowing his green eyes. "I don't know her, but you've mentioned her before. She was the woman you spoke with a couple weeks ago after golf. The one I said you were hot for?"

Hot for was right at the time, but it's changed a ton since then. It started as attraction. It morphed into lust. It veered into something stronger, and now, the more time I spend with her, the more time I *want* to spend with her. She fascinates me, and she intrigues me. Every time we talk, I gobble up all the morsels I learn about her. They feed me and yet make me hungry for more at the same time.

I answer my brother with complete honesty. "I like her."

Trevor wraps up the wire for the camera as he tucks it away in a bag. "She kicks ass. She's doing a great job with Paleo. Everything is moving along as it should, and Liam seems happy. He enjoyed meeting with you earlier in the week at the winery shoot, and the marketing team has been drawing up plans for your campaign. If this goes well, Ford thinks we can get you the quick-serve restaurant company soon. Organic Eats is the name."

"Everything is happening quickly. But that's the thing. Everything is happening quickly with her, too. When I said I like her, I don't mean just for work stuff. I like her *a lot*."

Trevor straightens his spine and holds up his hands as the full meaning registers. "Whoa. You're involved with her now?"

I shake my head. "No, and I have no idea if she'd even want that."

He rests his palms against the counter, meeting my eyes. "But you'd want that?"

I sigh heavily. "Yeah. And it would probably be a huge mistake, right?"

He claps me on the shoulder, shooting me a sympathetic smile. "If you're asking me if it's a good idea to get entangled with the person who's supposed to be making sure you move beyond some of the mistakes of the past, I feel like you probably know the answer to that already. I'm not saying you should be celibate. I'm not telling you to never date because one dinner or one picture can be taken out of context. I'm just saying maybe now isn't the time. You're trying to turn things around in that facet of your career, and I wonder if maybe pursuing something with the woman tasked with helping you is the wisest move."

I scratch my chin, wishing for a different answer. "But is it the worst thing in the world?"

He huffs. "Jones, you're making this hard. It's not the worst thing in the world, but what happens when it goes south? What happens when it ends in a few weeks, or hell, a few nights?"

I start to protest, but he holds up a hand. "I love you, bro, but your attention never strays that far from the field. You've never had a relationship last longer than, what? A month?"

"If that," I grumble. I've dated here and there, but it's been a long time since a woman was known as my girl-friend. My entanglements have run short and hot. I like Jillian a hell of a lot, but I'm not entirely sure what I'd do with any woman after more than a few nights together. It's uncharted territory.

"My point exactly. Even if something happened with her, even if you were all hush-hush about it, it's not as if you're going to settle down. Then it'll be over, and in a month, when you need something from her for the deal or just for the team, how's that going to be? That's a whole new level of soap opera drama—the player and the scorned publicist—and you do *not* want to have to deal with that fallout."

Fallout.

I force myself to stay on that word for a while longer, to picture it, to feel it. There would be a fallout. A massive, uncomfortable, awkward fallout.

And what matters more to me isn't the potential drama in working with her if things don't pan out. The bigger concern is *her*. Her job. Her reputation. I like her too much to risk messing up her professional life. If word leaked out that we'd had a fling, it could affect her credibility at work. It could change how management views her, and also how the team treats her.

I can't let that happen. She loves her job. She's great at it. She doesn't deserve to be tarnished.

"Things are turning a corner financially for you," Trevor adds. "We're getting you deals. This is what you wanted."

He sweeps his arm out to indicate our parents' home.

"Mom and Dad," I say, nodding solemnly.

I need the reminder. Taking care of my parents, buying them this house, giving them a comfortable retirement where my dad is free to grill on Sundays rather than head out for another long-haul truck route and my mom can sleep in rather than schedule extra shifts—that's what matters.

I need to do the right thing. Stay on the straight path. "Thanks, man. You're right. You're always right. You know what's best."

He shoots me a skeptical stare. "But you're not going to listen to me anyway, are you?"

"Of course I'll listen to you. Nothing has happened. Nothing will happen."

We join our parents on the porch for barbecued chicken, and I put Jillian out of my mind.

And the next day, I head to the airport and board a first-class flight to Miami with the very woman I intend to resist.

14

JILLIAN

I drink coffee on the plane. I down Diet Coke. I pop cinnamon Altoids.

Six hours later, I'm bouncing off the leather seats, hopped up on caffeine, but I've successfully avoided drooling in Jones's lap, sleeping on his leg, or even doing a head-flop onto his shoulder.

I'm winning at resisting him ever since he took off from my room sometime in the wee hours a few mornings ago.

One fully-awake plane ride later, we check in at our hotel. Both of us are on the third floor, but that shouldn't be a problem since I don't plan on spending time in his room, or vice versa. Heck, it might even make things easier when we head out for the photo shoots, since we have one every morning, including the day we leave. And after this trip, we'll be done with the calendar photography so goodbye temptation, thy name is no longer *Sleeping on Jones*.

As we turn away from the front desk in the sleek, teal-blue lobby of the Blue Dreams Hotel on South

Beach, the moment of truth arrives. Will we do that awkward "should we have dinner" thing that business traveling companions do, or can I pull off another dart and dodge to avoid the dangerous five-foot radius around Jones that usually reduces me to unexpected cuddling, snuggling, and flirting?

I wish my friend Andre was free tonight. He lives here and works for the local NBA team, but he has a date this evening, so I can't use seeing him as an excuse to keep my distance from Jones. I'll need to be strategic and find ways to maintain space between that man and me for the next three nights.

I take a deep breath.

Here goes.

"I'm going to hit the gym," he says, at the same time as I utter, "I'm going to take off for an evening walk."

He shoots me a grin. "Jinx."

"Jinx," I say with a laugh.

See? I'm pulling this off with panache and humor. Almost as if we never entwined our bodies in the middle of the night.

I drop off my bags in my room, telling myself it's better that we don't hang out. It's better if I feel zero temptation to curl up with him. Besides, the shoot tomorrow with the local shelter is a sunrise one, so I'll need to be up early.

I leave the boutique hotel and make my way to the ocean to take care of business. That business involves my phone, my bare feet, and the beach. Because tonight, the thermometer reads in the high seventies, a rarity for late July in Miami. The beach is my kind of bliss, with sand that's soft and sugary and water that's crystal clear and calm. I drop my big silver shades with rhinestones on the frames over my eyes, and drink in the tropical contrast to San Francisco. Back home, I'm surrounded by water and beaches, too, but the Pacific is colder, harsher, and our beaches are better suited for melancholy, solitary strolls while wearing jackets and thinking deep thoughts.

Here, even at seven in the evening, the Miami coastline is a brochure for bikinis and stylish trunks, suntan oil and toned muscles. Gentle waves lap the shore, and sleek white boats glide across the water. I can't deny that the view is quite lovely as I walk along the coastline, returning work calls to the West Coast, making sure I'm on top of my job.

My last call is with my boss.

"I'm going to need a bigger fan in my office," Lily declares as we chat.

I'm not really sure how that's an agenda item, but she's in charge, so I go with it. "Why's that?"

"Because these pictures of Jones Beckett are hawt, as in H-A-W-T. I'm looking at the calendar drafts so far, and I might be pregnant from them."

Cracking up, I manage to answer, "Be sure to take pre-natal vitamins, then."

"Don't worry. I have an appointment tomorrow with the OB because, holy smokes, the May photo might be giving me twins."

I smile. "That's the one of him and the greyhound mix. He was so lovey with this dog that had been abused, and I nearly melted watching the pooch warm up to him."

"Good thing you handled this shoot. I might have been tempted to break my golden rule of no player relations had I gone along."

No player relations—that's a good, solid rule, and I pat myself on the back since I didn't break it, either. Falling asleep in bed clearly doesn't count. "Let's hope men and women buy it in droves. I've already started the publicity for it, teasing fans that it's coming."

"And the early buzz is excellent. By the way, how is everything going with Paleo Pet? Even though it's not part of your regular assignment with the team, I think it will definitely look good when you talk to the general manager for the promotion."

"You do?" I hadn't considered that aspect of the deal, to tell the truth. I said yes because I wanted to be helpful, and because I knew I'd learn new and useful skills. But if it gives me a leg up, that would be a nice bonus.

"Absolutely. It shows everything you're capable of doing in terms of massaging, presenting, and turning around a reputation. I've been doing some monitoring of what the public thinks of Jones and it's already on the uptick," Lily tells me, and I pump a fist. "And when it's time for you to interview for the promotion in September, I'll prep you for it. I want you to nail it."

And I want to nail Jones.

Whoa. Where did that thought come from? Oh, right. My primal, animal brain. Time to reset. "Thank you so much, Lily. I appreciate everything you've done."

When we hang up, I'm reminded that *this* is what I want, and *this* is the next step in my career. I've been lucky enough to move up quickly in the job of my dreams. Though my mother would say it's not luck, it's focus, and she taught me that. While my father and I came first with her, she also balanced work and family with uncommon grace. She was home for me every day after school, but when I was in class she gave her all to her job. Every morning when she left for her psychology practice, she was energized. She liked to say her client sessions were her own form of caffeine. "Find something you're passionate about. Nurture it. Cherish it, and watch it grow. But always tend to it," she told me.

When she and my dad gave me the cherry earrings after I nabbed the Renegades job, she said, "A reminder to keep making your own luck."

That's what I've tried to do, by working hard, by giving my best every day.

That's one of the reasons I call my dad next—to get him up to speed on the latest at work and to ask for his advice in handling a thorny email I received from a reporter inquiring about training camp coverage. My dad offers his best tips for prickly journalists, and I thank him as a seagull swoops past me, hunting for french fries on the nearby picnic tables.

"And how is that young man you're smitten with?" my dad asks after we finish our work conversation.

"I'm not smitten with him."

He chuckles. "You always did make me laugh. Next thing you'll be telling me he doesn't fancy you."

"Don't be ridiculous. He doesn't like me like that."

"Denial is so entertaining. Can you do more of it? I find it amusing."

I snort-laugh but hold my ground. "Dad. Stop."

"Oh, please. Baby pictures? Who asks to see baby pictures?"

I furrow my brow as my feet sink into the soft sand. "Everyone? Isn't that normal, to want to look at baby photos?"

"Nope. A man who is keen on a woman wants to see

baby pictures. I know because I used that same trick with your mother back when I was courting her."

I weave around a group of women taking selfies in their microscopic bikinis. "But he's not courting me," I point out. "And just because I might have told you once that I thought he had a pretty face doesn't mean anything will happen."

"Want to know what I'm doing right now?" he asks in a leading tone.

"What are you doing?" I ask carefully, though I know he's setting me up for something. I duck out of the way of a volleyball whizzing past me. A fit, dark-haired guy in a painted-on pair of yellow swim trunks jogs after it, winking at me as he runs.

"Sitting at the desk that the man who is keen on my daughter made for me," my dad declares, sounding thoroughly satisfied with his pronouncement.

I shake my head, amused at my dad's persistence. No wonder he was a top journalist in his day. He's a dog with a bone. But I'm not a queen of spin for nothing. "He helped out. It was that simple. Nothing more to it."

My dad scoffs. "He helped out because he's a nice guy. I'll give you that." He clears his throat. "But he's a nice guy who happens to be quite fond of you. Mark my words. Sooner or later, Jones Beckett is going to make his intentions clear."

I swallow, and a spray of nerves hits me in the face. Or maybe it's the water from a water gun. Oh yeah, that's it. Yellow Swim Trunks Dude is now spraying his buddy with an orange Nerf gun, and I'm collateral damage in the battle. I wipe the drops from my cheek as Swim Trunks mouths *so sorry*, but he's smiling as he says it.

"I love you, Dad. I'll look into having you checked into the sanitarium soon," I say, and I put the conversation inside a box then stuff it in a far corner of my brain.

But after I hang up, some hopeful part of me wonders if there's a chance my father is correct. Does Jones have a thing for me? That doesn't compute. But as I search for the holes in my dad's logic, my mind flashes to all the times Jones has touched me—from his arm around me as we walked along the craggy shores of Stinson Beach, to his fingers laced through mine in the elevator, to his body curled around me in bed.

Do those moments mean Jones is keen on me?

I flip through them once more, hunting for clues. Even though I've felt the outline of his erection against my rear, that's not the moment I keep returning to. It's the feel of his hand on my hair in the car while I slept in his lap. He stroked my hair. Was that romantic?

I plop down on the beach, reflecting on what I'd do if he made his intentions clear. I'd say no. Of course I'd say no. Wouldn't I?

I nod to myself, answering my own question.

I'd say, "Thank you very much, but it's a bad idea to go on a date with you, no matter how sweet and kind and good with animals and thoughtful you are, and no matter how helpful you are with my dad, or how much I love all our conversations."

Groaning in frustration, I run my hands through my hair, my head falling against my knees. I wish I didn't like him so damn much.

But no matter how deep my affection tunnels, this is an exercise in futility.

He won't *ever* say any of those things.

But he touched your hair so tenderly.

A whoosh runs through my body, like a ribbon of desire unspooling from head to toe. Is it possible that he's into me and I've been denying it? Have the signs been there all along, and I've never let myself see them?

I can't rely on a father's opinion. I could ask Andre, but he doesn't know Jones.

There is only one person to turn to. I fire off a text to Katie.

Jillian: Be brutally honest. No smoke up my skirt, hear me?

Katie: Yes, you can buy me tickets to the new Adele show, and it will, in fact, make me love you more.

Jillian: Oh good, I was worried you'd be annoyed if I snagged first-row seats. Same apply to Ed Sheeran, too?

Katie: Do not ever joke about Ed Sheeran tickets. If you had them and kept them from me, I would divorce you.

Jillian: Yes, your love for him runs deeper than your love for me. As it should. :)

Katie: As it clearly should. Also, I love you madly and more than Ed—just don't tell him since I don't want the future father of my children to know you outrank him. But what do you really want me to be brutally honest about?

Jillian: Did you mean it when you said you thought there was something up with Jones?

Katie: How can I make this clear??? YES! YES! YES! Also, does that mean something is happening? I NEED DETAILS NOW!

Jillian: No. Nothing at all. Just thinking . . .

Katie: You're thinking about it? About him? About taking him for a ride around the block? For the record, I'm at my desk, officially squealing as I stop my review of IMPORTANT THINGS like the length of skirts for the spring. Because this is FAR MORE INTERESTING.

Jillian: Nothing will happen. There are all sorts of HUGE obstacles. Also, care to spill on the upcoming length of hemlines?

Katie: There is always a way around obstacles. There's always another path. Haven't you learned anything watching football? If Jones pulled off that crazy catch where he went nearly horizontal, his hands inches from the turf in that playoff game, you can pull off some equally big play. Also . . . short. Very, very short.

A smile spreads as I recall that play. I see it in slow motion, him leaping, grabbing, diving, then grabbing the ball as it careens toward the ground. It was a heart-stopping catch.

Jillian: Good to know regarding skirts. I'll stick to pants, then.

Katie: Pants, skirts—whatever you wear, Jones will check you out. I told you he was looking at you!

Jillian: But isn't that just what he does? Watch people? He's like a hawk. That's his job.

Katie: He looks at you because he likes looking at you. Same reason you look at him.

My chest swoops like a pirate boat ride at an amusement park. Up, down, around.

I stand, brushing sand off my tank dress as I fire off a goodbye text. I turn to head to the poolside entrance to the hotel, when the guy in the yellow trunks jogs over to me, flashes a gleaming white set of teeth, and says, "Hi, I'm Marcus. Want to have a drink with me?"

Boldness and confidence are quite appealing. So is his toned, trim body and his fantastic grin. He's probably twenty-two, and even though it's nice to be hit on by someone six years younger than me, I say, "Thank you so much, but I'm here for work."

"Can't fault a guy for trying," he says with a huge smile as he jogs backward, his arms out wide.

No, I can't fault him at all.

I float a little bit to my room, buoyed by the date request, as well as by Katie's insistent proclamation.

But then, on the elevator ride up, reality hits me. If Jones was going to make his intentions clear, he'd do what Marcus did.

Ask me out.

He never has, so I don't need to waste time pondering what-if scenarios.

Jones and I aren't a scenario. We aren't a thing, and the way we look at each other is meaningless.

In fact, looking at him is exactly what I try not to do

the next morning at the photo shoot. Because I can't let on that I think about this often. Too much is at stake, and the more I look at him, the more my stupid feelings cloud my brain.

That's why I resolve to keep everything light between us. That should be easy since he's shirtless on the sand, posing with a long-haired dachshund.

When we're done with the shoot, Jones ambles over to me, stroking the wiener dog in his arms. "Want to pet my wiener?"

Playfully, I wag a finger at him, doing my best to keep everything between us breezy. "There will be no wiener petting today."

He arches a brow. "But maybe tomorrow?"

I look away, laughing. The laughter reminds me that we've always had a fun professional rapport, one where we freely tease each other. That's the relationship I need to maintain. Sure, the idea of avoiding him at night during this trip has its appeal. But I'm a grown-up, and I can't hide from a tough situation. It'll be good for me to practice focusing solely on business with him.

I meet his eyes. "Do you want to have dinner tonight? We can strategize next steps with Paleo Pet and how to tackle social as the marketing campaign rolls out, as well as review some of the calendar publicity."

See? That sounded so professional. Because it was. I can absolutely zero in on business and just business with the guy.

"Um." He makes that sound. That sound guys make before they turn you down. That groan of regret-but-not-regret. "I'm hanging out with some of the guys from the Miami Mavericks. Sorry."

My heart skitters to the sidewalk like a top spinning

until it falters. I plaster on a smile, hiding my disappointment. "Oh, that's great. Have fun."

As I leave, I believe he's made his intentions clear after all. He has none for me.

I scroll through my phone, find Andre's name, and ask if he wants to have dinner poolside.

He says yes.

15

JONES

I slam the plastic ball across the net, watching defensive tackle Connor Washington dive for it on the sand, reaching as far as he can with the paddle.

But he swings and misses.

"Ah, too bad the little white ball eludes you," I say, since that's how we roll. I've never played a game of table tennis, Xbox, foosball, or golf with a fellow athlete where we didn't trash-talk each other.

"I wouldn't dish it out so fast," Connor warns, his dark eyes sparking with determination as he returns a punishing serve.

He's right. I miss it.

I fucking miss it. The ball skids past me, hitting the beach.

Because my mind is on Jillian.

Again.

It has been since I saw her at the pool, lounging in a luscious black triangle bikini, drinking a fruity drink, and laughing with a Henry Cavill look-alike.

I've no clue who he is. And hell, I never gave much

thought to her seeing other guys. Which is stupid as shit. Of course she dates. She's gorgeous and funny and witty and generally awesome. She's a catch.

The white plastic orb screams in my direction, and I lunge to the right, smacking it hard. Connor returns it fiercely with a grunt. We trade off like that, back and forth, and the focus exiles Jillian from my mind.

For a few minutes, until the game ends and I've lost. Connor's teammate Malcolm steps up to the table, pointing his paddle at me. His thick beard points at me, too. "You keep that shitty play going all through the season and we will clean up against your sorry ass in the conference."

"I save all my best moves for the field. You watch out when the third Sunday of October rolls around."

Connor smacks Malcolm's arm. "See that? He's scared of us. He already knows when we're playing so he can prepare to be whipped."

"Assholes." I laugh. "I know the schedule because I like to be prepared to destroy my opponents."

They shake their heads in unison. "We will ping-pong your ass back to the West Coast," Malcolm taunts.

I raise my hands to the sky. "Why do I hang out with you clowns when I'm in town?"

Malcolm makes his way around the table and taps his chest. "Because we're fun. So fun, in fact, I say it's time to ditch this Ping-Pong table. What do you say we hit the clubs?"

I shake my head. "Early bedtime for me. No more partying."

Malcolm lets out a dejected, dramatic sigh. "Man, are you serious? I know places where we can clean up like that." He snaps his fingers.

The offer is tempting. I wouldn't mind a night out, some dancing, chatting up some women. But that's not what I signed up for this year. That won't suit the new image, or sit well with the new sponsors. That doesn't sit well with me, either, because there is only one woman I want to chat up, and she's off-limits.

Connor holds up his index finger. "Training camp starts in one week. Then, no GFs, no bunnies, no girls stopping by for blowies."

Malcolm wiggles his eyebrows. "One night, JB. How can you resist?"

Easily, actually.

I tip my head toward the hotel. "I have a pillow calling my name and a movie to watch. Not to mention a brand-new contract with a pet food company as an incentive to keep squeaky clean."

"Nice," Connor says, holding up his palm to high-five. I smack back.

"Smart move. You need to keep that shit locked up. I'm going to unlock mine," Malcolm says, and the ironic thing is, he can, because his deals are different. His biggest sponsor is a vodka brand. That doesn't mean he can get roasted and show up on a YouTube compilation of blitzed athletes. The contrary. He doesn't drink when he's out, and he follows strict rules about where and when he dips his wick with women he meets at clubs. Those are the lines that suit him and his business partners.

We wander across the sand toward the pool. The sun has fallen below the horizon, and night is settling in. I say goodbye to the guys and head through the pool area to go into the hotel. I spot Jillian in the shallow end, her elbows on the side of the pool, chatting with the Cavill dude.

That unpleasant sensation stabs my chest again. My jaw clenches and my muscles tighten as jealousy crashes over me.

Jillian spots me and waves.

"Hey," I grunt, tipping my forehead in her direction as I stalk past them, since that's all I can manage. Once inside, I stab the up button for the elevator, and when it arrives I want to punch the panel.

I don't.

I curse under my breath as the doors whisk shut.

I can't fucking believe she's hanging out with that guy in front of me. I march down the hall to my room, fumes of jealousy in my wake.

In my room, I strip out of my shorts and T-shirt, crank up the shower to scalding, and wash away the sand. But as I scrub soap over my skin, all I can think is Superman is peeling off her bikini tonight.

Tossing it on the floor of her hotel room.

Kissing her neck. Making his way down her body.

Envy burns in me like a wildfire. This is not okay. In a heartbeat, I rinse off the shampoo, get out of the shower, and towel off. A minute later, I've yanked on swim trunks and a T-shirt, and I'm on my way to the pool.

I'm going to crash her party.

When I arrive, they're on the deck. Superman is giving her a hug. It's going to take every ounce of my restraint not to grab that arm of his and rip him off her.

Because she's mine. Even though I can't have her, that guy sure as hell can't, either.

I walk closer and key in on his words.

"Love you, Jilly. So much."

Jilly? He calls her by a pet name? I clench my fists.

"Love you, too, sweets," she says, dropping a kiss to his cheek. Her back is to me, and I stop in my tracks at the edge of the deep end, watching some other man hug the woman I want. Everything is wrong with this picture.

"Sorry I have to go, but I just got a text about this elementary school we sponsor. Some problem with the water pipes I need to figure out."

"Go, go," she says, shooing him off.

"Thank you so much for making time for me, and you know I will see you whenever you are in town," he says. "You just call me, and I'll come running."

She has a boyfriend in Miami? What the hell?

Red. I see red. It billows from my eyes, and I shut them for a moment and think of Cletus. As I picture his too-adorable Chihuahua face and how he likes to give me slobbery lap-dog kisses, the jealousy fades momentarily.

I open my eyes as Superman waves goodbye then blows her a kiss.

When he leaves, she hooks a towel around her waist, her gaze wandering around the pool then skidding to a halt when she gets to me. She jerks her head back, like she's surprised to see me, and maybe a little bit guilty, too?

I close the distance between us. "Hey."

Her voice is cool and even as she twists her hair into a slick ponytail. "Hi, Jones. How was your night?"

She says my name with distance, as if she's pushing it away from her, pushing me away. Maybe I deserve it for turning down her dinner invite.

"It was good," I say tightly. "How was yours?"

"Great." She flashes me a smile and keeps her shoulders squared, her eyes fixed firmly on my face. They don't stray at all, as if she's practicing perfect posture.

"You had fun with *that guy*?" The words come out like acid on my tongue.

Her brow pinches. "Andre and I always have fun."

Deep breath. Cletus kisses. He's wagging his tail.

The jealousy subsides again. "That's. So. Great." Each word comes out robotically.

She glances down at her towel, then points her thumb in the direction of the hotel. "I'm all wet, so I should probably go change."

She's doing her posture exercises again, and it irks me for some reason. "Why do you do that?" I blurt out.

"Do what?"

"You stare straight at my face when you talk."

She narrows her eyes. "Where am I supposed to look?"

"Anywhere."

"Should I talk to your belly button? Maybe your elbow? Or would you prefer if I addressed your feet?"

"No, obviously I'm not saying you should talk to my feet." I cross my arms. "I just don't get why you do that."

"I'm trying to be polite. Professional. Because we work together. That's why I look you in the eyes. And speaking of work, it's getting late, and we have another shoot in the morning, not to mention a few interviews about the new deal. I should go upstairs and do some planning. I'm glad you had fun with the guys."

I shake my head quickly, correcting her. "I didn't say I had fun with them."

"Sorry." She adjusts her ponytail again, raising her

chin, talking in that modulated, publicist voice. "Did you have fun?"

I swallow. "Yes and no."

"Yes and no?"

I'm dangerously close to admitting I want her. The words tango on the end of my tongue. *I want you. I need you. I can't stand how much I think of you.*

In this moment, I crave her more than a sponsorship deal, and I want her to know the reason I had a shitty time tonight is that she was out with some guy. But I trip on the words, and they fall out of my mouth like blocks tumbling. "I thought you were seeing someone. Like a boyfriend. That guy."

She's silent at first, then a sly smile spreads on her face, wider and wider still, until it turns into a belly laugh. "Andre and I bat for the same team."

All my jealousy drains in an instant. I try to cover up my glaring misread with a forced and sheepish chuckle. "Well, that's good to know."

I push out another laugh so she knows I'm not the jealous ass I was seconds ago. But my laughter ceases when she speaks again.

"We were admiring the same scenery tonight, if you know what I mean." She wriggles her eyebrows, and that's it. Evidently, I'm still the jealous ass, because I hate the thought of her admiring any scenery belonging to another man.

I'm *this* close to spilling my guts, but a scan right, a scan left, and a pool full of people swimming and lounging is the reminder I need to zip my lips.

She is controlling what these people think of me. She is helping me keep the sponsorship deals my agent lines up—deals that fund my parents' retirement. My dad doesn't have to drive a truck. My mom doesn't have to work extra shifts.

"I need to go for a walk."

I turn around and leave. If I stay near her, I'll try to kiss her in public. I'll haul her over my shoulder and carry her to my room, tell her I can't take this wanting anymore. It's miserable craving a person this much and not having her.

I walk down the beach, and I try to burn off this frustration, but thirty minutes later I'm no closer to finding Zen without her.

There's no Zen without her.

I go inside, take the elevator, and walk down the hallway, banging my fist on room 302. When she answers, I pose a question I've been dying to ask for a long, long time.

16

JILLIAN

His right arm rests against the doorframe. His big body fills the doorway.

Nerves skate over my skin. My throat is dry. I want to tell him he behaved like a jerk tonight at the pool, grunting out words like a caveman.

But I also want to know why he's come calling at nine at night, and why he seemed so upset over Andre.

The need to know is stronger than the urge to tell him off.

I try to manage a *hi, what can I do for you*, except he gets the first words in.

"What would it be like if we didn't work together?"

His words hang in the air like sweet smoke.

Like possibility.

Inside, I'm shaking—with want, with hope, with an anticipation that thrills and scares me. He's here at my hotel room, and his blue eyes are blazing. There's a fire in them, a heat I haven't seen before. Or maybe I just never noticed. But now, I can't *not* notice it. He stares at me with an intensity that's ferocious.

Briefly, I glance down, trying to see me as he does—I'm wearing only a tank top and pajama shorts. My hair is blow-dried, since I just took a shower. I had to wash off the chlorine, along with my frustration over how he behaved at the pool.

I should still be annoyed with him, but it's hard to stay that way since curiosity is eating at me. Carefully, in a low voice, I ask, "What do you mean?"

Blue lights along the floorboards glow faintly in the stylish room behind me, as Sam Smith plays from my phone. "Stay with Me" floats in the air like a call to him, a request for him to spend the night.

He leans a few inches closer, making me dizzy.

"What I mean is . . ." He takes his time answering, his voice full of a need I've never heard from him before. "What would things be like with you and me if we didn't work together?"

My voice is breathless as I answer, and I'm sure it betrays my heart. "What do you think they'd be like?" I ask quietly, but my wariness over prying eyes runs strong, so I shake my head. "Don't answer." I peer down the hall. No one's around, but whatever he's going to utter is best said behind closed doors. "Come inside." I open the door wider, and he enters. When the door slides closed with a *thunk*, the sound reverberates.

It feels like a line in the sand.

A line I shouldn't cross.

It marks the before and after. But I want to know what comes next. I want to venture into this dangerous territory.

He runs a hand through his hair and sighs heavily. His voice is vulnerable when he speaks. "Why don't you look at me, Jillian?"

A spark of anger burns in me. "Why were you a jerk at the pool?"

He huffs. "Because I thought that guy was with you."

"So you were dismissive and barely said a word?"

He nods. "Yes. And then when I talked to you, you just stared straight at me, but you didn't look at me." He takes a beat, breathes hard, then seems to let go of his anger. "And all I want is to look at you."

That dryness in my throat? It's vanished. I'm burning, everywhere. I'm hot and wet and electric. Heat flares low in my belly, settling between my legs.

"I do look at you." I wind my hands behind my back and lace my fingers together to keep from launching myself at him.

"Do you look at me the way I look at you?"

"How do you look at me?"

He steps closer. He's a foot away. I've never been so aware of space in my life. "Like it drove me crazy you were with that guy. Like it made me act like a jerk, and I'm sorry."

A wild thrill rushes through me at his admission. I've never experienced this sensation, this absolute intoxication from knowing the person you long for is longing for you, too. My friends and family have told me he feels this way, but I hunted for every reason to disavow what they said. Now, I'm floating on this cloud of disbelief, and it feels so good to fly this high. I don't want the real world. I don't want consequences. I just want him.

"You're not a jerk. But I told you—he's a friend, and that's all."

His shoulders rise and fall. "It drove me crazy to see you laughing with him. To see him hugging you."

Since honesty seems to be the theme tonight, I toss out another kernel of truth. "It drove me crazy that you didn't have dinner with me." It's a relief to finally give voice to my own jealousy, and taking the first step frees me to say more. Emboldened, I add softly, "I wanted to have dinner with you."

He steps closer. Inches separate us—that's all. "I was trying like hell to stay away from you."

I should tell him to go, but his words are everything I've longed for. Everything that's a terrible risk. I swallow harshly as my bones buzz. "Why?"

"Because I don't want to mess things up for you or for me. I don't want to ruin anything. But when I saw Liam chatting you up at the winery, and then your friend Andre tonight . . . it was too hard to keep this all inside. It was too hard to act like I don't totally fucking want you."

A gasp dares to escape my lips. I'm crackling everywhere as he continues, "I know you're beautiful, I know you're smart as a whip, but I want them to look at you and feel like they can't have you."

He lifts his hand and lightly, ever so gently, runs his fingers across my shoulder. I spark from that touch. I'm a live wire, and I could power whole cities tonight.

"Because you're mine."

I'm flying through the stars. The man I want is laying bare his desire, shedding all his pretenses, and I can hardly believe it's happening. He's making his intentions clear. I want to hear every word, imprint them on my memory so I can replay them when I'm on the other side of this, so I can remember why I'm about to do something foolish. Why I'm going to take a risk.

Somehow, I manage to speak. "What would you do if I was yours?"

He erases the distance, the inches, and lines his body up with mine. This is the point of no return, and I've passed it.

Willingly.

Gladly.

"Let me show you." Cupping my cheeks in his big hands, he dips his mouth to mine, and he kisses me.

This feels so unreal.

When you've dreamed so often of a person, when you've imagined every possible kiss, it's hard to believe when it happens that it's not another figment of your imagination.

Or that it could be better than a dream.

Jones has played the lead in so many fantasies of mine. I've pictured him moving over me, entwined with me, kissing me fiercely with everything he has.

That's how he kisses, and it's like a hot, dirty dream. It's both magnificent and terrifying, as if I'm on the cusp of waking up at any second and this fantastic dream will vanish. I want to stave off the alarm so I can float here in bliss. Every inch of my skin tingles; every molecule in my body vibrates.

His mouth slides over mine with lips that are soft, yet determined. The press of his hard body is delicious. Even though I'm taller than the average woman, I'm tiny next to him. Jones is so much larger than me, broader, bigger, and I love it.

I love everything about how he kisses me, most of all that he's not quiet. As his big hands grip my face, he makes the sexiest sounds—moans and groans and murmurs that all add up to sheer masculine desire. *For me.*

It's shocking to be wanted like this after all the time I thought the opposite. But it's a shock I crave. I want him to shock my system with his lust.

All my notions of right and wrong, limits and off-limits, have left the premises. I've surrendered to the choice I'm making, and there's no room inside me for regret. There is only space for lust, for desire, and for this need to go deeper with him.

To go deeper into the night.

My hands shoot up into his hair, threading through his soft dark locks as I curl my fingers around the back of his head. I can't get enough of him, and I kiss him harder. Soon our tongues are wild and frenzied, searching and tangling as our teeth click and our lips devour.

He is a hungry man. It's a whole new sensory experience as he kisses me with more passion than I ever imagined was possible. I know now what it means to be wanted in a raw, primal way. I don't think I've ever been wanted like this before, and it's the highest high. He kisses me as if I'm what he's fantasized about for days, for weeks, for months. As if he wants to kiss me everywhere, every inch of my body, and that thought sends a shudder through me, a wave of obscene pleasure that crashes between my legs where I'm hot and wet and needy for him.

It should be criminal to feel this good, to be this aroused.

If it is, I'm guilty and loving it.

A restless energy claws at me, a desperate desire to get closer to him, to climb him. I rub my pelvis against the outline of his erection. He's hard and long, and I'm dying to feel him fill me up.

"Ohh," I moan as the full awareness of his length dawns on me. The man is big everywhere.

I feel him laugh a little against my lips, then he separates from me, pressing his forehead to mine and whispering, "Are you trying to climb me?"

I laugh, too, answering breathlessly, "Yes."

"Let me help you out."

In a split second, he lifts me, wraps my legs around him, and carries me to the king-size bed. Low to the floor with a white lacquered platform, it screams *fuck me on this*. Or maybe I have a one-track mind tonight. I'm an open book right now, and I can't pretend any longer that I don't want him with every fiber of my body.

"Jones," I whisper as he lays me down under him. "This is just between us tonight."

He nods. "It'll always be between us."

There it is—the admission that we are secret. That we are illicit and lawless. But the risk won't stop us. I feel bold, brazen, like my mouth has been unlocked by his touch. "I want you tonight. I want all of you." It's such an awesome relief to say those words.

"I want you, Jillian. All of you. Don't you know how much?"

I kind of do, but I want to hear. "How much?"

He groans, hiking my legs tighter around his back. With one swift move he grinds against me, letting me feel the outline of his hard cock through my flimsy clothes. The sound I make is animalistic, like a tiger in heat.

"You make me so fucking hard. So fucking crazy. I

want you under me, writhing and moaning and calling my name," he says as he pushes against me, a tease of what's to come.

"I don't think that'll be an issue." Arching up into him, I revel in the feeling of his hard-on between my legs, knowing that soon there won't be any layers between us. I murmur in pleasure, breathing out his name. "*Jones.*"

He curses and thrusts against me. "Do you have any idea how attracted I am to you? I think about you constantly." His words come out in a rush, thick with emotion, brimming with heat and need.

I blink then swallow, trying to make sense of what he's just said. It feels like more than sex. More than lust. "You do?"

He nods vigorously. "So much, for so long."

Something bursts inside me, everything I've held back, and words spill free. "It's the same for me. It's exactly the same for me." My voice feels like it's breaking, but it's not tears—it's the emotion all stirred up with a desire that's been bottled and finally let loose.

He grins. "Yeah?"

"That's why it was so much harder not to look at you. I never stare at the guys anyway, but you—I wanted to see all of you, and I had to resist."

He crushes his mouth to mine, kissing me like it's a claiming, hot and fevered, sending me into a frenzy. My hips rock up against him, and we have to get naked soon or I will die.

He knows it, too, because he pulls away from me and stands, kicking off his flip-flops. He's only wearing a T-shirt and swim trunks that don't hide how aroused he is. "You can look at me now. I'm fair game."

"Take your clothes off, please. I'm begging you." I scoot back on the bed, resting on my elbows, gawking happily.

"This is just for you," he says, all rough and husky.

"Just for me," I repeat as if I'm in a trance, hypnotized by his body, which I can finally relish.

He grips the bottom of his shirt with crossed hands then strips it off in one quick move.

"Oh God," I gasp. "You're beautiful."

I've seen him shirtless before, but this is brand-new. It feels like an unveiling, a private show. I have the one and only seat, and it's front and center. I gaze at him with ravenous eyes, memorizing the firm shape of his pecs, the muscles in his arms, the grooves of his abs.

The V.

Dear God, the V. My mouth waters. I lift my fingers. I have to touch him. His lips curve in a grin. He knows I'm on the edge.

"Take your shorts off," I tell him, my voice like a feather as my eyes roam over him, finally free to enjoy the view. And, oh hell, do I enjoy him.

He cocks a brow. "Are you sure?"

I howl with frustration. "So sure. Please. Just please take your clothes off."

I'm begging, and I don't care. I want him naked. Every glorious inch.

He hooks his thumbs into his shorts and waggles his eyebrows. "More?"

"All. The. Way."

He laughs and pushes them down.

My mouth waters. His dick should be illegal. "Oh my God," I mutter in admiration as I stare at his hard, impressive length. Long, thick, and proud. It points at me.

Jones grips his length, stroking slowly, squeezing the head.

I spin around and crawl to him, a wild woman on her knees for the man she wants. Like that, I wrap a hand around him, and he growls. The skin is hot and smooth, like steel and velvet. The sound he makes when I touch him seems to reverberate in the room. I waste no time. I lower my head and take him in my mouth.

"Fuck, baby," he groans, threading his fingers in my hair.

I flick my tongue over the head, sucking him, savoring the salty, delicious taste of his cock.

"Jillian." My name is a warning. I don't heed it. I suck harder and tighter, trying to bring him deeper. But his hands push my shoulders, gently shoving me off him. "If you keep doing that, I'll come too soon."

"I want to taste you coming."

"I want that." He dips his face to mine. "More than you can know. And I want to taste you, too. I want to eat you, spread you open, and devour you. But I need to be patently honest right now."

I tense. "Yes?"

"I have wanted to fuck you for so long that what I want more than anything is to slide inside you and make you come like that."

Somehow, I'm even wetter. That heavy aching pulse throbs between my legs. I wrap my hands around his neck, yanking him close as I whisper my deepest wish, "Please fuck me."

17

JONES

My three favorite words ever.

Jillian begging me. Jillian asking me to take her. The woman I'm crazy for is wildly aroused.

Everything about her turns me on to an insane degree. But I find it incredibly problematic that she's still dressed, so I solve the clothing issue in seconds, stripping off her shorts and her panties as she takes off her top.

Then she's spread out and naked before me on the bed. "Jesus Christ, you're gorgeous. Hotter than I ever imagined." I savor the view of her perky tits, her trim, tight belly, her long, lean legs, and that thatch of dark hair that points home. My whole body is buzzed, bursting with adrenaline.

Faster than I can run a forty, I grab a condom from my wallet on the floor, roll it on my eager dick, and kneel between her thighs. "Spread your legs, baby."

There's no shyness in her. None at all as she lets her knees fall open for me. She's bold and confident, and it makes my skin sizzle. What makes me even hotter is how she stares at me—but now it's *all* of me, with wide eyes and permission. It's fucking awesome, not because I'm so vain I need the confirmation, but because it's *her*. There's nothing sexier than the woman you want admiring you as if you're the object of her fantasies. She can objectify me all night long if she wants.

I love what I'm seeing, too. A groan rumbles up my chest as I learn how wet she is, how slippery she feels when I glide two fingers over her pussy. She rocks up into my hand and parts her lips. *Please, please, please.*

I do as I'm begged, rubbing the head of my dick against her slick opening.

"Yes," she moans, and it's as if the word lasts for days.

I sink inside a few inches, shuddering as sparks tear through me from the first touch. This is better than all my dirty dreams of her, and I've had thousands. Hell, it's eons better than every time I've jacked off while imagining how it would feel to bury myself in her.

There is nothing, nothing at all, like the real thing.

She ropes her arms around my back, looks up into my eyes, and whispers, "All of you. I want all of you."

An obliterating wave of lust rolls over me as I sink into her, savoring the heat of her pussy, filling her completely. Sensations fire off in my body, like fireworks every-fucking-where. She's so warm, so tight, and I can't believe I'm finally having her.

This is where I want to be, and it's tremendous. Our eyes lock for a few seconds, and we're silent, but it feels like we say everything—*Finally. At last. I've wanted this. I've wanted you.*

The last unspoken word echoes between us. *You, you, you.*

Then, we fuck.

We don't go slow. We don't ease into it. We're off to the races, and she goes wild beneath me, arching and thrusting. She drags her nails down my back, scratching me.

It makes my blood run hotter. "Leave marks, baby," I urge.

She scratches harder, and I love the wildcat in her. Love that she wants to claim me in her own way.

I love, too, how she gives herself to me so openly. How she has no hang-ups now that we're finally tangled together. Swiveling my hips, I push deeper into her. She moans her approval. I do it again. She moans even louder. Her nails dig into me.

"Like that," she pants.

"Just like that." That's the pace I keep up, the rhythm she seems to need, the angle that sends her pitch rising.

And it makes my name rush from her lips in a filthy moan.

I hear my name said all the time. It's announced during games. It's uttered on TV. It's mentioned constantly on sports radio.

Never has my name sounded as good as it does tonight. "Jones . . . so close . . . I'm so close."

The fact that she's nearly there already triggers a fresh round of lust in my veins. Unleashing several hard, fast pumps, I drive into her, and she cries out, louder each time.

Raising her knees higher, she opens herself more. I wrap a hand around one knee, pushing up her leg, making even more room. She quivers, her shoulders trembling, her eyes squeezing shut. Her mouth, her lips, her beautiful face—I can't stop watching as the beginning of her orgasm radiates through her.

Another gasp. Another groan.

Then, the barest whisper from her—*coming*—and it sends a bolt of heat to my groin as I give her everything she needs, taking her to the edge.

The sound of her climax is the hottest thing I've ever heard. It's hotter when she digs her nails in as she keens. That trips the switch in me. Pleasure barrels down my spine, and I don't hold back. There's no need to anymore. My vision blurs, and my world spins out of orbit as everything turns white-hot.

I come hard, my orgasm reverberating with an intensity that feels like the end of time. Ecstatic oblivion, and worth every goddamn second. I collapse onto her, her arms still banded around me as we both breathe as if we've run a race.

Her hands move up my back with gentle strokes. She runs her fingers through my hair. She dusts a kiss to my sweaty forehead, whispering my name once more, a quiet murmur in the night.

As she glides her hands over my skin, the part of my brain that can still construct sentences is telling me that I could get accustomed to this, to her.

I don't want this to be a one-night stand.

18

JONES

"Hey."

The word is soft, but insistent. I'm still in an orgasm haze, even though I've already disposed of the condom. "Yeah?"

She runs her hand down my arm, and hell, do I ever love that she's using her permission slip at last. She can keep those hands on me all night long. I fucking love how she touches me, how much she wants to explore. She makes me feel like a cat, arching, purring, asking for more.

Turning to her side, she props her head in her hand, resting on her elbow. "We should talk. Don't you think?"

"Sure." I still sound groggy, but it's just the drug wearing off. The drug of her. Sobriety doesn't interest me, though. I need another hit. I kiss her neck, inhaling her clean skin.

She wriggles against me, gliding her hands over my belly. "Mmm. You're distracting me."

"I'm good at that." I nibble on her earlobe, flicking

my tongue against her red cherry earrings. "These are sexy."

"Thank you."

I run my hand through her silky hair. "Your hair is sexy."

She smiles. "Thank you."

"You're sexy."

She smiles, then wiggles her eyebrows. "And to think I was positively sure you were pretty much a blonde or bust type of guy."

I scoff. "Well, you were wrong."

"I suppose I was. What a surprise. A welcome one, since I didn't think you were into me."

Time to roll my eyes like I've never rolled them before. "You find it surprising that I like you? After we just fucked each other's brains out?"

A faint blush spreads over her cheeks. "Maybe." She shrugs.

"Fine. One roll in the hay isn't enough evidence for you, so clearly we'll need to do it again."

"Well, duh."

"But maybe you're right. Maybe fucking each other senseless isn't proof enough, because I sure as hell thought you would never give me the time of day."

"Seriously?" Her voice goes soft. "I was never mean to you."

"I know. You were always good to me. But you were also so tough when I tried to flirt with you. When I did things to get your attention. You were so impervious. So professional."

"I thought it was all just a game. Just you being your playful self."

"You did?"

She nods. "I figured the towel drop and the flirty comments were just who you were. And if I let myself think they meant anything more, I'd have been an idiot."

"They meant more," I say.

"But I had no idea." Vulnerability flashes in her irises. "I had to be strong. I had to be professional around you."

"Why?" I prop my head in my hand, mirroring her.

"I couldn't risk letting on how I really felt."

A cocky grin spreads on my face. I poke her shoulder. "Admit it. You do like me."

Nudging my side, she whispers, "Obviously." She winks. "I mean, *obviously* I like the orgasm you just gave me. That's what I wanted to say."

I flop my head dramatically on the pillow and mime stabbing myself in the heart. "I'm wounded. She only wants me for my dick."

She bends her face to mine and brushes her lips over my jawline. "I like you and your dick, and I'd like more orgasms."

"Good, but I'm still filing a report on you."

Flinching, she pulls back. "For what? For sexual harassment?"

I laugh, my head shaking vigorously. "No. God, no. I wouldn't even joke about that, not in this climate, and not ever. And it's a damn good thing we work *together*, not as one person under the other."

"But I was just under you." She gives a sly little wink, and I'm loving this new side of Jillian. It was there all along, and even though she's been professional, she's definitely been playful with me at times. But now with the clothes off, the sassy flirt I've seen hints of has fully emerged.

I move over her, pinning her beneath me, my palms planted flat by her shoulders. "And you will be under me again," I say, and she lets out a sexy little murmur. "But mostly I was going to file a report to put myself on the injured reserve, because I think you sent me into an orgasm coma there."

"One orgasm is all it takes to induce a coma? You're easy."

"Easy? Hardly. I still can't function fully because of the magnitude. It was like a nine-point-eight on the Richter scale."

If I thought Jillian had a great smile, I was wrong. She has a magnificent smile. She has a heart-stopping smile. Because now I'm rewarded with the biggest grin in the world. "Hmm. That does sound rather intense," she says. "Is there anything at all to do to revive you?"

I pretend as if I'm devoting deep thought to the topic. "More sex, for starters. A blow job, possibly. Maybe let me go down on you."

"I don't believe I was stopping you before. I think you're the one who wanted to skip straight to the main attraction."

"Woman, are you challenging me? I will go down on you right now."

"You will?"

I nod. "Why do you act like that's surprising?"

She quirks up an eyebrow. "Because I probably taste like a condom?"

"There's really only one way to find out."

I slide down her body, bring my face to her sweet paradise, and give her a kiss then a lick. There is a faint taste of rubber, but it fades in seconds and I'm left with the delicious taste of her. Sweet, salty, sexy. She tastes like the woman I've wanted to touch so badly. The woman who just came hard underneath me. She moans and moves, arching her hips against my face as I flick my tongue, as I lick long, devouring lines up her hot, wet center.

Twisting and writhing, she's like a belly dancer as I eat her. She can't lie still, and it's fucking fantastic because it makes me work harder, it makes me keep up with her as she rocks into me, tangling her hips and legs around my face. I swear by the time she's nearing the edge, she's practically on her side in some bizarre new position.

"Oh God, oh God, oh God," she cries out in a chant, yanking me closer, coming on my lips.

Afterward, she murmurs for several long seconds as I untangle from her, rolling her to her back. "Damn, you get into it."

She flashes me a satisfied smile, her eyes still glossy and hazy. "What can I say? I kind of like everything you do to me."

"Kind of?"

"Kind of a lot."

"Good, because I'm going to do that again, and soon. You taste like perfection. But I also would like to fuck you."

I bring my hand to my dick and stroke. Her eyes drift down and she stares hungrily. "That's so hot," she whispers as I run my hand along my length. "I want to watch you do that someday."

"Yeah? You do?"

She nods. "I've gotten off to that."

My eyes bulge. "You have?"

"Sometimes I picture you touching me, but one of my go-tos is imagining you're doing the same. That you're jerking off to thoughts of me. I imagine you in your shower, getting off as you picture me. And that pretty much makes me come in seconds."

I swear my dick grows impossibly harder as she says that. Harder and insistent. I let go and yank her up on all fours. "Then I will make sure you get to watch it someday, you sexy, pervy, perfect woman. But right now, I need to get inside you again."

She lowers herself to her elbows, lifting her fantastic heart-shaped ass high in the air. Damn. "You have the best ass I've ever seen," I tell her, swatting her cheek.

She lets out a sexy yelp, and I bite down on the soft flesh. My reward is a long moan, and I find another condom quickly.

Once it's on, I grab her hips and shove into her. We groan at the same time.

"You look so fucking hot like this," I tell her as she turns her face, watching us from underneath me. That sends a wicked charge down my spine as I pump into her, setting a relentless pace.

"So do you. You look so good on your knees fucking me deep."

"Jesus. What a filthy mouth." I'm burning up. Her shamelessness turns me on even more, makes desire prickle all over me.

I fuck her like I've always wanted to. With her offering her body, giving herself over.

Soon enough, she grabs at the white sheets, curling her fingers around the fabric, losing control in a beautiful orgasm that lasts for ages. Mine stretches on and on, too, as I join her on the other side.

Minutes later, she's still breathing hard as she runs a hand through her hair. "You're like an animal."

I blow on my fingers and rub them across my chest. "I will take that as a compliment. And I'm sweating now. And thirsty. Thanks for the workout."

I head to the bathroom, pour a glass of water for myself then one more for her, and return to the bed, offering a cup to Jillian. As we drink, my mind trips back to earlier in the night, something I heard her friend say.

"What was the deal with your buddy and the elementary school? The water pipes or something?"

She scoots up against the pillows, setting her glass on the nightstand. "He does press for the local NBA team and they pay for sporting goods and things like that at one of the inner-city schools. From what he was hearing, it sounds like the water pipes burst and the summer program for the fourth-grade kids who go there will be closed unexpectedly tomorrow. They have teachers to supervise the kids, but nowhere to go."

I furrow my brow. "That must suck for the parents. I remember when I was younger and schools had to close. My parents scrambled without any day care."

Jillian nods thoughtfully. "It's a real problem for working parents, especially with little kids."

"Do you know if Andre figured out what to do? If there's anything to do?"

She shakes her head. "I don't. Do you have something in mind?"

The cogs are turning. I tap my temple. "I do, actually."

I tell her my idea, and she beams. "You'd do that?"

"Of course. It's hard to be a working parent. That's one of the hardest things in the world."

She flashes a sweet smile and reaches for her phone. "Let me call him." Before she unlocks the screen, she clears her throat. "Do you need to go?"

I narrow my eyes. "Are you kicking me out?"

Her hair whips back and forth as she shakes her head. "No, but I don't want to be presumptuous."

I flop back down on the bed, full monty–style, and park my hands behind my head. "You can presume all you want with me. For instance, presume I want to give you more orgasms. Presume I want to spend the night. Presume I haven't remotely had my fill of you."

As she makes her call, I down the rest of the water and flick on ESPN, checking out baseball scores and pre-season reports as she talks to her friend. She covers the phone a few times and asks me questions. I nod and tell her yes, yes, and yes.

When she's done, she sets a hand on my chest. "You have the biggest heart."

"Tell me something else that's big."

She laughs, spreading her fingers over my pecs. "You're so ridiculous."

"But it is big."

Reaching for my dick, she squeezes it. "You know it is." Letting go, she tiptoes her fingers up my belly. "I might need to take you for a ride again. I presume you can go for a third round."

I scoff. "Yes, you really ought to take me for another test drive."

She wriggles her eyebrows, and I lean closer, pressing a quick kiss to her lips. When we separate, I run my fingers down her bare arm. "Hey, what did you want to talk about before? I got a little distracted by your pussy in my mouth. A good distraction."

"Yes, and I was distracted by petting your wiener."

I pump a fist in victory. "I knew the wiener was irresistible."

A soft laugh falls from her lips before she goes quiet for a moment. She motions from me to her. "But seriously. We need to talk about this. About what it means." She pauses and raises her chin as if she's toughening up. "What it doesn't mean."

I don't like the sound of the second half, but I know she's right. "Okay, talk."

She exhales. "I'm not going to massage words. We both know this is incredibly risky for my job and for your deal. You're aware of that, but it has to be said."

"It's not like we're banging in public."

"Of course not, but secrets are hard to keep these days. Brands drop athletes like hotcakes for the slightest transgression. For a wrong word, for an old comment dredged up. Paleo Pet signed on for single Jones, and then Ford brought me on to help." She holds up a finger, her eyes laser sharp. "But Paleo Pet *didn't* sign on for the Jones who sneaked into his publicist's room in Miami and screwed her all night long."

I drag a hand over my jaw. "Fuck," I mutter, hating how this time with her would be seen.

"Right now, you're the wholesome, dog-loving, squeaky-clean guy. You don't want to be the guy boning his colleague. *Such a scandal.* That's how it would be framed if it got out. As a *workplace scandal.* There's no other way for the gossip press to spin it."

I cringe at the way she puts it so bluntly.

She runs her hand along my arm, her voice softening. "You can't be too cautious when you're playing that kind of high-stakes game. We could be caught. I'm pursuing a promotion, and I'm trying to rehab your image, but I just did exactly what we're trying to avoid."

I furrow my brow. "That's not entirely true. No one said to go on a sex diet. Just to be careful."

"Fine, true. But I'm your publicist."

"Does the team have rules against you dating players?" I ask, genuinely interested. I've no clue if she's crossing some sort of formal line in an HR handbook.

She shakes her head. "No, there isn't a specific rule against it. The only fraternization rules involve getting involved with direct reports and vice versa. I can't date my boss or any of the PR supervisors who report to me. We're not forbidden from dating players, though."

I curve up my lips. "Well, that's good, right?"

"Yes, technically, but there's so much more at stake. Even if I'm not violating a rule per se, think about how it would look, especially while I'm up for a promotion. While you're trying to land new deals. While we're working on those deals together. Here I am, trying to craft a good-boy image for you—one you rightfully deserve—and meanwhile, I'm on my hands and knees as you slam into me."

Against my better judgment, I groan, "I like you on your hands and knees." But then I turn more serious. "But I hear you. It's risky."

"It's dangerous."

Scrubbing a hand over my jaw, I ask, "Do you think it shouldn't happen again?" Part of me is hoping she'll laugh and say, *No, take me again now and tomorrow and over and over.*

"Do *you* think it should happen again?"

"I want it to," I answer honestly, because as far as I'm concerned, everything is in the open tonight. I don't want to play any more games with Jillian, and I won't toy with her emotions, or my own. Given the way I've stored everything until now, like a pressure cooker that only needed the smallest spark of jealousy to spill over, I've no interest in keeping my feelings private. "I know you might find this hard to believe, but I like you. Really like you. If I could, I would date you. I would take you out. I would romance you. I would do all the things I haven't done before."

Her breath flutters over her lips, and her eyes shine. She wiggles her body closer to mine. "Really?"

"Would you want that?" I ask softly.

She nods, that flash of vulnerability back in her brown eyes. "Of course I want that." Taking a deep breath, she looks away, swallowing tightly. "But we can't have it."

My shoulders sag. My chest is heavy. "We can't, can we?" I say with a sigh, an acknowledgment that she's right. That Trevor was right. That I need to focus on football and business only. That Jillian needs to do the kick-ass job she's always done, without a guy like me complicating her life. Trevor's words blare in my ears, the reminder of my track record. I've never had a relationship last longer than a month, and I detest the thought that her reputation could be called into question if she dated me. I care about Jillian far too much to let her be a question mark everyone has about me.

Her fingers trace my chest. "If we did that, we'd have to sneak around, and sneaking around is lying. No good can come of it."

"Then we agree that this can't happen again?"

She screws up the corner of her lips, clearly thinking. "As a publicist, I'm always looking for angles, so maybe we agree that when we go back to San Francisco, we can return to being player and publicist."

I grin wickedly, liking her clever mind. "Your angle is sharp. And since we return in two days, that means tomorrow I can get you on your hands and knees again so I can fuck you like the animal you say I am?"

"*Jones . . .*" It comes out like a purr.

"I'll take that as a yes."

She nods. "Yes, then we go back to how it was." Her expression turns apologetic. "I love what I do, and I don't want to chance losing it. My career has always been important to me. It was that way for my mom, too. I learned it from her."

I can't help but smile when she mentions her mom. I love that she's such a family gal. "Why was it that way for her?"

"She always said that true contentment comes from what you do. She'd say don't go looking for happiness in a man or in a relationship. Find it in your work. Find it, and when you do, it'll feed your soul."

"Does publicity feed your soul?"

"This might sound weird, but it does. I love sports, and I love using the platform the team has to do good. Sometimes, athletes get a bad rep," she says, and I huff, knowing that reality too well. "But in most cases, the public just needs to see the other side. And with so many young people looking up to athletes, it's great to show them doing amazing things for the community. I love that I can do that. I love that the great work you do on and off the field can inspire some young boys and girls to work harder, to be better, to be the best they can be. That does feed my soul, in a way, and I think I'm good at it."

Running my fingers through her soft locks, I nod. "You're not just good at it. You're great at it." I slow my strokes, making sure she meets my eyes. "I love knowing there's a piece of your mom driving you on, even when she's not here."

Jillian whispers, "Me, too."

"You miss her, don't you?" I ask.

She bites the corner of her lips, nodding. "I do. I'm used to it, but I do miss her."

"How could you not?" Dropping my hand from her hair, I loop my fingers through hers.

"But sometimes, I think she lives on."

"In what way?"

"In my superstitions. My good luck charms. She was like that. She believed you make your own luck, but she also loved all the symbols of luck, too. She was so very American, but she really embraced the Chinese culture and introduced me to it. She wanted me to grow up knowing it, even if I wasn't there anymore."

"I love that. She wanted to honor where you came from."

"Exactly. They didn't go over the top and send me to Chinese school and all that, but they found little ways to bring it into their lives." A smile crosses her face, and her eyes twinkle. "Like, they gave me dollar bills in little red envelopes during Chinese New Year. I liked that a lot."

I chuckle. "That is a most excellent cultural celebration. Another good luck symbol?"

"It is. My people love their luck."

"Hey, my people love their luck, too."

"You mean the Becketts?"

"Yeah, but mostly me. I love hearing about all your lucky symbols, since I'm the most superstitious guy around. I'm going to have to eat a pomelo a day during the season now that you've hooked me on them," I tell her, and she smiles in a way that makes my heart thump harder.

"Were your parents superstitious?"

"Not really. But my dad has his own theory about luck. He's very much of the mindset that luck means sometimes you lose and sometimes you win. Growing up, he tried to teach me to keep an even head about winning or losing, to remind me that success on the field is about talent and effort, but also luck. The way the ball falls, how a foot lands, how the wind blows."

"Do you believe that?"

I lean back and rub a hand over my jaw. "I want to. But I also think if I'm not out there busting my ass every second, then I'm not serving my team or my fans or myself. That's probably why I follow different superstitions about the game. I give a hundred and ten percent on the field—that I *can* control. But I can't control the wind, and I can't control the refs, so I have my little rituals."

"You do serve the team every day. You give it your all. I love watching you play. I can tell football feeds your soul."

She's right on the last count. The game absolutely commands my heart and my head. But I like the *other* thing she said, too. I raise an eyebrow. "You like watching me play?"

She nods.

I take a deep, satisfied breath. "That makes me want to make a big circus catch for you. To be on the field and raise my hands in a *J* so you'll know when I dive for a ball, I'm doing it for you." I bring her fingers to my lips and kiss them. "Still can't believe you didn't know I wanted you."

"I didn't think I was your type."

I scoop my hands under her waist and tug her on top of me, meeting her gaze. "Jillian, my type is you. If we didn't work together, I would be doing everything possible to get you to keep seeing me every night."

"You would?" Her cheeks seem to glow.

"I would."

"Stay the night?"

"You want to sleep on me again, don't you?"

"I do."

After we brush our teeth, since the hotel has extra toothbrushes in each room, and slide under the covers, she whispers something to me that makes me wish this wasn't ending. "I like you so much. I have for so long."

And I wish I could have her completely.

* * *

As dawn rises, she stirs in my arms. I kiss her cheek, run my fingers down her arm, and breathe her in. This is what I will miss most.

Waking up with her.

19

JILLIAN

Twin shrieks of ten-year-old glee echo in the cavernous indoor pool area. Fourth-grader Charlie splashes vigorously as his classmate Emma raises her arms up high. "Me, me, me!" the girl squeals.

The man of the hour lifts a beach ball high above his head from several feet away in the deeper water. Taking aim, Jones tosses it toward the kids. Emma catches it and shouts once more in excitement as she splashes onto her back. When she pops up, she turns to the deck and waves at her mom, who stands next to me.

The trim, tired woman in a haggard ponytail smiles at her young daughter, snapping a picture of her playing in the pool at the end of the day.

"Okay to post online?" the mom asks me.

"Absolutely."

Emma dolphins her way to the side of the pool. "Mom! This is the best day ever." The girl dunks her head underwater, pushes off, and swims to find another ball, presumably to launch at Jones.

"She wants to be a kicker," her mom says, gazing admiringly at the young girl. "Crazy dream, I'm sure."

"You never know. Perhaps she can be the first female kicker in the NFL someday."

The mom nods, a dreamy look in her eyes but a disbelieving note in her voice. "Maybe someday."

It's unlikely, but you never know what might happen.

"Thank you again for all this." She waves at the pool and behind her to the rest of the rec center.

"It was all Jones," I say, giving credit where credit is due.

This was his brilliant idea. After I called Andre last night, he put things in motion to make this day happen, but Jones is the one behind it with his generosity. He rented out an entire rec center and invited the kids at the shuttered elementary school summer program to spend the day here playing board games, shooting hoops, and cavorting in the indoor pool. We arrived as soon as the morning's calendar shoot ended, since he had free time during the day. Jones has joined in on most of the activities, including a rousing game of Candyland, in which a group of fourth-grade girls banded together to utterly destroy him as they reached Candy Castle well before he did.

"This was a godsend, I tell you," the woman says, adjusting the strands of hair that have fallen from her elastic band. "I answer phones at an auto-repair shop, and I had no more time off. When I heard about the problem with the school being closed, I was completely backed into a corner. I needed this"—she pauses, as if hunting for the right word—"gift."

"I'm glad it feels that way."

That was Jones's hope, but he did more than simply let the quandary tug on his heartstrings. He *solved* the problem. I've spent the day here with him, hanging out with the kids, joining in as well—my hoops game is strong, and I led the girls to a victory over the boys, thank you very much—and making sure the kids had food and snacks, courtesy of Jones's pizza party order.

The day is winding down, and most of the parents have picked up their kids, snapping photos of them with the athlete. Though I could have invited local press today, I chose not to, in part because we'd have needed release waivers from the parents. Even so, one of the keys in publicity is to know when to turn on the cameras and when to shut them down. Press wasn't the point of this effort, nor did I want to turn this into a photo frenzy. But at the same time, we decided the kids and parents were welcome to take photos. In the age of social media, everything eventually ends up online, but I did want the photos from today to come from the parents rather than from reporters.

Though I'm pretty sure a few of the kids have Instagram and Snapchat, too, since I saw an Instagram pic of Jones, filtered so he was wearing a pair of panda ears as he languished by Gumdrop Mountain. Next to him in the shot were Malcolm and Connor, who fought valiantly to buy Park Place from a pair of industrious boys in a heated game of Monopoly, since Jones convinced his Mavericks buddies to stop by for a few hours. But mostly, it's been the former party-boy Renegade entertaining the kids on an unexpected day off.

When I see him like this, it's hard to imagine he ever had a questionable rep.

As I watch Jones swim to the steps of the pool with

Charlie, the last kid to be picked up, I'm reminded again of what's at stake if we were to be found out. *So very much.* Even though part of me is deliciously tempted to carry on clandestinely with him, to invite him over for a midnight tryst at my home back in San Francisco, to ask him if he wants to meet up somewhere, someplace, maybe out of town in another chichi hotel—that all feels like an illicit affair.

An illicit affair is precisely the opposite of what he needs right now.

I wish we could carry on out in the open, like he said he wanted to last night. Date me, romance me, take me out. My heart flutters just thinking of that.

But the risks are far too real for me to entertain it seriously. I can't take that chance with my job, and there's no way he could pull off dating me without it looking like I'm the next chick in a long line of his ladies.

That thought curdles my stomach. The notion that I could be an over-and-out girl, and the idea that people would see me that way. And see *him* that way.

As I look at him now, hanging out with the kids, I know *this* is what he needs, because this is who he is.

A guy who cares.

A guy who tries.

A guy who has a massive heart for families.

That's what I want everyone to know about him, and if I keep dallying with him beyond tonight, then I'll be risking more than my own job. I'll risk his reputation, and his reputation matters.

He's more than I thought he was a few weeks ago. Whether it's animals left homeless, families who need a little extra, or even a woman's dad trying to put together a piece of furniture, he has such a giving spirit. Seeing him toss a towel to skinny Charlie as the kid steps out of the pool is one more instance in a day brimming with moments that melt my heart and make me fall a little deeper.

A little later, as Emma and Charlie head for the exit doors, Jones gives me a big hug. "Thank you so much for doing this with me. I'm sure you had a ton of other work today, but I appreciate you being here."

"There's no place I'd rather have been."

"Smile!"

I freeze for a second at the sound of Emma's voice, but then remind myself we're doing nothing wrong. We're simply two colleagues hugging. As we break apart, we turn and grin for her as she lifts her mom's phone and snaps one more shot. Though Jones's arm is draped over my shoulder, I reassure myself there's no way to tell my stomach is flipping, my insides are melting, and I can't wait to see him again tonight.

The picture can't possibly capture all that, and it certainly can't photograph what's inside my heart for him.

Which is far more than I ever expected.

As Emma's mom waves goodbye, there's a tug on my purse. I turn, looking for the girl, in case she has something else to say. But she's out the door, and only Jones is here.

I give him a quizzical look, and he simply shrugs impishly.

* * *

"Rock star."

The praise comes from Ford Grayson. He's on the other end of the line, and I swear I can see his animated face, pointing at his screen, thrilled at the photos that have made their way across social feeds. "The world is seeing how motherfucking awesome this dude is. And check out the two of you." I brace myself as Ford whistles his appreciation while checking out our picture, clearly. "You look like such a great team."

I breathe a private sigh of relief, grateful that my feelings for the man were indeed shrouded in the image. All pro, that's the goal.

"He's been easy to work with, as he's always been," I say, pacing across my hotel room, checking the time. Jones said he'd text or call as soon as he finished his workout, and to say I'm an eager beaver would be an understatement. Though, it's not just the beaver that's eager; all of me wants to see all of him.

"When he gets back in town, Liam wants him to shoot some commercials and some online ads for Paleo Pet right before training camp," Ford continues, chattering away about the deal. "Then they can roll that partnership out big-time. The sky is the limit. And you know, I wouldn't have been able to do any of this so well without you. Jones says you're a dream to work with."

Dream. I fear that's what these two days will feel like when tomorrow comes and we go home. Nothing but a lovely, dirty, wonderful dream that's ended far too soon.

"It's been my pleasure," I say tightly, and once more the double entendre isn't lost on me. Everything with Jones has been more pleasure than I imagined.

And more pleasure than I should allow.

A frisson of guilt washes over me as Ford heaps on more praise for my work. But I bat the feeling away. I *am* a damn fine addition to the team. I *have* helped. I've done good work for Jones. I can't let my feelings for him obscure the reality that we are well and truly a great team professionally.

I thank Ford, and as I hang up, a lump forms in my throat. Dumb lump. Stupid emotions. I roll my shoulders like a boxer, trying to shake off the wayward emotion. Touching my cherry earrings, I tell myself to keep my head clear. There's nothing to cry over. Nothing to get all sad and mournful about.

Everything is going great for Jones. Everything is going great for me at work.

Work—the word clangs in my mind. My mother taught me to act with honesty and integrity in all endeavors. Perhaps that's why there's a lump in my throat and a churning in my stomach. Maybe I'm not behaving as I should at work.

I honestly believe Jones is a good guy. I truly want the world to see his real heart. That has to mean I'm acting with honesty and integrity, I tell myself, as I wring my hands.

I can't ask my mom for advice, though, and I don't know what she would have told me. Instead, I picture my dad's face—my sarcastic, sweet, lonely-but-dealing-with-it widower father. He'd understand, surely. He's been a fan of Jones. He's always been a softie, a romantic. He would side with the heart. He always did.

Even so, I can't expect him to fully understand all the risks. I can't trick myself into believing what I'm doing is okay, simply because my dad thinks we'd be a cute couple.

I vow to remain realistic, to make my own choices.

I'm a grown woman, and I can handle this brief and fantastic fling, as well as its inevitable ending.

I square my shoulders, grab my phone, and turn to my playlist. I love me some sexy music. Always have. That's the mood I want to be in tonight, so I find Zayn's "Pillowtalk" and crank the tune all the way up. Closing my eyes, I sway to the slow jam, moving my body to its languid notes, its sensual words, its filthy lines, too.

It's a promise of a long, lingering night rich with the kind of tempo I want with Jones. As I listen, I don't think about good ideas or bad ideas. Roles or places. Right or wrong.

I let go of the daughter I am, the hard worker I am, the career woman I am. Tonight, I want to be only one part of me.

The woman. The lover.

When my phone rings, I'm turned on before I hear his voice. I've already set my own mood.

"Can you meet me in five minutes?" His gravelly voice rumbles over me.

"Yes."

"Come down the hall to my room. You don't even have to knock."

"I don't? Are you leaving the door open?"

"No. There is a key in the side of your purse. I put it there at the pool," he says, and I remember the tugging I felt on my bag. That was him. "Let yourself in. You'll understand why."

20

JILLIAN

I slide the card key across his door, anticipation threading through me. Goose bumps rise on my arms. I don't know what he has in store, but the crazy beat of my heart tells me I want whatever is coming my way.

Badly.

As soon as I push open the door, I know.

Water from the shower pounds in a rhythm, signaling to me. A zing tears through me, racing across my skin, leaving tingles in its wake.

I shut the hotel room door behind me, locking the chain.

I tiptoe, not because I need to, but because I want to. The lights are low, and when I enter the large, white-tiled bathroom, only the mirror lights are on. They illuminate him just enough. I see his reflection first in the mirror, and heat rushes to my core.

He's naked in the shower.

He's giving me my fantasy. Discovering him all alone.

As I walk into the room, I turn my gaze to stare

directly at his carved, muscular body through the glass shower wall. He doesn't look at me as he runs soap over his skin.

He's bathing, and it's erotic.

So much more than I dreamed.

That big left hand runs over his right pec, down his side, and I murmur, as if I'm watching a naughty video.

This is my filthy fantasy.

His private time.

As I watch him rub soap across those powerful thighs and legs, he doesn't acknowledge me. I've become a voyeur, and I hope he's saved the best till the audience arrived.

I walk past the enclosed shower, heading to the counter in front of the mirror. The shower is behind me now, and my back is to him as I stop at the counter. My view in the mirror reveals everything, shows every move he makes. He glides the bar of soap over his body, lathering up his arms, his stomach, and now his erection.

His hand slides over his hard-on.

A murmur falls from my mouth. He's in silhouette, his hand washing his dick. He lets go of the soap, places it in the dish, and leans under the stream, rinsing the shampoo from his head. Both hands rise, giving me a view of those powerful arms as he drags them through his hair, the suds pooling at his feet.

With his eyes still closed, he lowers his hands, the right drifting down between his legs again.

His palm slides over his cock and strokes once, absently, as if he's testing whether he wants to pleasure himself, as if he's curious if he's even in the mood.

I moan as a wild pulse beats in my body, heat rising in my core. As he runs a hand slowly down his shaft, desire rockets around inside me, flooding every square inch of my body. I'm dying to touch myself, to slide my fingers inside my panties and feel how slick I am.

But I don't want to miss a minute of this private show. The pace of the water is relentless, insistent. The patter of the stream against the tiles is the soundtrack of his seduction as he grips himself, stroking his length. I can't help but start to rock my hips. I'm dying to move my body against his, to find some relief for this absolute ache in my center.

Instead, I stare unabashedly in the reflection as he tugs on his cock, his other hand cupping his balls. His palm moves faster, his fist sliding over the head now, squeezing, then back down to the base. I'm so jealous of his hand. I want it to be my hand, my mouth, *me*. But I want this even more. I want this movie that he's not acting in—he *is* in—to keep playing on the screen in the mirror.

I've never been more aroused in my life. He squeezes harder, his hips moving now, rocking, thrusting, and my God, he's truly fucking his own fist.

I'm liquid. I'm a pool of heat. My skin flames red-hot, and my bones dissolve.

A loud groan echoes from the shower, and it triggers a wave of molten pleasure. The fact that he's so turned on already is killing me. I jam my palms against the counter, gripping the edge, watching him, craving him, wanting to know what he looks and sounds like when he comes alone while thinking of me.

But tonight, he's alone with me. His hand shuttles faster, up and down his erection. He still doesn't meet my gaze, and I love it. I love that he's showing me what he does when I'm not here.

His lips part.

A harsh breath comes.

A jerk of his hand.

A thrust of his hips.

A visible shudder.

"*Jillian.*"

My name is a dirty word. I break. I can't take it anymore. I've become a bonfire, and I'm going to burn alive if I don't get in there with him right now. Swiveling around, I strip in a frenzy, tossing my sundress on the floor along with my shoes, panties, and bra.

He turns to me, his eyes blazing with heat, even in the shadowy light. "Get in here."

I nod. I'll do anything he says. He opens the door, and I step into the shower with him. He doesn't stop what he's doing. His hand flies over his cock, and I'm on edge. So aroused. So wet. So needy.

His expression is marked with a lust that I want to experience for a long, long time. "You're gonna make me come." His voice is a growl.

I'm desperate as I answer, "I want to taste it. I want to taste you. Let me."

He tips his chin. "Get on your knees."

In a second, I'm on the floor, my knees digging into the tiles, my hands grabbing his hips, my eyes watching his.

He stares down at me as he jerks his length. "This what you pictured?" His hand is a blur. His words are rough.

"Yes, but it's so much better."

"Fuck, baby. The real thing is so much better with you." His hand moves faster than I knew it could, and he grunts my name. His next words are one syllable only. Tinged with desire. "Yeah. Now. Fuck."

He yanks his shaft to my lips and I open, but he doesn't fill my mouth. He rubs the head over my top lip as he trembles and comes on my lips, rubbing it across my mouth. My tongue flicks out, licking it off, tasting him.

He pants and groans and swears again and again.

Like this is too much for him to take.

Like he can barely comprehend how hard he's come, how much I want him.

He reaches for my shoulders and pulls me to my feet, wiping his hand across my mouth before he kisses me like a mad, hungry man. As our lips lock, his hand finds its way between my legs where he discovers how insanely wet I am there.

He breaks the kiss, murmuring in my ear, "You're drenched, baby."

I nod. I can barely speak now. I only want him to put me out of my misery. My sounds are wanton and wild as he strokes. It won't take long at all. I'm practically there. He pushes two fingers inside, his thumb rubbing where I want him most, and all the nerve endings in my body sizzle at once, then crackle. An instant and shattering burst of exquisite pleasure overtakes me, and I come on his hand while his lips devour mine.

Afterward, he dries me off, carries me to his bed, finds a condom, and spreads me open once more. I'm still wet and eager for him, and he's hard again, ready to go.

He sinks inside me, and we screw like the desperate creatures we are. But even as we pant, as we scratch, as we thrust, this time feels different. He brings me closer, wraps his arms tighter around me, lowers his mouth to my ear.

Becomes gentler.

More tender.

Needier.

His words hook into me, surrounding me, warming my soul.

Want you.

Want this.

Wish I could have you again.

He takes me to the edge, talking dirty, talking sweet.

I'll keep wanting this. I won't stop wanting you.

Before I can even start to think about what this all means, I'm yanked under by another epic climax. He's right behind me, flying in this land of ecstatic bliss by my side.

We spend the night together, and the morning comes far too soon, the dawn a cruel reminder that sultry, sexy Miami is nearly behind us and that we're heading home to San Francisco, where our brief and explosive secret affair will become a fiery memory, one I will revisit over and over.

Endlessly, I'm sure, because I don't know how I will ever get him out of my system.

But I'll have to find a way.

21

JONES

Training camp is brutal. It's supposed to be brutal. Exhaustion is my sole state of mind and body at the end of every day as Coach Greenhaven works us to the bone. We run routes like we've never run routes before. Last year, we went as far as the championship game, but we were knocked out by our biggest rivals, the Los Angeles Devil Sharks. This year, the goal is to go all the way to another ring.

Better, faster, stronger. That's my motto as I rise at dawn, hit the weight room, then run drills and sprints on the practice field all afternoon.

During training camp, I'm all football all the time, and I love it.

Except when I see Jillian.

We train at a university an hour from the city, and she's here regularly, since training camp is a media fiesta. At least a few times a week, I see her. Standing against the wall in the back of the press conference room, scribbling notes in her notebook, tapping out replies to emails on her phone. Hanging out on the edge of the field, answering questions from reporters and bloggers. One afternoon as I grab water after an intense drill, I see a local sportscaster stride over to her. Kevin Stone is his name, and he dresses sharp. As he approaches, Jillian crosses her arms and raises her chin, a slight shift in her demeanor, as if she's protecting herself.

Awareness slams me like a linebacker.

She used to date him. I remember her seeing him a year ago. Holy shit. Is he the asshole who detests room service? Wait. His crime is way worse than hating a great meal option. He's the shithead who cheated on her. For a second, this feels a little like jealousy because it tightens my muscles and makes me grit my teeth. But I feel zero envy for that ass. He'll never have that incredible woman again. Not after he broke her trust.

That's what pisses me off. That's why I'm wound up. That jackass hurt my woman, and I have half a mind to march over, shoot him a withering glare, and tell him he lost out on the greatest chance ever.

But I don't do that. I snap my gaze away and down another water. I lost a chance, too.

For vastly different reasons, but I'm in the same boat as that fucker.

She's not my woman, either.

* * *

On the second to last day of training camp, Jillian asks the marquee players to sit for a news conference. That's Cooper, Harlan, Rick, and me.

At the end of the presser, a sports blogger tosses out

the final question in my direction. "Jones, how do you feel about your chances this year?"

The question has been asked every day, countless times, in press conferences all across the NFL and in every professional sports league. Reporters and fans have a bottomless appetite for pondering how far any team can go. Can we go all the way? That's what everyone wants to know. Hell, that's why we play.

As I clear my throat and prepare to answer, my eyes drift to Jillian, standing against the white wall near the front of the room. I've seen her in this pose hundreds of times before, dressed to the nines, her brown eyes taking in the whole room.

She wears a black skirt and a candy-apple red blouse with white polka dots. She's so fucking business-sexy that it's impossible for me not to want to strip those clothes off and fuck her against the wall.

But that's what I shouldn't think about.

Except, she's looking at me now. Not in the way she used to before Miami, but really looking at me. Seeing me. *Knowing* me.

The question hangs in the air as that loaded word—chances—takes on a brand-new meaning. *How do you feel about your chances this year?*

Our eyes lock. A connection seems to pass between us, as if she knows what's on my mind. *She's* on my mind. *She's* the chance I wish I could take. I repeat the question, buying myself time. "How do I feel about our chances?"

The reporter nods, an expectant look in his eyes, his phone pointing in my direction, recording my answer.

"If we play hard every day, we have a shot. And isn't that all we can hope for?" My eyes drift back to her for a fleeting second. "To have a chance?" I add one more word, so she knows I mean her. I'm not entirely sure what I'm hinting at. Or if I'm merely expressing a wish. But I say it anyway. "*Presumably.*"

She dips her head, and a smile spreads across her face, even as she tries to rein it in.

After the press conference ends, I drag my feet, taking my time leaving. I make sure I'm the last player to exit, and when I'm the only one in the hall, she comes out of the room, shutting the door.

"Oh. Hey." She sounds startled to see only me in the long, empty hallway.

"Hey." It's the first time at training camp when it's been just the two of us.

"How are you?"

"I'm good."

"Are you enjoying training camp?"

I step closer, dangerously close. "You can presume it would be better if you sneaked into my room at night," I whisper into her ear.

Her eyes float closed, and a visible tremble moves down her body. She murmurs my name, then she opens her eyes. "You are far too tempting."

My gaze roams over her from head to toe, thinking of those two days and nights in Miami when she was all mine. "I could say the same about you. Especially in this red shirt. Red is lucky, you know?"

A faint smile spreads. "I wish."

"I wish we were getting lucky."

"Me, too." She glances down the hall, and even though the coast is clear, she tips her forehead to the door at the far end. "I should probably go. Someone will show up here any second."

"Are you worried you'd be tempted to do something if you stayed here in this hall with me?"

She shakes her head. "I'm not worried. I'm absolutely certain of what would happen if I stayed near you for another five seconds."

I grab her wrist, the need to touch her overruling any reason. Stroking my finger across her skin, I move closer. She'd better stop me, because I'm not sure I can stop myself. I'm not sure I want to.

She swallows, shakes her head. "Jones, you're making this hard." Her voice is wobbly.

"It is hard."

She sighs, and it comes out soft, so sexy and needy that it nearly shatters my already weak resolve. "I really need to go." But she doesn't make a move. She leans in close, almost as if she's inhaling me.

She's inches from me, and if anyone saw us, they'd be hard-pressed to believe any denials we'd utter.

That reality—how close I'm tangoing to fucking shit up—smashes into me, and I let go of her hand in an instant. "I know. I really need to let you go, but you have to know that's the part that's hardest. Letting you go."

Her brown eyes are big, beautiful, and full of something deeper, something I wish was in my life. The kind of connection I've never had before with a woman. The kind that lasts.

"I know," she whispers, her voice trembling, her eyes shining. She inhales sharply, waving her hand as if to shake off her emotions.

She walks away.

* * *

Later that night, in the room I share with Harlan, he packs his suitcase. "Hey, man, whatever happened with Jillian?"

I toss a shirt into my duffel. "Nothing."

"The cherry pie didn't work?"

I shake my head.

"What about Miami?"

I don't like lying to my buddy, but I promised Jillian that what happened in Miami was just between us. I have to keep it that way, even if I want what happened in Miami to happen again and again.

"Miami was . . . just work."

* * *

The crowd roars. The din of sixty thousand fans in Seattle vibrates across the field, a steady drumbeat. That noise is paired with insults from the D line, the usual trash talk, words about my mother, your mother, my dick, your dick. I tune it all out, narrowing on Cooper taking the snap.

My cue. Breaking to the right, I race downfield, hunting for an opening every step of the way. The score is tied, and it's the fourth quarter. There are two minutes left in the first game of the season in early September, against one of our division rivals on their home turf.

I have one job. Find the gap.

I dodge a speed-demon cornerback, racing into the perfect spot as Cooper launches the ball. All my senses zero in on one thing. My eyes track the pigskin like an eagle scanning for fish.

Crosshairs. Mine. I own that ball.

A linebacker appears out of nowhere, aiming for

me. A quick sidestep, a double back, and I'm right where I need to be, avoiding him as the ball arcs low toward the grass. That won't fucking do. No way in hell is this pass going incomplete.

I stretch my arms as I lunge for the ball, extending my hands. The football tap dances on the tips of my fingers. This is when the big hands count the most, and I grapple the edge, barely holding it before I reel that ball in like a big catch in the ocean, yanking it to my chest. In a split second, I'm off and running, sprinting hard. The end zone is twenty yards away. It's my destination—it's always my destination. A safety comes at me, trying to grab me anywhere. Arms flail at me. But I'm faster, and when I cross the goal line, the sounds truly become deafening.

The cheers, and mostly jeers, from the fans. The shouts. My heavy breath. The clomp of cleats, bodies slamming into bodies, big guys sledgehammering other big guys. Then me.

The safety wraps his arms around my waist, yanking me to the ground.

I'm fair game. I always am.

As a receiver, I know how to take the hits and how to fall, but there's always a moment when I could fall wrong.

Fortunately, it's not today as I land on the side of my ass. My padded ass, thankfully.

It still hurts for a second, and I wince. But then I shuck that off, the momentary hurt blotted out by the reward of six glorious points.

Thanks to a circus catch.

I raise my arms and form a *J*.

* * *

After the game, Sierra Franklin makes a beeline for me. One of the San Francisco sports reporters who travels with the team, she's quick and smart. Jillian is by her side as the redhead thrusts her mic at me, her diamond ring sparkling under the afternoon sun. "Great job in a tight game that went down to the wire. Tell us what you were thinking when O'Malley circled around you before you caught the ball," she says, naming the tackler who was aiming for me.

I answer her question the way I nearly always do. "I was just focused on finding an opening and getting in position to catch the ball."

It's that simple. Sometimes with sports, outsiders overthink what we do. Sure, it takes unusual talent, a larger than average physique, and a whole hell of a lot of work. But more than that, the secret sauce is focus. When I'm on the field, I'm not thinking of how my stocks are faring, what I'll cook for dinner, or if there are any good flicks out that weekend. I don't even think of women. My focus is one-track only. The ball—find the ball, catch the ball, run with the ball.

I block out everything else.

"You definitely made sure of that." With a wry smile, Sierra adds, "What about the gesture you made in the end zone? We haven't seen that from you before, but it looked like a *J*. Shall I presume that's a new calling card now for your name?"

My eyes stray to Jillian, waiting patiently. For a split second, mischief flickers in her eyes. I flash back to Miami, the night I promised I would send her a signal.

"All the best names start with *J*. Thanks so much,

Sierra. And congratulations again on your upcoming wedding."

"Thank you so much, Jones."

The redheaded reporter beams, and as the two women head off to find the next player to interview, Jillian says something about how she can't wait to see her walk down the aisle in a few more days.

Then, Jillian glances over her shoulder at me, nibbling on the corner of her lip.

A charge rocks down my body.

From that.

From her biting her lip.

I'm screwed.

When I turn to the locker room, I wonder why I ever thought it would be wise to fall hard for a woman I can't have.

22

JILLIAN

Katie pours me a glass of white wine. "How was it? Did you survive the first game?"

I motion for her to keep going with the chardonnay. "Let me put it this way. I'm ready to accept my medal in self-restraint. Have you made that trophy for me yet?"

"It's on its way, along with a plaque." She sets down the bottle and hands me the glass. "This enough for you?"

"Unlikely, but I'll try to make do," I say as I sink into my cushy couch and tuck my feet under me, taking a sip. "He made the *J* for me. *For me.* This is killing me."

Katie nods sympathetically. "I better leave the bottle with you."

"Leave a whole crate with me, 'kay? Thanks."

She pats my knee. "I will, but may I please point out how I'll soon be taking you out for ice cream and pepper, and proving that it goes together like you and Jones? And you guys obviously go together."

"We do not go together. Isn't it obvious that we don't?"

Bringing the wine to my lips, I guzzle. There is no way to mince words about how I drink it. After training camp, after seeing him every day, after still fantasizing about him every night, after the game today and the quick flight home from Seattle, I need a fat drink or two or three.

Katie shakes her head, her blond strands falling loose and long over her shoulders. "There really isn't a way for you to manage this? C'mon. Football is always about finding openings."

"No. I have my interview next week. I need to be focused on that. Being with Jones is too risky. I've gone over it in my head a million times, and there's just no way for me to make this work and not be the pot who called the kettle black."

"Oh, that's terrible. Who would want to be the pot calling the kettle black? That's like the worst thing anybody could ever say to you."

I sigh. "It's not that, Katie. It's just . . . I can't see this going well. Ending well."

"You're not Chelsea, who snapped his shot on Tinder. You're not that model Annika, who drank champagne with him in a dress that bared all."

My skin crawls thinking of his former conquests. I narrow my eyes, my nostrils flaring. "I hate them."

"Meow, kitty-cat."

"I know. It's terrible. But I don't know how to bring this out in the open and have it go well. All my work with him is predicated on this stuff not happening. Flings not happening. Risqué trysts not occurring. And he doesn't exactly have a track record with relationships. Even if he said, 'Hey, she's my girl now,' who's going to believe him?"

Katie shrugs and says softly, "I don't know the answer to that."

"That's the issue. The answer is that it likely wouldn't fly. We're trying to craft a more wholesome image, an image that helps him *keep* deals, not lose them."

Katie lifts her glass and nods thoughtfully. "Right, but you're only focused on work, Jillian. Not on the fact that you might have actual feelings for someone."

I give her a sharp stare. "But isn't that how forbidden relationships are always justified once you try to bring them out in the open? *But I care about him.* Like that exonerates people from responsibility. *We couldn't hide it anymore.*" I take another drink, trying to settle this tempest of emotions inside me.

"No, but maybe there are rules worth bending."

I shake my head. If I bend, I'll lose. If I bend even more, he could break my heart. I take a fortifying breath. I need to stay strong. "Even if we have actual feelings, it's too risky for both our careers to be involved. Too often we think emotions give us carte blanche to excuse ourselves from right or wrong. Have an affair? It's totally fine if you love the person you cheated with."

She arches a well-groomed eyebrow, her blue eyes zeroing in on me. "So you love him?"

I roll my eyes. "You know what I mean."

But later, after she leaves, I have to ask myself what *do* I mean.

Do my feelings for him run that deep? I can't believe they do. I know better. I'm smart and savvy, and I simply wouldn't let myself fall for a guy like him.

Like him.

That's the me of two months ago talking. That's the

me who only knew Jones on the surface. When we started working on the calendar, he was a pretty face, a delicious body, a flirt.

That was all.

He's so much more now.

So much deeper.

And yet, I've managed without him since we returned from Florida. That's damn impressive. If I can pull off several weeks, what's the rest of my life? It'll get easier. As I strip off my clothes and tug on a tank top to slide into bed, it's not easier. That's why I told Katie all about him. It's too hard to miss him like this by myself.

Maybe it's the two glasses of wine, or maybe it's the *J* he made on the field.

I take out my phone and send him a text.

Jillian: Hey.

Jones: Hey.

Jillian: I feel bad about something.

Jones: Don't feel bad about trying to distract me with your hotness after the game, wearing that blouse I wanted to rip off with my teeth.

A stupidly big grin forms, but I stick to my plan.

Jillian: I would like to know how strong your teeth are. But in all seriousness, I feel bad because I know we said we were going to keep everything that happened in Miami a secret, but I told my best friend, Katie.

Jillian: I'm so sorry, Jones. I feel terrible.

Jones: So terrible you'd let me spank the terrible right out of you?

I cross my ankles, laughing at his response. He's always made me laugh. His sense of humor is one of the things I adore about him.

Jillian: I guess I'm in very big trouble, then.

Jones: So big that if you were here, I would bend you over my lap and swat that gorgeous heart-shaped ass of yours.

I turn to my side, clutching the phone as if it's the source of all the happiness in the world—or maybe just in my world.

Jillian: I deserve it.

Jones: I would smack you on one cheek, then the other, and you'd probably tremble all over because I'm pretty sure you like to be spanked.

Jillian: Pretty sure? Don't you know? You already spanked me. Also, you're not annoyed?

Jones: Woman, if you didn't tell your best friend about me, I'd have been devastated. The fact that you told her makes me weirdly, stupidly happy.

Jillian: Why?

Jones: Because it means you like me enough to tell a girlfriend. Now, please don't interrupt my spanking fantasy again. Because I'd like to put you on all fours, bite your ass, and nibble my way down your legs. I'd nip your right ankle, then your left, then I'd lick my way up your other leg to that absolutely delicious spot between your thighs where I know you're already wet and aching for me.

More like on fire. I wriggle around on the bed, murmuring his name.

Jillian: How did you know the top two adjectives to describe how I feel right now? Wet and aching are shockingly accurate.

Jones: Because I've touched you enough to know what turns you on.

Jillian: What turns me on?

Jones: You like it when I kiss you like it's something I've been wanting to do for years. You like it when I go down on you like you're the hottest thing I've tasted. And you go out of your mind when I fuck you like there's nothing I want more in the world.

Like that, I've entered a state of reckless arousal. I moan so loudly I'm sure my neighbors can hear, and I don't care. I ache for him. I long for him.

Jillian: If you're looking for me, my phone officially caught fire and melted.

Jones: Good. So I was right?

Jillian: You're more than right, and I don't think we're doing a very good job at staying apart.

Jones: Are you in my house right now?

Jillian: Sadly, no.

Jones: Then, as far as I'm concerned, this is staying apart. No one ever said I couldn't send you a dirty text.

Jillian: That was a little more than a dirty text. That felt like sexting. Like more than sexting.

Jones: It's always felt like more with you. And now I can't stop thinking about how much I want to be inside you again. So, distract me. Tell me what you told Katie about me.

I smile now, a giddy grin that seems to light me up from head to toe. I start to type, but he texts again.

Jones: Besides the obvious traits of awesome I possess. That I made you come so hard you saw stars, planets, and galaxies, and that my cock is illegal. Your words.

Jillian: And I like when you use that illegal weapon on me. I told her you rocked my world in bed. I told her you made a difference in the lives of families. I told her you helped my dad. I told her you're very dangerous for me.

Jones: Dangerous?

Jillian: I told her you're the most intoxicating mix of rough and tender.

Jones: In bed?

Jillian: In bed and out of bed.

Jones: And do you like that mix? I think you do . . .

Jillian: You know I do. You're sweet and sexy. You're funny and kind. You're jealous and caring. You listen. And you also make my toes curl, my knees weak, and my—

I send before I finish the last word. My fingers went too fast.

Jones: What was the last my . . .?

You make my heart flutter. But I can't say that to him yet. Once those words make landfall, you can't take them back. I'd be putting that fluttering heart on the line.

Jillian: My belly flip . . .

There. That's safer.

Jones: I wish you were in my bed right now.

See? He likes the sex talk, too, and as I contemplate a naughty reply, he's typing back.

Jones: That's because the most dangerous thing to me is how much I like it when you're curled up in my arms and you fall asleep with me at night. Because that means you'll be in my arms when I wake up.

Jillian: That's my favorite way to wake up.

As I stare at the phone, the problem is clear. Miami wasn't a fling. Miami wasn't a no-strings-attached dalliance for either one of us. That trip across the country was the start of everything, and I want to take him back and make him all mine again, with no consequences, no risk, and no fallout. I want it all, without anyone getting hurt.

* * *

The next morning, I crunch on some toast and sip some hot tea as I work on the lineup for my Fire-Breathing Dragons. After I adjust my starting pitcher rotation, I check my email.

A message from Kevin greets me. I click it open, and it's the usual from him—an interview request. *Can Cooper come on my Sunday preview show?*

I'm about to reply that I'll check with the quarter-back, when I see his postscript.

P.S. See you at Sierra's wedding this Thursday! Be sure to say hello to Shelly and me! We can toast to Sierra together!

I groan loudly. I forgot he'd be attending the wedding.

I might be over the guy, but this is precisely why he irritates me.

Because he thinks I'd want to say hello to him and the woman he cheated on me with.

"You sure know how to pick 'em, girl," I mutter.

My spine straightens. Wait. Just because Kevin is a dickhead doesn't mean I have bad taste in men.

Of course not. Jones is nothing like Kevin.

My taste is not an issue.

But perhaps my judgment is. I did fall for a man I can't have.

Maybe I don't know how to pick them at all.

23

JONES

Cletus leaps through the air, chasing a Frisbee, landing like the agile dude he is with the disc in his mouth. The camera zooms in on me and I give my 100 percent honest assessment. "That's why I won't feed my little guy anything but the best." Next shot, Cletus retrieves a ball as I finish my ode to the dog food. "When your dog is worth the very best, that's when you give him Paleo Pet."

Ford points the remote at the TV and hits stop theatrically. "Bam. That is a dog food commercial if I've ever seen one. And look at Cletus. He loves watching it."

My agent gestures to my pooch, who I brought to Ford's office the day after the game for the "premiere" of the television spot. Wagging his tiny tail, Cletus stretches out in a downward dog.

He's also showing off for Jillian, pawing at her legs, but she seems distracted. She's still staring at the screen even though the TV is off.

Cletus whimpers, and that gets her attention. She

reaches down, scoops him into her lap, and strokes his soft brown and white fur.

"What can I say? He's a ladies' man?" I wink.

Trevor eyes me. "Something you're not anymore."

"Oh yeah." Ford stretches across the desk and high-fives my brother before turning his attention to Jillian. "Liam gave the okay to tease this on social media before it runs on Lifetime in a few days," he says. "Can you handle?"

Jillian nods crisply, back to her usual sharp-as-a-tack demeanor. "Absolutely. I have a plan for how to magnify this online."

"Excellent. Liam is thrilled with how it's all coming along," Trevor chimes in, since he's been handling a lot of the details with my sponsor.

"We all are. And don't you forget, you have a dinner with him later this week," Ford says, pointing at me.

"Dude. I know. You put it on my calendar."

"My job is to remind you, too. We'll all be there. And soon, we'll be having a dinner with the quick-serve restaurant because that deal is coming together with Organic Eats."

Trevor pumps a fist. "Great work, man."

We make our way out of the office. In the elevator, it's the four of us as Ford rides down. Jillian is quiet again, a faraway look in her eyes. I wish I could take her hand, haul her next to me, and ask her what's bothering her.

I wish I could talk to her the way I want.

Like she's mine.

I wish I could stop being so damn dishonest in front of these guys who I like and respect. In front of my brother, in front of my agent. I want to tell them the truth—that the woman standing across from me makes me want to say goodbye to the former ladies' man forever.

More than that, as she heads to her car, before she speeds off to the office, I want to drop a kiss on her cheek and tell her to drive safely. But I can't.

I head home with my dog, and after a long run, I crash on the sofa. He jumps on my lap and curls into a ball.

"What is wrong with me? It was just sex, right?"

Cletus lifts his snout, as if to say, "Keep going."

"You know what I mean. I've seen you hump the stuffed monkey from T.J. Maxx. Don't deny it."

Cletus waits for me to say more.

"You go crazy for that monkey. You guys are definitely having a no-strings-attached deal."

He doesn't say anything, but we both know he's a horndog. Except, as he rubs his little head against my arm, I don't think I've fooled him. I definitely haven't fooled myself. I know it wasn't just sex with Jillian. I miss her, and texting her last night wasn't enough. Texting her only made me want to see her again.

I pick up my phone to call my brother, to finally ask him how I can sort this out. But there's a message from Jillian glaring at me. It's not a text. It's from her work email.

I have a reporter wanting to talk to you about your new deals. It would be a good idea if we could prep. Would you have any time to meet with me today? My office?

Hell, yeah, I'd like to go to her office.

* * *

We take care of the phone interview quickly, handling it with ease, chatting with a prominent business reporter at a national magazine about my new partnership.

When we hang up, Jillian flips a pen around from her thumb to her forefinger, over and over. Her usual vibrancy is still missing. Raising my chin, I say what I wanted to say earlier this morning. "You don't seem like yourself today. You seemed distracted at Ford's office, and here, too. Is everything okay?"

Surprise flickers across her eyes. "I didn't think I was that easy to read."

I offer a small shrug. "Maybe you're not. But maybe I've learned how to read you." Her lips curve in a small smile. "I've seen you when you're much more animated. Kind of funny, because I know how guarded you can be, too. But you didn't seem guarded this morning. You seemed distracted, like something was bugging you. I hate the thought that something has thrown you."

"It's stupid," she answers quickly, as if she's trying to dismiss what's on her mind.

"Stupid or not, do you want to talk about it?"

She drops her pen on her desk. "My ex never noticed if I was distracted. He never asked if I wanted to talk about bad days. Why do you have to be so sweet?"

"Would you prefer me sour?"

"I would prefer we weren't so clearly ice cream and hot pepper that tastes surprisingly good."

I laugh. "I'd like to try that combo."

"Me, too," she says with a heavy sigh. Once she

blows out all the air in the world, she squares her shoulders and speaks in a rush. "Kevin's going to Sierra's wedding this Thursday, and he emailed me asking me to come say hi to him and Shelly, the skank he cheated on me with, and honestly, it made me wonder if I'm just kind of . . ." She slows down, the last words coming out dejectedly, "Bad at relationships."

I furrow my brow. "How does that make you bad at relationships?"

She shrugs sadly. "I don't know. Like I said, it's stupid."

I hate that she's down on herself, especially because of that guy. "Kevin is a dickhead douche ass-wipe who doesn't like room service and thinks he can still be your buddy. That doesn't make *you* bad at anything."

"Except judging character?"

I stare pointedly at her. "His mistake. His fuckup. Not yours. Don't let him get you down."

"You're right. I shouldn't let him bother me."

I point at her, nodding firmly. "Precisely. That jackass cheating on you makes him bad at relationships and unworthy of you. You not wanting to make small talk with him and his skank makes you normal."

She laughs lightly. "I guess his note made me feel foolish. But it also made me think about this other guy, too. This guy I really like . . ."

My ears prick. "The ice cream and pepper guy?"

"Yes. But I can't be with him, so that's a bit of a bummer. I suppose that's what bothers me more, to be honest."

My heart hurts a little. I want to reach across the desk and squeeze her hand in mine. "Would it make you feel any better if you knew he was bummed, too?"

She leans back in her chair. "We'll be bummed together."

Together.

That last word rings in my ears.

It's what I want. To find a way to be together with her. I don't have any grand plans, I haven't concocted some brilliant scheme for the long run.

But for the short term? I have one hell of an idea.

I drum my fingers on the wood of her desk as the wheels turn in my head. Faster, picking up speed, because this wedding is a chance for something else entirely. Something that's not about her ex and his stupid comments.

Something about us.

A plan forms as I imagine Jillian wearing a sexy dress, black heels, her hair all done up. She'd be stunning, like she is every time I see her. "Did I ever tell you about the time I was invited to Sierra's wedding, too, and forgot to RSVP?"

She lifts a brow in curiosity. "I don't believe I'm familiar with that tale. Go on."

"If memory serves, an invitation arrived a month or so ago, and I did this thing I often do with mail."

"You forgot about it?"

"Yes, but now I'm not forgetting about it. I'm thinking Sierra likes me. Sierra's a cool chick. Sierra probably wouldn't mind if I said I was so very sorry for the late response, but that I'd love to attend her nuptials."

"You would?" Her voice is breathy.

My gaze locks with hers. "I would love to attend. I hear one of the other guests is someone I've been trying to steal a moment with here or there."

"I'm going with Katie. She's my plus-one."

"Even better." The train rattles faster down the tracks. "I've no doubt I can convince Harlan to go with me." I smile wickedly, pleased with my plan. "Me with my friend. You with your friend. No one would think I was only going to see how pretty you'd look all dressed up. And maybe to sneak a dance with you."

Sparks dance across her eyes as they glitter with the thrill of a secret date in the most unlikely of places—a place where no one would suspect us. We'd be hiding a tree in a forest, and a date like this is much safer than a late night rendezvous at her place or mine, someplace where a photographer, a fan, a paparazzo might see one of us slipping in or out.

Lowering her voice, she speaks ever-so-softly. "I want a stolen moment with you. I want a dance with you. Do you think it's a good idea, though?"

I inch closer, placing my elbows on the edge of her desk. "I think not having a dance with you is a bad idea."

I'd like to grab her, kiss her across the desk, haul her next to me. I'd like to slam the door and get my hands all over her.

But our hazy, flirty moment severs when someone knocks on the door. I straighten in the chair, pushing farther away from her desk.

Lily strides in, her flaming red hair and big personality lighting up the room. One of her hands is positioned behind her back. "Jones! That was an epic catch yesterday. I saw it all over the highlight reels last night and today, too."

"Just doing my job."

"And love the *J*. Love it, iove it, love it. It's the perfect mix of cocky and cute."

"That's me. The two *C*s."

"I heard you were here, so I have a surprise." She whips her hand from behind her back to brandish a calendar. "It's a sample of the calendar for our approval, and it's stunning. The two of you did amazing work," Lily says, pointing from Jillian to me.

Jillian hurries around to the front of the desk, and the three of us crowd together as Lily flips through the pages of me with pussycats and puppies. Jillian's hair falls loosely over her shoulders, like a silky curtain, and I curl my fingers into fists to refrain from touching it. With her this close to me, it's a five-star feat of resistance that I somehow don't bend my nose closer to sneak a whiff of her shampoo.

As we flick through the pictures shot in Miami, Jillian's breath catches, and one syllable seems to escape in a faintly sultry, "Oh."

Lily cocks her head, her eyebrow arched in question.

A splash of pink races across Jillian's cheeks. "*Oh*, these are so fantastic," she says, her tone as cheery as can be.

Lily taps the November photo. "Yes! Fantastic! These are my favorites. You look so happy, so relaxed."

I chime in, speaking the full truth. "I was very happy."

Jillian's eyes flutter closed for a brief second. "They're all great."

When we reach the December shot, Lily shuts the calendar. "I want to have a little party in a few weeks to celebrate. Maybe a fun little photo op at a local restaurant. What do you say, Jillian?"

Jillian nods, her tone crisp and cool. "Yes, that sounds like a great idea."

Lily leaves and Jillian turns to me, her shoulders sagging, letting out a deep exhalation. "I felt like I was caught stealing."

"But you weren't," I say under my breath.

"I know, but it felt like we were close. And I don't know how much longer I can pull this off."

I can't argue with that.

24

JILLIAN

It's official. I've worn a hole in the carpet in my office from pacing from the window to my desk. It's a five-foot-long stretch, and the effort is all the more amazing considering it only took a day.

For the last twenty-four hours, I've mastered the art of pacing, along with stressing, along with worrying. I've also considered entering myself in a lip-synching contest because I've spent so much time mouthing words silently as I pace. For instance, consider these potential winners.

"Lily, I need to tell you something crazy . . ."

"Well, it's kind of a funny story . . ."

"Guess what? That player who's known for being a playa? I want him to play with me."

Ugh.

I sigh so deeply, the sound of my frustration burrows underground. They are all sucktastic. None fit the bill for broaching a touchy topic with my boss.

Touchy with a capital *T*.

But I meant it when I told Jones I'm not sure how much longer I can pull this off. How many secret dates, stolen moments, or hallway encounters can my nerves sustain?

Or my conscience, for that matter.

That's the bigger issue, and in the last several hours it's been an insistent drumbeat, telling me to do something, say something.

I don't know if Jones and I will ever amount to anything, but I admire Lily. I respect Lily, and I don't want to keep lying to her.

It feels all kinds of wrong. Lily taught me better. She mentored me better, and whether Jones and I can ever be together isn't the concern gnawing at my heart. What's eating away at me is the fact that I don't want to be a person who sneaks around.

I want to find a way to come clean, no matter what awaits with him—if anything—on the other side.

I sink down in my desk chair, swiveling to the window and the view of the San Francisco skyline, the cresting hills of Pacific Heights, the choppy dark blue water of the bay, and the brilliant rust-colored bridge that majestically spans the seas.

I'm lucky to have this view.

I'm lucky to have this job.

I'm lucky to have this wonderful life.

Am I going to risk it all for a guy?

How could a man be worth it? Is it even possible that this feeling in my chest—this sense of champagne and wonder when he's nearby—is worth gambling what I've worked so hard for?

My throat catches, and I swallow down another

lump as I reach for a framed photo on my desk—a picture of my mom and dad lifting wine glasses at the camera as they shot a selfie in Florence for me.

They went to Italy a few months before her heart attack, rode bikes across Tuscany, visited the Uffizi Gallery in Florence. When they learned of my very first promotion with the Renegades while traveling, they shot this photo for me. Running my thumb over the glass frame, I want to ask my mom what to do.

I wish I knew what she'd say. She was so wise, so smart, so balanced.

I could ask my dad for his opinion. But I'm afraid I know what his answer would be. When it comes to matters of the heart, he's a softie.

In the end, I need to make my own choice. My stomach hurts, like a stone is inside me, wriggling around, painfully pressing against my ribs.

You make your own luck.

Pomelos.

Cherries.

The color red.

Little envelopes.

Dragons.

I've always loved the idea of luck. I've held it tight in my hands, believed that if I honored its power, I could manifest good fortune in my life as long as I put elbow grease behind it.

But luck is capricious. Luck does what luck wants. Luck knows no consequences. And luck can turn south in the blink of an eye.

Luck can bring on a heart attack unexpectedly when you had no warning signs, when you weren't over-weight, when your blood pressure was normal, when you exercised. Luck, or more specifically, bad luck, can upend a perfectly normal life and a happy marriage, leaving one party missing his other half, his soul mate. I tear my gaze away from the photo before my eyes turn too watery.

If I can't turn to either one of my parents for advice, I'll need to rely on my own barometer.

I head upstairs to Lily's office, where she preps me for my interview next week. She reviews the projects I worked on over the last few years, as well as my accomplishments and my ongoing successes.

Rattling them off one by one until she runs out of fingers, she names the players' auction, the charity calendar, the consistent and fantastic coverage, my reliability when it comes to running the press conferences, the community work I've set up, the extra effort with Jones this past summer.

She shakes her head, visibly impressed. "I have to say you've done great work here."

I don't bother to rein in a grin. I smile widely and say, "Thank you."

I have to admit, she's damn right. I'm not only good at my job—I'm great at it. I'm driven, relentless, professional, innovative, and passionate. That has nothing to do with luck, and everything to do with hard work and dedication.

And, if I am all those things, will falling in love with a player change that?

I gasp under my breath, quickly covering my mouth, hoping Lily didn't notice. She's continuing to talk about the interview, so I'm safe.

On the surface.

But my head is swimming because *there it is.*

Reality.

Clarity.

I'm falling in love with Jones Beckett.

I'm absolutely crazy for him. I miss being with him like there's an emptiness inside me. Jones makes me feel like all my sexy songs. He makes me laugh. He makes me think. He challenges me. And he gives me so much of himself.

In this second, another blast of clarity lands in my lap—I must tell Lily. I can't hide this anymore from my mentor and my boss. I need her to know my truth before I march into that interview next week. I have to put my cards on the table, no matter what.

Once she finishes, I clear my throat, chucking all my practice words in the trash bin. Time to start fresh and speak from the heart, right here, right now.

Her desk phone bleats, a loud, shrill ring that insists on being answered.

Cradling it against her neck, she answers, waits, and then says, "Oh, fudge sticks."

More silence.

"It's in an hour?"

She's quiet again.

"Yep. I'll be there."

She hangs up the phone, bolts from her chair, grabs her purse, and declares, "Apparently, it's poetry workshop day. My daughter signed me up for it, since she thinks I'm a poet on account of writing press releases, and now I have to go spend the afternoon critiquing poetry from third-graders."

I wave to her door. "Go. Craft odes. Make words. And please let me know what you have on your agenda. I'll take care of all of it."

Snatching a sheet of paper from her desk, she thrusts it at me. "These are the calls I need to make today. You're an angel."

I don't need to possess the soul of an angel to know today isn't the day for confession.

25

JONES

Organic Eats is in the bag. Paleo Pet is rolling out its commercial campaign. The first check has cashed.

I plunked that slip of paper into my bank account faster than I cleared the end zone in Sunday's game, then I dropped a huge chunk of change into a college fund I set up for my sister's kids.

I texted her to tell her, and she called me back crying tears of happiness.

I also bought my mom a gift, one she's been coveting for a long time, and it's the equivalent of diamonds for her. A top-of-the-line top-loading washer. When we were kids, she'd joked that her greatest guilty pleasure was doing mounds of laundry. The washing machine and the dryer ran constantly, a regular soundtrack of spinning in our home.

She loved it because she listened to romance audiobooks while she sorted the laundry. "Just finished Sophie Kinsella while I folded the whites," she'd say.

I invested some of the dough, too, thanks to Trevor's

help researching mutual funds. No risky investments for me at all. But the process of hitting the online transfer button from my bank account to my mutual fund hasn't made me stop missing Jillian at all.

Imagine that.

Stashing money is great, but it doesn't pave the way for me to drive to her house on a Tuesday evening after I practice. It doesn't give me permission to wake up with her on a Thursday morning before I hit the gym. Nor does it make it possible for me to take her to see the next *Mission Impossible* flick when it's on the big screen.

And damn, do I want to share popcorn with her in a darkened theater.

That's both the truth, and a euphemism.

Mostly, though, I want to hold her hand as we walk into the cinema, searching for the best stadium seats, not giving an ounce of worry that someone might capture a picture of us.

My thoughts snap back to the here and now as the waiter brings me my flank steak and sautéed broccoli, and sets down plates for the rest of the guys. Liam raises his fork and knife to slice his strip steak, casting a glance at me. "How are your parents doing, Jones? I saw them on the TV during a pre-season game. They seemed quite pleased to be watching you."

I'm grateful for the distraction. "They're doing great, and Mom loves the new washer that I bought her."

Trevor cracks up. "She always said it was her dream come true. A new washing machine and a son in the NFL."

Liam chuckles deeply. "Excellent. Love that you're close with them. Family is what it's all about."

My heart craters a little bit. Liam needs me to be a good boy. He loves the new image we've crafted of the reformed playboy.

As I slice my steak, I ask myself what it means to be good—how could falling for a woman like Jillian be anything *but* good? She's smart and classy, and so damn caring. I don't see how she could possibly be bad for me. Isn't this what Paleo Pet wants? A guy who's committed to a woman? A guy who treats his woman like a family member?

"I can introduce you to my parents at the game this weekend if you'd like," I say to Liam, returning to the topic at hand. "They'll be at the stadium."

"Fantastic. I'd love to meet them, and you must be busy this week getting ready for the first home game, so thank you again for fitting me in."

"No problem. Happy to do it, no matter how busy the week is." I'm about to add that I'm going to make time to go to a wedding tomorrow night to see Jillian, but I swallow those words whole, as if they're made of dust and they're choking me. Instead, I push them out in a different formation. "Harlan and I are going to a wedding tomorrow night. Sierra Franklin, a local reporter, is getting married, and she invited the two of us."

Best to put it out there, right? That way, no one will be surprised to see shots of Harlan, Jillian, Katie, and me hanging out together.

Ford chimes in, "Ah, Sierra Franklin, tying the knot on a Thursday night so she can be on the sidelines on Sunday, reporting on the game."

I manage a small laugh. "She's dedicated. That's for sure."

Liam spears a piece of steak, a thoughtful look in his eyes. "That's admirable. That kind of dedication to work and a relationship."

I want to tell him I can be like that, too. I can be dedicated to football, and Paleo Pet, and Jillian.

My shoulders tighten in frustration because I want to leave this restaurant and tell the guys I'm heading to her place. I want to wander down the street with her during her lunch break tomorrow, and duck into stores or coffee shops if she wants. I want to walk my dog with her.

When dinner ends, Liam, Trevor, Ford, and I weave our way through the restaurant, passing a young dude at the bar, who raises his phone and snaps a shot of me.

Out with the guys. Out with my brother. Out for business.

It's all good. It's all permissible. It's all photographable. As Ford pushes open the door, I have to wonder what would be so bad about being out with Jillian? What would the press say if that guy captured a shot of me holding the door for her? What would Liam, Ford, or Trevor say? I once thought being with her would be terribly wrong. I once thought it was far too dangerous.

But when I think of Jillian now, the possibility of us leaving a restaurant hand in hand only seems right.

I want these guys to be on my side—to believe in their hearts that Jillian and I are right together. Only, I'm not a starry-eyed dreamer. I'm a realist and I *get* that it's naive to think a simple declaration of my feelings is all it'd take.

I don't know what it will take, though. That's the trouble. But I need to start figuring out how to have Jillian *and* the contract.

If I can have both, that is.

At the valet stand, Liam takes off first, telling us he's heading to the airport to catch a red-eye to the East Coast for the next few days. Once Ford is gone, the attendant pulls up with Trevor's ride. I slide into the passenger seat and buckle in, and he drives me home.

We stop outside my house, and my brother knits his brow. "Are you okay? You've been quiet all night."

"No. I'm not okay."

He cuts the engine. "Talk to me."

I tip my forehead to the house. "I have to take my guy for a stroll."

Three minutes later, we're out walking Cletus. "So there's a girl," I begin.

Trevor drags a hand through his hair. "It's always about girls, isn't it?"

Part of me wants to defend myself, but he's right. When a man wants to make big changes in his life, it's nearly always on account of a girl. Because when a man feels this strongly for a woman, it makes him want to transform his priorities. It makes him want to take chances he never thought he'd take before.

Still, I correct him. "*Girl*. As in one. Not girls."

"Okay. What's the story with this girl?"

"She's different. She's not like anyone else I've been with," I add as we turn the corner, Cletus leading the way around the block.

"It's Jillian, isn't it?"

I nod.

"Dude, you need to be careful." His tone is a stern warning.

"I am careful, but look, I like her. I like her a lot. I'm fucking falling for her."

Stopping in his tracks, Trevor stares at me, his eyes wide, his mouth hanging open. "Are you kidding me? You're falling for a woman? For real?"

I shake my head, because that's not correct. It's well past falling. Everything I pictured earlier tonight clicks into place. I want the freedom to be with Jillian because I've fallen in love with her. My heart thumps a little harder as the thought shifts from bits and pieces of emotion to a fully formed certainty. "No, I'm not falling. I've *fallen*. I'm in love with her."

"Whoa." He holds up his hand like a stop sign. "In. Love?" He points at me, incredulous. "You? In love? For the first time, ever?"

"Don't act so surprised. It was bound to happen."

He shakes his head in disbelief. "I never thought you'd say those words," he says, like he's still processing the sheer magnitude of the bomb I dropped on him.

"It's the truth. And listen, I know you think I can't sustain a relationship for longer than a week, let alone a month, but I've had feelings for her for a while. I didn't act on them because of what we talked about, and your concerns, but when we were in Miami . . ."

"You hooked up in South Beach?"

Anger flares through me. "Don't you get it? I'm trying to tell you it's more than hooking up. It's way more than that."

"Okay, it was more than hooking up. Fine. I get it. Are you still . . . doing whatever this more than hooking up is?"

I shake my head. "We've been behaving since we returned more than a month ago. The thing is, nothing has changed, and I still want her. I like her. I'm in love with her, man."

He breathes out heavily through his nostrils as we turn back onto my block. "Don't just chase a piece of ass, Jones."

Faster than I captured the ball last week, I grab the neck of his shirt with my free hand and yank him closer. My eyes are full of fury. I stare hard into his irises, my jaw tight. "She's not a piece of ass."

He holds up his hands in surrender. He knows I'd never hurt him. But he also knows I'm so much bigger than he is.

I shake my head. "Don't call her that."

He doesn't say anything at first, but soon he smirks. Laughs. Smiles.

I narrow my eyes. "What the hell?"

"You really like her, don't you?"

I drop my fist from his shirt, letting my hand fall to my side as Cletus whimpers. "I told you I love her."

"I had to test you, though."

"You called her a piece of ass to test me?"

Trevor grins sheepishly. "It worked. You made your feelings for her crystal clear. That was all it took."

"Dick," I mutter as we resume walking Cletus.

"Yeah, but I love you."

I drape an arm over his shoulder. "I love you, too."

"What now? Are you going to tell Ford? Tell Liam? How are you going to pull this off? This is a big risk you're about to take, dating your publicist."

"I know that."

He claps my back. "Just want you to be aware. Brands are cautious these days. They drop athletes for the smallest of reasons. That could happen to you. You do know that?"

"I'm aware, and I'm also well aware I don't have a track record to stand on."

He shoots a rueful smile, his tone shifting now to brotherly concern. "You don't, though I understand where you're coming from. You want Liam to believe what you know in your heart to be true." He taps my chest. "There's a first time for everything, and you're feeling it, so you want him to line up behind you. But you need to know that Liam might not see things the same way."

I sigh heavily. "I know."

"He might not be convinced as easily as I was."

I scoff. "You were easily convinced? We might have different definitions of *easily*."

He stops, looking me square in the eyes. "I do believe you. I know you wouldn't put your neck out like this with me if you weren't in love. But I'm your flesh and blood. I'm on your side no matter what. And that's why I want you to be realistic about how other people—people who haven't stood by you since Mom and Dad brought you home from the hospital and all your big brothers and sister had to help give you a bottle and babysit you—"

I raise a hand to cut him off. "Bottle? Are we back to bottles and babysitting?"

"When you're the baby of the family, it's always going to come back to bottles and babysitting. Point being, I'm on your team. And part of why you wanted me to work closely on your business is to make sure someone you trust implicitly is always looking out for you. I'm looking out for you when I say I'm behind you one hundred percent." He slows and takes a beat. "And I also want you to be realistic, too."

I rub a hand over the back of my neck, heaving a sigh as we resume our walk. "Yeah, I get it. I can't assume that just because I feel this way about her, everyone else is going to clap their hands in glee and say *oh, we've been hoping you'd fall in love, Jones.*"

He laughs. "If only it were that simple."

Nothing is simple in this situation. I haven't proven myself when it comes to relationships, and that's the risk I'd be asking Paleo Pet to take—to stand by a guy who's never gone the distance. "They'll worry it'll end in a few days, a few weeks."

Trevor nods. "Yeah, they might. They might also worry it'll blow up into a huge mess. They won't want to be collateral damage."

"They'd worry it'd look like a scandal," I say, thinking of Jillian's words in Miami. No matter how deeply I feel for her, I can see how the press would twist the two of us to suit a narrative. "I need to think carefully about how to broach this with Liam when he returns this weekend."

"I'll help you brainstorm, but I think you know what to do," Trevor says.

I complete the thought. "Be honest."

That's who I want to be—the guy who handles things right. I want to do the hard work to earn the rewards. That's what my dad taught me.

In this case, the hard work lies in communication, being open with people I care about, people I do business with.

But that also means that if Liam cuts me off, I have to be willing to let the deal go. Saying the words out loud tonight for the first time—that I'm in love with her

—yields a stark and beautiful kind of clarity to the dilemma.

I might want both Jillian and the contract. But if I can't have both, I choose her.

First, though, I have a wedding to attend.

26

JONES

It's like prom, only so much better because I like Jillian way more than Cassie Perkins, the girl I took to the dance. We had a fun time, danced to a couple songs, laughed at a few jokes. But I didn't feel this stirring of excitement down to my bones when I picked her up.

The limo Harlan and I rented stops at Jillian's home in Hayes Valley. Dressed in my dark navy tailored suit, I bound up the steps and ring the bell. A minute later, Jillian appears at the door, and I'm speechless. I drink her in, and I want to eat her up.

Sexy but classy, the black dress she wears clings to her, hugging her curves alluringly. The V of her neckline offers the tiniest peek of her cleavage, a hint of flesh. I groan my appreciation. "I want to take that off. Kiss you from head to toe, get my mouth all over every square inch of your skin, skip the wedding, and spend the night with you." I lean closer. "Inside you. Exploring you. Having you."

Her lips part, and her breath comes in an unsteady rush. Her hand moves to her chest. "If you talk to me like that, I don't know how I'll make it through the wedding."

"If you keep looking at me like that, I don't know how I will."

"How do I look at you?"

"Like you want all the same things."

Gripping the railing in one hand, she answers in a soft, sexy voice, "You know I do."

Somehow, I muster the strength to tear myself away from her porch and the possibility of what's behind door number one—her, alone with me, tonight. I offer her an arm and walk her to the car.

Harlan lounges in the back, tipping his imaginary hat as he says hello. I don't know if it's a blessing or a curse that I picked him up first. I decide on blessing for now, because maybe he's the roadblock I need.

We pick up Katie next, and as she slides into the car wearing a pale pink dress, it's safe to say Harlan's eyes pop out of his head. "How do you do?" He extends a hand as if to shake hers, then dips his head to kiss the top of her fingers.

"My, my, what a gentleman," Katie remarks.

"I can dance, too."

"You don't say," Katie tosses back.

He shrugs and shoots her a lopsided grin. "I enjoy dancing. It's one of my many talents."

"What are your others? Besides running, blocking, and tackling."

"I can bake pies like nobody's business."

Katie's eyes light up, and she hums her approval. "I'll be saving a dance for you, Mr. Pie Maker."

I glance at Jillian, and she simply shrugs happily. I

have a feeling this won't be the last I hear of Harlan's interest in Katie.

* * *

In front of three hundred friends, family members, colleagues, and professional athletes in a swank hotel ballroom overlooking the Pacific Ocean, Sierra's fiancé tells her he'll love, cherish, and honor her for the rest of his days. A few rows in front of us, Kevin leans in closer to the woman he cheated on Jillian with, and dusts a kiss on her cheek.

I seethe inside. He never deserved Jillian. But I let the anger fade because his actions gave me this chance. Seated next to Jillian, I lean in and speak softly. "I'm glad Kevin's with that skank."

She laughs quietly. "You are?"

"Because that means he's not with you."

She smiles at me, and it's an arrow straight to my heart. It hits me hard and fantastically, and I want to keep earning the right to all her beautiful smiles. "Also, you look beautiful tonight," I say in a low voice. "Stunning."

I tell her because I want her to feel as beautiful as she is. But I need her to know something else, too. Something more important. That there are guys who would never violate her trust. How I'm one of those guys. I want her to know that even though I might've started as a player, I'd never do what he did. When the ceremony ends, and the bride and groom walk down the aisle to the wedding march, I grab Jillian's arm and whisper, "You have to know that even though I might have a past, I would never do what Kevin did."

She turns her gaze to mine, that vulnerable look I love flashing across her brown irises. "I'd never think you would."

Even with all these people around us, I can't stop looking at her. "I need you to know I'm a one-woman kind of guy."

As the guests clap and cheer, she mouths words just for me. *I'm a one-guy kind of woman.*

All my instincts tell me to pull her close and seal this moment with a kiss, but once more, I'm painfully aware we can't. We're a secret—one-time clandestine lovers attending a mutual acquaintance's wedding for a quick hit of one another's company.

I hate that I can't kiss her in public, or at all.

We're ushered into the reception room. People chat and snap photos, and I get pulled in a few different directions, posing for shots with fans, with Sierra, and even with Kevin. He yanks Harlan next to him on the other side. I have no doubt Kevin is going to post this picture everywhere. Bumping into two of the Renegades at Sierra's nuptials. Isn't he oh-so connected?

"So good to see you two," his baritone voice booms, and I want to punch him and thank him at the same damn time.

But most of all, I don't want to *be* him.

Because I don't want to lose her.

And I don't even have her.

After the pictures, I keep trying to snag a private moment with the woman I love, but it's a fool's errand since this is a crazy-ass public event. I don't know why I thought this would be a good idea. I'm running into the same wall everywhere I see her. I can't talk to her the way I want to. I can't be with her the way I want to. But

I'm relentless, and I don't stop hunting for an opening, just like I do on the field.

Harlan must sense it. He's no dummy, and he has to know what I said at training camp is a lie. He also doesn't care that I fibbed to him, since once the dancing begins, he says, "How about I take the first dance with Jillian, and you take Katie for a whirl. You feel me?" His eyes pin me.

"I fucking feel you. And I love you for it."

He smacks my shoulder. "I know what's going on, and it's cool with me. I've got your back. I always do."

"I know, man."

Harlan holds out an arm and asks Jillian for a dance. They dance as two colleagues do. Nothing more. They maintain a professional distance while I join Katie on the dance floor, her hands chastely on my shoulders.

"You better treat her well," Katie says, shedding formalities instantly.

My answer is true and honest. "I will."

But her blue eyes brook no argument. "I mean it. If she goes out on a limb for you, do not let her down. I know that you're a foot taller than me and probably one-hundred-fifty pounds heavier, but I don't care. I will kick you in the balls if you hurt her."

I flinch instinctively, wanting to cup the goods. "Damn."

Katie isn't done with me yet. "She is the best person I know, and she tries to live her life with honesty and integrity. If you make a move for her, you better make that play for real. Be prepared to put your whole heart into it." She pauses, softens her expression, and flashes the biggest smile. "Or you will answer to me and my steel-toed cowboy boots."

My balls wince just thinking about it. "You will never need to break those out with me. Also, I can see why you're her best friend."

When the song ends, we switch partners, and Harlan seems none too sad to have another chance to chat with Katie.

Once Jillian is in my arms, I struggle mightily to resist bringing her close. But what I can't say with my body, I say with words. "Jillian," I rasp out. "Something's gotta give."

Her voice is soft, overflowing with emotion. "I know. We can't keep looking for stolen opportunities like this."

"I need to find a way to be with you. I want that more than anything."

Her breath hitches. "I want that so much, too. I nearly told Lily the other day."

My eyes pop out. "You did?"

"Almost, but I didn't have a chance to. I was tempted, though, because I don't want to keep pretending."

"I don't like it, either. All I want is to pull you close and stop pretending right now."

"Me, too."

Her hands wind more tightly around my neck, and I groan.

A soft murmur escapes her lips.

My gaze roams her gorgeous face, and I can see in her eyes, in the tightness of her jaw, in the rush of breath from her lips, that the fight is real for both of us.

Real and painful.

I want this fight to end. I want us to give in. "Do you have any idea how hard it is for me not to kiss you senseless right now?"

"As hard as it is for me?"

I laugh softly, then the laughter fades. "I need to be with you, baby."

"I need that, too."

"I don't know why I thought coming to a wedding with you would be a good idea. I feel like a starving man. I'm just trying to get crumbs. But now I have these crumbs, and I want to gobble the whole pie."

She laughs. "A cherry pie."

"Don't say words like cherry. It's too sexy. It turns me on. They make me think of all the things I want to do to you. You're like a cherry, and I want to eat you up."

"I want you to eat me up like a cherry."

"You're. Killing. Me. We need to get out of here."

Worry flickers across her face. "Don't you think it would be obvious if we left together?"

"Yeah, but I kind of don't care anymore."

"Sneaking around is risky," she whispers, caution coloring her tone. "You know it's dangerous."

"I know, but we can pull this off. We have to."

Her eyes flash with the same desperation I feel. "Are you sure?"

"I can't stand not having you tonight. Are you with me on this?"

She glances around briefly, as if she's debating her options. When her gaze returns to me, she nods. "I'll say my goodbyes and leave first. Then you stay behind ten minutes or something, so it's not obvious. I'll wait in the car until you make it out."

I nod approvingly. "Look at you, making plays, devising strategies."

"Finding openings," she adds, with a lift of her eyebrows.

"Hell, yeah. That's my favorite thing to do. I'd like to find one with you."

"I have an—" Jillian freezes, her gaze locked across the dance floor. "Lily's here." She whispers the warning, creating distance between us. "She must have come for the reception."

Jillian fixes on a smile, waving as she makes eye contact with her boss, who's chatting with a small girl by her side. I recognize the kid as Olivia, Lily's daughter. I've met her a few times. She's nine, and she told me I was her favorite Renegade, so I take a chance. After I say hello to the head of the publicity department, I bend down and ask her daughter if she wants to dance.

Olivia beams, and we head to the dance floor to cut the rug to a fast tune.

She shimmies. She shakes. She laughs.

I do the same as Sabrina Carpenter's "We'll Be the Stars" plays—perfect music for a dance with a third-grader.

"You're a good dancer," she says.

"Not as good as you."

"But you're better at catching the football."

I wipe a hand across my brow as I move my hips, bopping along to the beat. "Boy, am I glad to hear that."

When the dance ends, Olivia gives me a bear hug, but the one from her mom is even bigger.

I didn't dance with her kid to win her over. I didn't do it to smooth the path for Jillian. I did it because I wanted to, and I hope *that* desire is what matters most in the end.

Not my past.

Not the dumb stuff I've done.

Just the things I've done lately.

They have to outweigh the mistakes.

* * *

An hour later, I nod at Harlan as I leave. He gives a crisp nod in return. He said he'd catch his own ride and take Katie home.

Once I'm outside, I find the limo, grab the handle, and open the door. I've made my great escape.

The car door slams shut behind me, and it's her and me, alone at last. The partition is up. Total privacy. I toss my suit jacket onto the seat.

The driver pulls away from the hotel, and Jillian launches herself at me.

Fuck yes.

She grabs my face and crushes her lips to mine. Everything in my body screams yes the second she makes contact. Our tongues tangle, our lips devour, and our hands are everywhere.

She grabs at my shirt, plays with my hair. My hands fly down her sides, over her ass, up to her neck.

"It's been too long," I mutter, then slide my lips over hers again. I have to have her. Must consume her.

This is everything I missed. This is everything I want. Electricity lights my skin, and my brain is a static haze of lust, desire, and something more.

Something I don't want to give up.

We kiss like a wild homecoming, like I've been away for months and she can't get enough of me. Climbing on top of me, she straddles my lap, hikes up her skirt, and grinds against me. She goes to town on my hard-on, and I can't stop kissing her. Can't stop wanting her.

This is fire and heat, and I need more of the blaze.

I fumble around in the pocket of my jacket, finding my wallet and grabbing a condom.

"Need to be inside you," I grit out, and she nods, panting a yes as she reaches for the zipper on my pants and slides it down.

My eyes stray to her hands undressing me, and hell, this is perfect. This is the view I want for a long time.

I want her hands on me.

I want her owning my body.

I want her to know that she's the only one I want touching me.

She's the one.

It's staggering, the realization that she's the end of the line for me. She's the one I want. It's been hitting me all week long, over and over, in different ways.

I knew it earlier in the week at the game. I was sure when we texted. I felt it again in my agent's office, then at dinner, and now once more tonight.

And I need to feel it in a physical way.

Need to know what it's like to connect deeper than I ever have before. I cup her cheek, meet her gaze. "I need to make love to you."

"*Please.* Please, make love to me."

Quickly, I rearrange us, laying her down on the leather seat, then roll on the condom. She slides off her panties, and I groan in appreciation of the stunning view of her perfectly wet pussy. "Fuck, you're beautiful. I missed you so fucking much."

"I missed you, too. Now, *please, please*. We're going to be at my house soon, and I need this."

I slide inside her, and I shudder. It's unreal. It's bone-shatteringly good. She grabs my neck, pulls me closer, and kisses me harder, rougher than before.

"Yes," I groan as I swivel my hips, filling her completely, thrusting deep inside her.

The sounds she makes send me into a frenzy as lust spreads all over my body, but it's so much more than that. As I go deeper, she cries out, "So good."

I wrap my arms around her. "I can't get close enough to you, baby."

She digs her nails into my ass. "I know. I feel the same."

"I can't stand being without you."

"I can't take it, either." She brings her mouth down on my shoulder and bites. Hard. Leaving marks. Setting me off, because I fucking love her orgasms, and she has to be close. I give her what she wants—hard, deep strokes—because I know what she wants, and I want to be with her like this. Always.

Soon, she flies over the edge, falling apart in my arms, biting down on my flesh, and it's as good as it's ever been.

No. It's even better. Because I know what I want.

After I follow her there, coming hard, I meet her gaze. Her eyes are blissed-out. The words that come next are so damn easy to say. "I'm in love with you."

The sigh she makes is soft and happy, but also a little sad, as she whispers, "I'm in love with you, too."

This should be a defining moment in the playbook of my life. This should be when the quarterback launches the ball and I run clear to the end zone to score a touchdown.

The trouble is, I fear I'm going to drop the pass, or worse, get slaughtered by a hit I don't see coming.

We all have a blind side.

But I don't know how to anticipate a problem I can't

see, so I hold her face and kiss her, a little soft, a little desperate, as we drive the last mile to her home.

When we turn onto her block, she breaks the kiss and sets a hand on my arm. "I want to spend the night with you. You have to know that."

"Yeah, I know that, and I want to spend the night with you, too, but . . ."

"But the longer we keep sneaking around, the worse it's going to be." She brushes a kiss on my cheek. "I need to go through with it this time. I need to tell Lily."

"And I need to tell Ford and Liam." I brush my lips against hers once more, as if we're finalizing our plans. Sealing them with a kiss before the night ends, and the hard work begins tomorrow.

When she's gone, I tell the driver to take me home.

* * *

The next day, I'm up bright and early, the morning fog snaking through the hills of San Francisco as I run. Along the way, I focus on the words I'll say to my agent and to my new business partner.

When I've crested five miles, I head for the gym near my home to lift weights, and forty-five minutes later, I'm energized and ready to make the call.

But as I head for the exit, I bump into my old teammate, Garrett Snow.

27

JILLIAN

My stomach is a skydiver, executing loops and flips that I didn't know it could do. I'm pretty sure that at some point it tries to crawl up my esophagus.

Nerves can suck it. I need to be made of steel.

I lift my chin and continue my march down the hall to my boss's office. My high-heeled shoes click along the floor as I picture my patent leather pumps giving me power, giving me the strength to say what must be said.

To the judge, jury, executioner.

Like everyone, I've felt nerves many times. Before my first-ever press conference, before my first time on the field, before my first interview. I've experienced them, too, when I've had to handle thorny situations with the media, and when I've had to make uncomfortable announcements about players being let go.

The worries whipping inside me are different now because it's *my* job, all twisted and turned and wrapped in a huge red ribbon around the most precious organ —my heart.

I can't separate my head and my heart in this case.

My job and the man I love are inextricably linked, and I don't control my fate. But soon, I'll know it, at least, and the prospect is terrifying and strangely electrifying, too.

Taking a deep breath, I smooth a hand over my red blouse, touching my earrings next. I need all the luck in the world. This might not be what my mother would've done, and though I can speculate what my dad would do, I didn't ask him. That's because it's *my* situation, and I'm certain what I must do to be the kind of person I want to be.

Be truthful. Be honest. And be prepared for the fallout.

My knuckles rap against the door once before Lily calls out, "Come in."

I enter, shutting the door behind me.

She glances up from the pile of papers on her desk, her pen scribbling across them. "Fun wedding," she remarks, still writing. "I saw some great pictures online today. Harlan and Jones looked so sharp, even in that photo with Kevin. And then you and Harlan on the dance floor, and you and Jones. You guys get along so well."

I take the seat across from her, opting out of the small talk and diving straight into the rocky waters. "I need to talk to you about that." My tone is serious, all business.

"Of course." She sets down her pen.

I straighten my shoulders, willing myself to ignore the fresh wave of acrobatics in my belly. "There is no delicate way to say this, but I want you to know. I'm in love with Jones Beckett."

She laughs, shaking her head. "So is half the female

population of the city. More will be when they see the calendar." She chuckles, pushing out another laugh.

But I don't join in. "No, I am in love with him." My expression is serious; my voice is clear. There is no laughter in my eyes because this is no laughing matter.

"Oh." The note of surprise hangs in the air like thick perfume. Rising from behind her desk, she walks around it and takes the chair next to me. She reaches for my hand. "Oh, sweetie, I'm so sorry. That sucks. Unrequited love is the worst."

I squeeze my eyes shut, shaking my head. I can't believe I'm botching this. I open my eyes. "Lily, we're in love with each other."

She drops my hand, letting it fall onto the wooden armrest. Her expression meanders through a myriad of emotions, mostly along the surprise spectrum. "That's a horse of a different color. Do you want to tell me more?"

I rip off the Band-Aid. "I've had a crush on him forever. But nothing happened, and I never did anything about it because I wanted to stay professional and true to my job. Then, we worked on the calendar, and I learned he really is the guy we have shown to our fans," I say, and a smile dares to appear on my face as the memories snap into focus. "He's the guy who cuddles with dogs. Who helped my dad build a desk. Who rented out an entire rec center on his day off and helped families who needed it."

"Those are admirable traits," Lily says, her tone even.

"They are, and as I spent time with him, I grew to like him more, and then, to fall in love with him. I know this probably sounds cheesy," I say, and I wish I could read her eyes, but her face is thoroughly neutral, "but you're not just my boss. You're my mentor, and I feel terrible that I wasn't honest with you when it first happened, so I need to be honest now. I understand that I might be risking everything. My job. Your respect." I take a deep, fortifying breath, and speak aloud the toughest words of this confession. "Do you want me to tender my resignation?"

Saying it hurts, but it's what I have to do. It's the chance I have to take.

I wait for her answer.

28

JONES

As I say goodbye to the fan who works at the gym's front desk, telling him that, yes, I will do my very best to kick ass this Sunday, I do a double take when I see a familiar face.

"Hey, Garrett. I didn't know you worked out here," I say.

Garrett flashes me a smile, his gleaming white teeth shining. "I don't just work out here. I work here."

The strangest sense of déjà vu crashes into me, and I'm knocked off-kilter into a sort of twilight zone. "You do?"

"Just got the job." He holds up a hand to high-five. I smack back, but I'm not entirely sure why we're high-fiving a job at the gym. There's nothing wrong with honest work, but Garrett is a left tackle. He's supposed to be working on the gridiron.

"You just started here? What do you do?" I ask, since maybe I heard wrong. Maybe he means he landed a job on a team and he's working *out* here.

"I'm a personal trainer."

And I'm wrong. Way wrong. "That's great," I say woodenly. This has to be a way station. This has to be temporary. I cling to that notion. "Before you go back to the field?"

He laughs. "Wouldn't that be nice? I've been putting out feelers about a job in broadcasting, or coaching, maybe even at the high school level, but until something comes through, I'm here, and I can't complain."

My feet feel unsteady, and it's the oddest sensation, as if I'm not quite sure how to stand anymore. There's only one reason why he'd be working as a personal trainer, or *putting out feelers*. Because he doesn't have a job playing football, and he'll never be able to have a job playing football.

I shove past the strange dryness in my throat that almost makes me not want to ask the next question. But morbid curiosity pushes me forward. "What happened with your knee?"

He shrugs. "It's not going to get better."

"It's not?"

He shakes his head. "Tough break, but that's how it goes."

I grab hold of the counter, and it feels like someone yanked the carpet out from under me. Garrett's life is my worst nightmare. I've played against guys who've had their careers curtailed by injury, but I don't usually bump into them at my gym. Maybe I misunderstood him. "That's it? You can't play again? You can't rehab?"

He chuckles deeply, sounding as warm as Santa Claus and just as wise. "Let me tell you something, brother. I did nothing but try to rehab my knee for the last two years. I did everything I could. I went and I tried out for Baltimore, made it through training camp this summer, and then in the first preseason game, my knee gave out again. God was trying to tell me something."

I blink. "God was involved in this?" I ask, trying to make sense of the unthinkable.

"I suspect the big guy was telling me it was time to focus on something else. It's not happening for me in football."

Words that don't compute. Words that make no sense. Words I never want to have to say.

"I nabbed the first job I could find. Because of this." Garrett smiles, a big, authentic grin. Reaching into his shorts pocket, he grabs his phone, clicks to his camera roll, and shows me a picture: a tiny baby with bright eyes and a mess of dark hair.

"This is my baby daughter, Gabriela. My wife gave birth three months ago."

"Congratulations. That's fantastic. I'm so happy for you," I say. The words sound genuine coming out of my mouth, and they are. But I'm not happy. Not at all. I'm more sad for his knee than happy for his kid. "Sorry about your knee, though."

"Me, too. But what can you do? It happens. You do your best. You move on. You do something else."

But there is nothing else, my brain screams.

"What about the money you lost?" I ask, bracing myself for the onslaught of more bad news from him.

"I'll be okay. I was smart enough to sock at least some of it away, so I'm not going to be hurting. We'll get by. That's really all that matters, right? To be okay."

Is he convincing himself, or is he telling me? I'm not entirely sure. "Do you want to get something to eat? Breakfast, maybe?"

"I wish. I have a client coming in ten minutes. Let's do it another time?"

"Definitely."

I leave, but I can't shake this cloudy feeling from my head for the rest of the day. Like it's full of static and confusion. I try to train my thoughts back on Jillian, try to think about calling Liam and Ford. But as I head to the practice field, running routes and reviewing plays, all I can think about is Garrett Snow. Everything that's in front of me is gone from his life. Every single thing.

I know what the déjà vu sensation is. It's déjà fear.

What happened to him could happen to me.

29

JILLIAN

Lily frowns. "What?"

I try again, to let her know I'm aware of the consequences of my choices. "I understand that I may have lost your trust. That you might not want me in the department anymore. And if I've lost my job, I'm prepared to accept that."

The sound she makes is like a train whistle meeting a big fat ball of *no*, and she shakes her head so vigorously I'm worried she'll bring on a headache. "No. No. No. I don't want you to resign. You're the best thing that's ever happened to this department. You've done amazing things for this team."

I breathe a deep sigh of relief, one that spreads to my bones and feels like silver and gold.

"But I'm shocked," she adds. "Honestly, I'm probably surprised for the reasons you'd expect. I didn't think Jones had it in him to fall in love."

"I thought the same, too. But now that I know him, I don't see him in any other way." My heart warms, and a sense of contentment flows through me. Jones surprised me, too, but now I see the parts of him that have always been there, just hidden from public view, and I'm thrilled that he has so much love in him. More than that, I'm grateful that I'm the one he's giving it to.

Lily's not done with me, though. She pins me with a sharp stare. "Are you prepared for what this means?"

"What do you think I should be prepared for?" I ask carefully.

"It means you'll be in the public eye in a whole new way. You won't just be a woman introducing a press conference. You won't just be somebody who's casually known to a few reporters. You're going to a whole new level. This means you're potentially going to be out in the public as the girlfriend of a Super Bowl–winning, all-pro receiver who's one of the best players in the National Football League."

I gulp. When she puts it like that, it sounds so big and terrifying. But it also sounds like exactly what I've known all along. What I'm ready to tackle. "I'm aware of that."

Lily points at me. "People will take pictures of you. You'll have to pose for pictures with him. You'll be known as Jones Beckett's girlfriend. People will speculate about you. They'll want to know what you have that attracted him. They'll want to know how the ultimate playboy finally settled down." She stops and expels a harsh breath. "Are you ready for that?"

Squaring my shoulders, I answer her truthfully. "I am." The last several years have trained me. Managing a life in the public eye is something I've done for others, and I can do it for myself, too.

"And what if it goes south?"

A pebble wedges itself under my heart, pushing and

prodding, a reminder that this could fall to pieces. "I'm prepared for that. And if it does, I won't let that affect my work. Look at Kevin—I still treat him with respect, the same way I would any other reporter."

She leans back in her chair, nodding a few more times as if she's taking this all in. "I've known you for nearly eight years and admired you the whole time. And if there's one thing I believe in, it's your ability to make good decisions. If you have fallen in love with Jones Beckett . . ." I can't help but smile, because it's such a relief to have said it aloud to someone other than my best friend, and Lily continues, "And obviously you have, based on that ridiculously goofy look on your face, then it is clearly the right decision for you. I hope he knows how lucky he is to have won your heart. He better protect it like it's as precious as the football he carries to the end zone. And if he doesn't, he will have to answer to me."

I smile like an idiot in love. "So this means you're not firing me?"

She rolls her eyes. "You'll have to quit for me to let you get away."

I laugh. "Then neither one of us needs to worry."

I leave as if I'm walking on a ray of sunshine, and nothing can ruin my mood.

Not a thing.

As soon as I reach my office, I text Jones to tell him the good news.

I tackle some calls to the media, then check my phone an hour later, but he hasn't written back. He's probably practicing. Today will be a busy day for the guys, so I carry on, flying high on hope, eager to see him again.

Later that night, when I'm home catching up on the news on my phone, his name flashes on my screen. Butterflies soar in my chest, and my fingers fly to scroll open the message.

Jones: That's great. I'm thinking of you.

"What?" I blurt to my phone, my brow furrowed.

But that's all he wrote. The butterflies crash-land in my belly. I read the message once more, trying to find the true meaning behind words that feel terribly empty. But I can't. Because that's the most un-Jones-like message he's ever sent. He's not an *I'm thinking of you* guy.

He's all-in, or he's not in at all.

But I'm not the type of woman to pressure, or to cling, so I take a deep breath and tell myself to let it go for now.

I click back to the news. It's more reassuring right now, and that's really saying something.

* * *

Katie hunts through a rack of silk blouses. Once she locates her prey, she grabs it and brandishes the soft teal-blue shirt, positioning it over her chest and arching an eyebrow as she turns her lips into Betty Boop's. "What do you think? Is this going to be perfect for you coming out as the receiver's girl?"

I offer a faint smile. It's hard for me to focus on

shopping since I've only heard from Jones once, and that was the abysmal text last night. "It looks great. Do you really think I need a whole new wardrobe now?"

"There's never a bad time for a wardrobe revamp." She eyes me from head to toe in the Hayes Valley boutique where we're shopping on Saturday afternoon. She fancies herself my personal dresser. She taps her finger against her chin. "But I wonder if we should put you in dresses more?"

"No."

"Do you hate dresses now?"

I roll my eyes. "Oh yes, that's it. I've developed a deep hatred for dresses. I simply prefer blouses and skirts."

"That's fine. We can work with that. You'll keep up the look as the office doll who nabbed the guy with the ball—"

"Wherever that rhyme is going, it should retire."

She pouts as she riffles through more clothes. "Must find you a sexy new skirt now. Aha!" Nabbing a short black number, she thrusts it at me.

"It's thigh-length."

"It's hot."

"It's inappropriate."

"That's totally the rage. You could be fashion forward. You could maybe even help set standards."

Laughing, I put the skirt back on the rack, drawing an imaginary line above my knee. "Must hit here."

"Fine, I'll find something else, but you have to look the part every time. You're going to be a very big deal."

I want to believe her, but my phone has been quiet all day. I scan the store quickly, lean in, then whisper, "He's barely been in touch."

She waves a hand dismissively. "No biggie. He's probably distracted playing *NBA 2K* or working out with the guys. I bet he gets back to you tomorrow after the game. Besides, you know how they are before they play. It's all game focus, all the time."

"True," I say, but it sounds half-hearted. It feels that way, too.

My phone buzzes and my heart skips a beat as I fish it eagerly from the back pocket of my jeans with the hope that it's Jones sending a sexy text, a romantic text, a good news text. Something that says he's talked to his guys, and he's ready to tell the world that he's in love with me. Like I've done for him.

I deflate when I see it's my dad.

Dad: Can't wait to see you at the game tomorrow! Stop by and chat with the old man, will ya?

Jillian: Count on me. :)

As I close the message, I wish I felt like I could count on Jones.

I remind myself to stay cool. There's no reason to think anything's changed. He's busy, he's playing tomorrow, and tough talks take time.

I'm not a football floozy. I'm not a one-night stand. I'm the one he wants to be with.

I cling to that as the day goes on with no word.

"I'm a dick." I wait for an answer that doesn't come.

"Come on, buddy. You can tell me. Am I an asshole?"

From his perch on the couch, Cletus drops one ear and cocks his head. His tail flicks back and forth.

"Total ass?"

An excited whimper sounds from his snout as he jumps on my chest. And we have a winner. Total ass, it is.

But even assholes must take care of their pets. I roughhouse with Cletus, rubbing his belly and pretending to box with him. After he play-growls for a bit, I take him to the yard and run him through the weave poles, then in and out of tunnels on the agility course.

After twenty minutes, he's panting hard, but he's happy. I rub his head and scoop him up in my arms. "You're a good boy."

He rewards my compliment by licking my cheek. "That clearly means you don't think I'm a dick at all."

Another lick.

"I knew it. I'm not."

But winning a dog's love is easy. A woman's is much more complex, and I wonder if Jillian thinks I'm an ass, since I've been dragging my feet. I should've called Ford, should've tracked him down this morning, because I sure as hell didn't do that yesterday. We had a long practice, but that's just an excuse.

I *chose* not to call him.

Because I'm fucking afraid.

I'm afraid like I've never been afraid before, and there's no room in my life for fear since tomorrow is game day. I need to be in the zone, and only in the zone.

Even though the game is at home, we always stay at a hotel the night before, so I head to Trevor's house to drop off the little dude. Cletus whines with excitement when he sees my brother. "Hey buddy, you want to hang out with your favorite Beckett tonight?" Trevor asks the pooch.

"I'm still his favorite person." That came out more defensively than I intended.

"Just messing with you." Trevor lifts his chin. "You okay? You look out of sorts. Did you talk to Ford yet?"

"No," I spit out.

Trevor studies my face. "Are you having second thoughts?"

I shake my head. "No. No. No."

He arches an eyebrow. Obviously, that was too much denial.

I'm not having second thoughts about loving Jillian, but I'm having truckloads of doubt about everything else in my life and how the hell to make it fit.

Seeing Garrett was a flashing neon sign that I could

lose everything I've worked so hard for. Is dating Jillian a risk that could send me on the path to *putting out feelers*? Not directly. But I could lose other things if I'm with her, and I need to get some clarity on how to move forward with her and with football.

I need to be prepared for a worst-case scenario, but how the hell do I prep for that? Trouble is, I'm shaken to the core, and I don't know how to put one foot in front of the other after what I learned about Garrett.

"Just a ton of stuff on my mind," I mutter. "I'll call Ford when my head is clear."

Trevor claps me on the shoulder. "Good plan. Focus on the game and only the game."

"Exactly."

I take his advice, because if I let this weigh on me—what to say, how to say it—I'll risk a fuck-up on the field tomorrow, and I can't afford mistakes.

My secret sauce is focus, and in the last twenty-four hours, that skill has been slipping to an alarming degree.

At the hotel, I check in and shut myself in my room, guiltily grateful that Jillian's not here tonight. Sometimes she stays at the game hotel, but the manager of PR is on duty tonight. That means I won't be tempted to find her in her room, because God knows if I did, my remaining focus would be shredded like a credit report.

But total ass or not, I can't leave her hanging. When I slide into bed, I tap out a text.

Jones: Haven't been able to reach the guys. But I'm thinking of you. I promise.

* * *

I lace up my cleats and adjust my pads. Rolling my shoulders back and forth, I repeat under my breath, "Ready. I'm ready."

Harlan grabs his helmet from his locker. "You ready?"

That's the question.

"Always."

That's the only answer.

He gives me a look. "Are you sure? You're quieter today than usual. You haven't busted my chops about a single thing."

I could give him shit about being sensitive enough to notice my silence, but I'm in no mood. Instead, I blurt out, "Do you ever think about getting hurt?"

He tips his forehead in the direction of the stadium. "During a game?"

I nod.

"Of course."

"What do you do about it?"

"Don't write checks I can't cash. Don't make plays that are too risky. Do everything I can to make sure I don't get in harm's way."

"But what if it happens anyway?"

"Then you deal with it, man. You just deal with it. Do I want it? Hell no. Do I think about it? Sure. Do I get out there and play as hard as I possibly can because that's what I signed up for? Yes. Yes, I do."

I let out a frustrated groan. "My head is a mess right now."

"It's game-time, man. That's not a good state to be in."

Pushing my thumb and forefinger against the bridge of my nose, I try mightily to shove away this awful feeling. If I thought jealousy was bad, it has nothing on sheer dread. "I ran into Garrett Snow. He's done. Finished. Can't play anymore."

"That sucks," Harlan says with a sympathetic sigh. "But it happens. It's a risk we take. You have to find a way to get that out of your head right now." He grabs my shoulder and squeezes, even though I can't feel it through the pads. "We have a game to play. Just know I'm your brother-in-arms out there. I have the same worries."

Some of the tension in me loosens. Maybe I needed to give voice to these fears to let them go.

He points to the exit. "When you go through that tunnel, you check them at the door. You leave it all behind because you put everything on the field. That's our job. Let's go do it."

Offering a fist for knocking, I smack back. "Let's do it."

All I can do is what my father taught me. Give more than 100 percent. Give everything. This is what I've done my entire life on the field, and when I'm playing ball, I don't have to worry about what to say or how to love a woman for the first time in my life. I do love Jillian. I'm madly in love with her.

But for the next sixty minutes, I have one job, and that job is to move the ball.

As soon as I run through the tunnel and onto the field, where I'm greeted by the cheers of our fifty thousand hometown fans, I leave everything behind.

It's game-time.

31

JILLIAN

"Sushi!" my father declares from his spot at the fifty-yard line. "I still can't get over the fact that you let them serve sushi here."

He gestures dismissively at the aproned guy peddling California rolls in our section while the teams take a time-out in the second quarter for a commercial break.

"You do know I don't have any control over what they serve at the stadium?"

He flubs his lips. "Next thing you know it'll be barbecued kale."

"Dad, you live in California. They serve wine here, too."

He scoffs, lifting a cup of beer. "I have my beer, and I'm good to go with my foam finger," he says, waggling a blue number one on his hand. "And look, I even put a number eighty-six on it for your beau."

Beau.

Is Jones my beau?

I wish I knew.

The sound of the fans drumming their feet drowns out my sad, pathetic sigh. I thought we were doing the whole let's-be-together thing. But so far, we're doing the same thing we were doing before. *Nothing.*

I try to tell myself it's timing. It's the weekend. There's a game. I have to understand that. Hell, I should understand that better than anyone.

My dad leans in closer, bumping me with his shoulder. "What's going on with the two of you?"

It's like he can read my mind.

I squeeze my eyes shut as a sob works its way up my throat. "I feel so stupid," I mutter, and I didn't plan to say that, but he's my dad. He's the one who has comforted me my whole life over bruised knees, bad days at school, and my first teenage heartbreak with a boy named Randall. A flash of fear cuts through me. Is this going to be my newest heartbreak?

He sets down his beer and wraps his arm around me, foam finger and all. "Why do you feel stupid, honey?"

Because I'm going to cry.

Because I want more than two texts.

Because I want to know if Jones has done the same thing I did. "I put my heart on the line, my job on the line, and I've barely heard from him," I say, my voice breaking. Behind us, a woman waves pom-poms and cheers. "All he said yesterday was 'I'm thinking of you.'"

"Give him time."

I nod, biting my lip. "It's just hard."

He squeezes my shoulder and drops a kiss to the top of my head. "It's hard when you love somebody. But sometimes, a man has to figure things out in his own time. Man-time does not equal woman-time."

A small laugh escapes me. "Truer words..."

"I wish it did, for your sake, but it doesn't. You're a quick thinker and a problem solver. You act. You know your heart and your mind. Some men do, but some men take longer to figure it out. Especially when a man falls for a woman for the first time. It's like trying to start a car with a leaf. The engine sputters, and warning lights flicker all over the dashboard."

I laugh loudly at his insane analogy. "Who has ever tried to start a car with a leaf?"

"I hope no one, because I don't think it would work. Maybe it's like trying to assemble a desk with a spoon."

"I love your metaphors. They're wonderfully awful."

"I aim to please." Patting my knee, he adds, "And don't lose sight of the fact that you did what you needed to do for you. You did the right thing even without the reward in your pocket. Sometimes, we have to take a chance, even if the odds are we're going to fall."

I want a soft landing, though. But I haven't been getting one this weekend, and I suppose I'll have to be okay with it. "You're right. It's only been a few days. I'll wait patiently."

"Have faith. Now, let's watch the game. We don't want to miss a big play, do we?"

"No way."

My attention returns to the game as the defense forces a punt. I'll need to head to the press suite shortly, but I stay with my dad for one more play as the Renegades take possession. When there are eight minutes left in the half, Jones makes a spectacular catch. As his hands cradle the ball, my heart flies up my chest. Once he lands safely out of bounds, I'm on the edge of my seat, waiting.

Waiting for my special signal.

He raises his arms. I cross my fingers.

Cooper rushes to him and they smack palms, then race into the next play.

There is no *J*, and I don't have a clue if he even intended to make one before the quarterback high-fived him.

32

JONES

The lead slips through our fingers as the Indianapolis offense attacks with ferocity in the second half.

Their quarterback marches downfield, earning first down after first down, launching beautiful passes that turn into even more beautiful catches. They pull in front by six.

With crossed arms, I stare at the action on the field, searching for a way for us to regain the lead. Cooper is by my side, and Coach Greenhaven reviews the upcoming play—his plan of attack for when we get the ball again.

Once we do, we trot out to the field, ready, absolutely ready. As the noise in the stadium rises to deafening levels, Cooper drops back in the pocket and I cut across the field in a new route the Indy defense hasn't seen from us before. Cooper's arm is a gun, and he takes aim.

My eyes zero in on the ball. All I know is the hunt. Hunt that ball, haul it in, and take it to the end zone.

Scan left and right, watch for predators. Dodge this way, dart that way, the target in my crosshairs.

As the ball soars through the air, I race for it. It's ten feet away, five feet away. It's in my hands.

A surge of energy lights up my chest, powering me like an electric grid. It barrels through my legs, and I race, blinders on, the end zone in sight, my guys blocking for me. At the five-yard line, a touchdown seems a foregone conclusion, but a safety catches up from out of nowhere, slamming into me.

Clutching the ball like the precious cargo it is, I take another huge step, and one more, until all the air spills from my lungs as he hits hard again.

My ears ring.

My bones rattle.

The collision echoes through my body as I crumple. My knee slams against the grass, then the rest of me smashes to the earth in a crush of limbs.

The safety's legs tangle up with mine, and the heavy weight of his body shoves my knee harder against the ground.

Harder than I've felt before.

Then, everything turns into déjà vu.

This must be how Garrett felt when he fell.

33

JILLIAN

My heart jams my throat.

Fear attacks every cell in my body.

A player's down. But not just any player. *My* player.

My guy. My man.

A brand-new sensation courses through me as I rush to the window of the press suite where I've been watching. I press my fingers to the glass, and my veins flood with a primal, wild fear.

Jones lies on the field, grappling with his right leg.

"Oh God." A tear streams down my cheek, and I snap my gaze to the TV screen as the camera zooms in on him. The trainer's already there—the coach, too. Harlan kneels next to him, offering a hand.

The shot of his face shows Jones wincing. The pain seems to ricochet through him, and I wish I could take it on for him. My feet are glued to the floor and my eyes to the screen. I can't look away.

"We don't know what happened to Jones Beckett, and whether he can walk it off or not. But that was one tough fall as Collings rammed into him right at the end zone," the announcer says. "I've seen these kind of falls before, and sometimes you get right up, and sometimes you don't."

Shut up, I want to say. He'll get up.

To the screen, I mouth, *Get up. Please get up.*

Jones rolls to his side, his big, beautiful hands clutching his right knee.

Harlan slides an arm under him, the trainer on the other side, and all the tears in the universe streak down my face as Jones hobbles off the field with them.

I run like hell from the suite, down the hall, and to the elevator that'll take me to the locker room. He's not even going to the sidelines medical tents. They're taking him to the locker room, and that means it's serious.

"C'mon," I mutter as I wave my ID tag at the card reader, and I wait and I wait and I wait. Grabbing my phone from my pocket, I try to find some information, but that's stupid. That's pointless.

ESPN has no more data than I do.

This is happening in real time, and I need to get to him.

34

JONES

They say all good things must come to an end. They say anything can happen any given Sunday.

But I'm not thinking about football as Miles, the trainer, becomes my crutch, taking me to the lower floor of the stadium where the team doctor waits. Harlan stays behind to play.

This is my biggest fear—a career-ending injury—and as the very real prospect of never playing football again hangs in the balance, a new terror races through me—the horror that I've royally fucked up.

I'm on the cusp of losing it all, watching everything I've worked for splinter to pieces, but I've forgotten one important thing—to tell my woman I love her before the game started.

I'm a great and terrible idiot.

"You doing okay, big guy?" Miles's arm is under me. Hell, his whole upper frame is under me, since he's probably all of five foot, nine inches.

"I'm okay. I didn't need a cart to go off the field," I say, since I can walk still. But everything hurts with every step. My muscles are sore. My bones ache. I ran into a truck, and it knocked me to the ground. Collings is made of titanium, and it hurt just as much to collide with him. I tread gingerly, carefully moving one foot in front of the other.

"You can do it. You're going to be fine. We can figure this out," he says, offering encouraging words, since that's his job.

I have no idea what we'll figure out. I have no idea if this is how Garrett felt when he was hit so hard his career ended, but I know one thing—the biggest mistake I made today wasn't running all-out to the end zone.

It was half-assing things with the woman I love.

I was a dick. Cletus was right, and I hope to hell Jillian can forgive me like the little guy did.

"Slow down," Miles says gently as we near the locker room.

"Was I walking faster?"

"You were. You need to take it easy. Don't exacerbate anything. Okay?"

"Okay." Then I add, "I'm okay." This time it feels a little truer as we turn into the locker room.

One of the PTs is waiting with the doctor, and he offers to lift me onto the exam table, but I wave him off, hopping up there on my own power.

The bespectacled doctor gets to work quickly, cutting my football pants along the knee.

"Does this hurt?" The doctor wiggles my kneecap.

Oddly enough, it doesn't hurt as much. I let my mind wander as he does his job, and maybe this is what it means to have an out-of-body experience, since I'm not feeling much pain any longer.

My mind circles again to Garrett, the picture of his little girl, the mention of his wife, the smile on his face.

A razor-sharp awareness zings through me, piercing my heart.

I was wrong.

Garrett might miss football, but his life is far from over.

His happiness is not dependent on the game. His heart is with his family. Friday morning, I only saw what I feared. I saw what was lost, not what he'd found.

But I see clearly now—he's a man who has what matters most.

The doctor asks a question. I blink and make eye contact. "What did you say?"

"Does this hurt at all? Does anything hurt? You didn't answer me."

I look at the doctor. "I love her."

He quirks up an eyebrow. "Excuse me?"

Louder, in case he didn't hear, I announce, "I love Jillian Moore. I want you to know, Doctor Miller."

He laughs, his gray eyes twinkling through his glasses. "Did you hit your head, too, Jones?"

I shake my head.

"Let's focus on one thing at a time, then." He moves my ankle. "Does this hurt?"

Before I can answer, Ford bursts into the room in a flurry of Armani and wingtips.

"Dude, you can dress down for a game," I say, laughing.

He glares at me. "Never. Also—"

"—I love Jillian," I cut him off.

He shoots me a look like I'm high, waving a hand

dismissively as he strides to the exam table. "Is he on morphine already?"

The doctor shakes his head. "Of course not."

"Then what the hell is going on?"

I grab Ford's arm, getting his attention till he looks me square in the eyes. "I'm in love with Jillian. All I care about right now is that you know that. Do you get it? I love her."

"Sure. You love her. Okay, great."

Another slam of the door, and Trevor strides in.

"Tell him," I shout to Trevor, pointing at my big brother. "He knows! I told him the other night. Trevor, tell them I'm in love with Jillian."

My brother stops in his tracks and laughs. "But how is your knee?"

I hold my arms out wide. "Do you people not get it? Listen to me. I. LOVE. HER."

But they don't get it. They look at me as if I've gone mad.

My heart stops when the most beautiful sight appears at the door. Long black hair, beautiful brown eyes, red cherry earrings. Tears stream down her face as she runs into the locker room. She races to me, puts her hand on my shoulder, and with concern asks point-blank, "Are you okay?"

I smile dopily, happiness whistling a happy tune inside me as I meet her eyes. "I love you. I love you so much I want everyone to know that I'm love with you."

She dips her face closer. "Did you get hit on the head?"

"No! Why is everyone asking me that?"

Dr. Miller clears his throat. "Jones—"

I know what's coming, so I slide off the table,

landing on both feet without wincing. I take a few steps around the locker room, my arms out wide, showing off. "There? See? Everyone happy? It hardly hurts. My knee is fine. I can probably even run a mile right now."

Dr. Miller and the PT each grab hold of an arm before I can show them my speed.

"No," the doctor says sharply. "No running."

I shake them off and walk the few feet. I stop at Jillian, cup her cheeks, and say once more, "I'm in love with you." I plant a kiss on her lips. She kisses me back, so softly, so tenderly it makes me tremble.

We break the kiss, and I spin around. "My knee is fine, and I love this woman. Do you all hear that?" I stare at each and every person in the locker room. "She is mine. I'm with her. We're together. I'm going to take her to dinner and kiss her in public. I'm going to the movies with her, and I'm going to hold her hand. I'm going to spend the night at her house and leave in the morning. I'm not going to hide."

I turn back to her, my words for her now. "I want a career, I want deals, and I want to play for a long time, but I want you more. I should've told you last night. I should have told you the night before. I should have sent more than two texts. I should have called Ford yesterday, and I didn't because I was afraid of losing everything. I was scared of this very thing happening, but once it happened, I realized you're what I can't afford to lose. Even if the deals all fall apart. Even if this ends today. I'm not going to give up loving you for any of those things, and I'm sorry it took me getting clocked to see the light, but sometimes it takes—"

"Man-time," she supplies with a smile. Tears slide

down her cheeks, but they sure as hell look like happy tears now. "It took you man-time."

I laugh. "Yeah, I suppose it did. Do you forgive me?"

She runs a hand through my hair. "That's already done."

I grab her, pulling her close, lifting her up and then kissing her once more. When I set her down, I'm greeted by slow claps from the audience. "See? They're happy I love you."

Jillian shrugs. "I think they're happy because you walked and you lifted me, even though ten minutes ago you were wincing in pain."

I look down at my knee. "Holy shit. It doesn't hurt anymore. She's a miracle worker."

The doctor laughs, then clears his throat. "Be that as it may, we still need X-rays."

"Listen to the doctor, Jones," Jillian says. "Go."

"Don't leave?"

She crosses her arms. "I'm not going anywhere."

* * *

Thirty minutes later, Dr. Miller studies the X-ray film and makes his declaration. "You're one of the lucky ones. Sometimes you fall and you fracture your tibial plateau. Sometimes you tear your ACL, and sometimes it hurts like hell when you get clobbered and it turns out to be nothing."

"This is nothing?"

He nods. "This is nothing. Right now, I see no reason why you can't play next weekend. But come back tomorrow to check in, and you know the drill for tonight – ibuprofen and ice if you need it."

As I leave with Ford and Jillian, I tell my agent once more, "I'm not having a secret relationship with this woman any longer. I'm having a relationship that's out in the great wide open, and that's exactly where I want to be with her. We need to tell Liam."

"Tell him yourself. He's chatting with your parents."

We find them on the field, and my mom clasps me in a big hug, reaching up to circle her arms around me. "They told us you were going to be fine. Thank God." Her voice is laced with the relief that I suppose only a mom can ever feel this deeply. Liam takes a few steps away, giving us space.

"I'm great, Mom. I'm all good."

We separate, and she pats my chest. "You be careful." Her blue eyes are fierce and full of love.

"Mom, I want you to meet someone." I squeeze Jillian's arm, and she smiles at my mom. "This is Jillian Moore. She works for the team. She's my girlfriend. Can she come over for dinner sometime?"

My mom freezes for a moment, then turns to Jillian and shakes her hand. "You're welcome anytime, sweetheart."

"So great to meet you. And thank you, Mrs. Beckett. I'm looking forward to it."

My mom swivels her attention to me, wagging a finger. "And thanks for telling me you had a girlfriend."

I shrug happily. "Everyone is kind of finding out at the same time. But I've wanted to introduce her to you for a long time."

"Good. Now, let's have you meet his father," my mom says to Jillian then takes her to meet my dad.

Ford brings Liam to my side, and my agent's voice is

deep and firm. "I believe you gentlemen have some things to chat about, and I'm happy to help."

"Thanks. I can take it from here," I tell him, since this is my job—to man up. Like my dad taught me—success on the field is about talent and effort, but also luck. This is the effort part.

I look at Liam and waste no time. "I'm dating Jillian. I love her. And if that causes a problem with the contract, I'm sorry. Please know I enjoyed working with you. But I love this woman."

Liam blinks, surprise registering in his eyes. He's quiet at first, scratching his jaw, swinging his gaze down the field. He takes a breath then turns his attention back to me. He hooks his thumb over his shoulder. "I met your parents."

"Good to hear," I say, not sure why he's mentioning what I already know.

"They're good people."

I smile. "They are."

"Your mom couldn't stop talking about how worried she was about you, but how she knew you were going to be okay."

"Yeah?"

Liam nods. "She said she watched the replay over and over. Said it was like a fall you took in high school, but you walked that off, too."

"Those are the best kinds of falls."

He's silent again, and I have the impression he's the type of man who's fine with the quiet. Who takes time to process. When he speaks again, his words surprise me. "I see you introduced Jillian to your parents."

"I did," I say, then add, "sir," because he feels like one right now.

He laughs lightly as he tucks his hands into the pockets of his slacks. "And you invited her to dinner at their home."

Damn, he has good ears.

"I bet that's not something you've done a lot before."

I shake my head. "Never."

He rocks onto the balls of his feet. "Listen, Jones. I appreciate you telling me about Jillian now, before it gets out. It's always good to know these things. You can never be too careful these days. With the climate we operate in, we've both seen how brands and companies have to be sensitive about the slightest things—a wrong comment here, a remark out of context there, something that sounds far too insensitive . . ."

His observation is spot-on, and exactly why I've been cautious with Jillian. But it's his turn to speak, not mine. So I wait.

He heaves a sigh. "But you're in love with her, and I don't have the sense you're going to go carousing down Fillmore Street with a bottle of Jack Daniels before you screw her in an alley, to be frank."

I jerk my head back, startled by his bluntness. "No, I don't plan to do that."

He claps my shoulder. "Just keep doing things the right way. Be good to her, treat your fans well, and keep loving on that pooch of yours. That's all I can ask for. If you do that, we'll keep doing business together."

My muscles relax, and I smile. I was willing to let him go. More than willing if I had to, and maybe that's the biggest reason he's keeping me. "Count on it."

He nods. "I will." He screws up the corner of his lips, as if he's thinking. "Also, I'm happy for you. You chose well."

"Thank you. I think so, too."

* * *

A little while later, I tug Jillian close and whisper in her ear, "Come home with me tonight."

She arches an eyebrow. "That's presumptuous of you."

"I'll make it worth your while. *Presumably.*"

And I do. I make it very worth her while indeed.

Three times, in fact, including once with her bent over the bed. Yeah, my knee is just fine. Sometimes, I suppose your luck doesn't run out after all.

EPILOGUE

Jones

The sizzling rice soup with shrimp is delicious. The pepper steak is some of the tastiest I've ever had. And the company is unequivocally the finest—my girlfriend. When I offer her a taste of the pepper steak, she opens her mouth and I feed it to her. In public. At a Chinese restaurant she loves.

Someone might snap a picture.

Someone might not.

Both options are fine by me.

If anyone did capture our date, they'd have a gallery of images of one of the happiest guys in the city, walking into House of Nanking with his arm wrapped around the woman he works with, one who now happens to be VP of publicity for the San Francisco Renegades. They'd see me hold her hand at the table as we ordered. They'd see her reach across to ruffle my hair when I made her laugh.

After we finish, the waiter brings a plate of fortune cookies, and Jillian grabs the one pointed at her, cracking it open. Her eyebrows wiggle as she reads. "Ooh, this is a good one."

"What does it say?"

"It says, 'You have the hottest guy in the city wrapped around your finger.'"

"Sounds less like a fortune and more like the truth."

"I speak no lies."

"What does it really say?"

She takes a breath. "It says, 'Good things come to those who wait.'"

I scoff. "That's kind of vague."

"I don't know. I waited for you."

"Did you?"

"You know I had my eyes on you for a long time."

"I had my eyes on you for even longer. So much so I was always getting naked in front of you. Why didn't you have your eyes on that?"

She laughs. "I'm making up for lost time," she says, then tips her chin at my cookie. "What's your fortune?"

I break the cookie and fish out the white strip of paper, reading the red words aloud. "'May your life be as steadfast as the mountains and your fortune as limitless as the sea.'" I nod, taking in the sentiment, letting it roll around in my head. "I like that. In fact," I say, folding the slip of paper and tucking it into my wallet, "I'm keeping it with me."

"Like a good luck symbol," she says knowingly.

"You know luck and me are like this." I twist my middle and index fingers together.

That's why before every game, I follow my ritual. I eat a pomelo, whether home or away. So far, it's been working. We're only a few games into the season, but we have a winning record.

The record that matters most to me, though, is the one I have with Jillian. Every night I tell her I love her. Every morning, too, and usually several times during the day.

What can I say? I text her a lot. Many are naughty. Many are not. But she's never far from my mind, or my body, since I've convinced her to spend nearly every night with Cletus and me. I have a big appetite, and I find the one streak I don't want to break is having her every damn day.

That's what I plan to do tonight, and as we leave and walk past a laughing Buddha statue, she stops, rubbing its head. I do the same. She grabs her phone, asks me a question with her eyes, and I say yes.

She takes a picture of us rubbing the Buddha and posts it to my Instagram, tagging it with #luck, #good-fortune, and #love.

Out on the street in Chinatown, I pull her in close and kiss her as we wait for a Lyft. Someone walking by mutters my name. Maybe that someone takes a picture. Maybe it'll show up online. Maybe it won't. Whatever happens is all good because I don't have to worry anymore. I've learned the best way to rehab a reputation is to be a good guy and to fall in love with a woman who makes you want to be even better.

* * *

Jillian

My boss was right. Being involved with a ballplayer means you're under scrutiny. A lot of gossip papers wanted to know *why her*? What does she have that the model, the actress, the Tinder chick didn't have?

Let the press speculate. I know what I have—a guy who declared his intention for me, and then declared it again and again and again. I have a guy who has a heart as big as his hands.

And, well, a certain other part.

I do love when he uses that part on me.

And when I watch him use it for himself.

I still have my fantasies.

But now, they're my reality.

Like tonight, when I told him I wanted to come home from a long day at the office to find him in bed, a sheet riding low on his hips, a hand wrapped around his hard length, stroking absently. I drop my purse in his living room, kick off my shoes, say hello to Cletus, and head to the bedroom.

The light is low. Only the rays of the moon streak through the window. I stand in the doorway, and a shiver runs through me as I savor the view.

His eyes are closed, his muscles ripple, and his right hand grips his erection. I bite my lip as I watch him, like the voyeur he lets me be. Everything about this turns me on wildly, especially the sounds—his groans, his grunts, his heavy breathing. The pants as he strokes faster. The moan as he grips tighter.

Most of all, how he always says my name.

That always breaks me.

Tonight, when he utters it in a raspy, needy voice as his hand shuttles up and down, I strip off my skirt and yank off my top.

My panties are gone in seconds, and I climb on him.

I know why this turns me on so much.

It's because he's getting off to me, even when he's by himself. I think that will always turn me on because it makes me feel so wonderfully wanted.

Right now, I want to show him how much.

He lets go of his dick, grabs my hips, and brings me down on him. I draw a sharp gasp as he fills me completely.

He's completely bare.

I'm on birth control, and he's safe, and I love the feel of us like this. Together. No barriers. He moves me up and down, and with every stroke, I moan. I breathe out hard. I shudder.

I'm not sure how sex that's been this good can become even better, but as he runs a hand up my back and into my hair, I'm given the answer.

It comes as he brings my face near to his. "Need you closer to me."

He's never held back in bed. He's always made it clear where he stands between the sheets. This man has the biggest appetite. He wants more of me, as much as he can have. And I love giving myself to him. He makes me feel beautiful, sexy, and alluring.

He makes me feel like I'm all he needs.

As he draws me closer, telling me to ride him harder, faster, rougher because it's so fucking good, it's all so fucking good with me, I know he's all I'll ever need.

A little later, as we lie in bed, sated and sweaty, he positions us so I'm in the crook of his arm. "You know you can sleep on me anytime, right?"

"I do know that, since I sleep on you every night."

"Sleep on me, sleep with me. I love it all," he says,

then he shifts to his side and drops a kiss on my nose. "I love you. Have I told you that today?"

"Maybe ten times?"

"Let's make it eleven." He kisses a trail up my neck to my ear, and I tremble again, then I shudder as he says, "I'm so in love with you."

Cletus jumps on the bed, wagging his tail and plopping down between us.

"He's also in love with you," Jones says as I rub the dog's little head.

"I love him, too. And the other guy as well," I say when a soft paw swipes my shoulder. I crane my neck to see Smoky sitting on my pillow, purring.

Cletus and Smoky are good buddies now, ever since we adopted the orange kitten as soon as he was ready for his *fur-ever* home.

The four of us fall asleep.

When we wake up together the next morning, Jones whispers in my ear, "Told you I like waking up next to you."

Then he shows me why it's my favorite way to wake up, too.

* * *

Jones

A week later, we're at another restaurant, and Jillian's boss holds up the charity calendar before the crowd.

"And look at February," Lily says, showing off the cat and me at the winery.

The crowd cheers, and I wave from my spot next to her.

"And how about March?" That's the shot from Stinson Beach.

More hoots and hollers abound.

When we make it to the Miami shots, my heart beats a little faster, and I look to Jillian, standing at the bar. *Love those*, I mouth to her.

Me, too, she replies.

They remind me of the best play I ever made. The one for her heart.

ANOTHER EPILOGUE

Jillian

Several months later

Jones's mom doesn't need any help in the kitchen, but I offer anyway. I always do, since I'm so often here in the off-season.

"Yes, if you could grab the salad from the fridge, that would be great," she says.

"I can do that," I say, snagging the bowl and setting it on the dinner table.

It's Sunday supper, and Jones, his siblings, his dad, and his mom are here. Oh, someone else is here, too. My dad. He doesn't live far away, and he's not terribly busy, so I picked him up on the way, and I love that he's become part of these get-togethers.

He and Jones's parents get along well. They talk about politics, sports, and the state of the world. Sometimes they do that thing the older generation does—

they chat about how much harder it was when they were growing up. Those of us in the younger generation laugh and roll our eyes.

As I sit at the table with some of my favorite people, I mostly listen. I listen to my dad ask thoughtful questions about local town issues, I listen to Trevor share details of his beer show, and I listen to Jones's dad as he compliments his wife on the dinner, and on how pretty she looks.

In moments like these, I see where the gentleman in Jones came from—from his family. From these people he loves to the ends of the earth and back. As I raise a glass of iced tea and take a sip, I remember the night in wine country when I wished that someday I would be able to come here and bring wine and flowers. Now I have, and now I do, and it fills my heart with so much joy that I know my mom would say all the choices I made that brought me here were the right ones.

They were. They absolutely were.

As the meal ends, Jones clears his throat. "There's something I wanted to bring up."

"Yes, my dear?" his mother asks.

"And since everyone is here, this seems as good a time as any."

My dad looks deliberately away from me, as if he's avoiding eye contact. I'm not sure why, but he doesn't look at Jones, either. Not as Jones rises, not as he walks to me, and not as he takes my hand.

"What is it?"

"Jillian, I love you madly, and I have loved nothing more than taking you out on dates, showing you off, making you happy, and making sure the world knows you're spoken for."

"You've done a pretty good job of that," I say, wondering why he needed to get up from his chair to say it. Then, a possibility flashes before my eyes. Fireworks light up inside me, bursting with a daring, crazy hope.

The hope is answered as he drops down to one knee. I gasp and bring a hand to my mouth as he takes a blue velvet box from his pocket. "The only thing I want more is for you to be spoken for always. For the rest of our lives. Because I want you to be the rest of my life. I love you so much, baby. Will you marry me?"

The fireworks crackle. They spark. They fill the night sky with a brilliant display of all the colors, all the brightness, and all the wonder as I say yes. "You're my good luck," I whisper, and he whispers back, "You're mine."

He slides a huge diamond solitaire onto my ring finger and kisses me in front of his family and in front of mine, and this is more than I could ever have hoped for long ago, and now it's all I want.

Him with me, always.

That night, as we head to a local hotel, I can't stop staring at my ring. "You are absolutely getting lucky tonight."

He pumps a fist. "Then I'd say I've scored."

THE END

Want more Jones and Jillian? Sign up at https://www.subscribepage.com/MLTS-bonus **to**

receive a bonus scene of this sexy, fun couple sent straight to your inbox! If you've already signed up for my list, be sure to sign up again! It's the only way to receive the MOST LIKELY TO SCORE bonus scene, but rest assured you won't be double subscribed to the list! You can also sign up directly for my newsletter http://laurenblakely.com/newsletter/ to receive an alert when these sexy new books are available!

Author's Note: The details about Jillian's adoption from China were taken directly from my own experience adopting a Chinese daughter! The "lucky baby" and "baby is cold" comments were things I heard while in China with my little girl! I hope you enjoyed this aspect of Jillian's character!

Want to know what's next? In March I'll release WANDERLUST, a breathtaking new standalone romance set in Paris! This is an epic romance that will steal your heart! Here's a preview! You can find WANDERLUST   here   at http://laurenblakely.com/wanderlust

Griffin

"Bonjour." The greeting comes from the woman behind me.

I turn in the direction of the voice. The American voice. The confident, strong American voice.

"Je voudrais un croissant chocolat."

But she's all wrong, so I jump in. "It's *pain au chocolat.*"

She furrows her brow. "What did you say?"

I repeat myself. I can't help it. In my line of work, it's a natural reaction to offer up the more appropriate translations for Americans. I ought to tune out conversations.

But *this* American? I don't want to tune her out.

She's so very . . . red.

Rich auburn hair spills down her shoulders, landing in the kind of big, soft curls that look like they take hours to achieve, with loads of potions and lotions and many fights with heated devices that do all sorts of things to hair. But she hardly seems the high-maintenance type, since she wears a red-checkered bandana like a headband. Jeans hug her legs, a pretty maroon blouse accentuates her lovely assets, and boots make her even taller. Cowboy boots.

She's statuesque.

Good thing I like tall birds.

Good thing I'm even taller.

Wait. Am I really thinking of picking up a woman in the bakery?

Of course I fucking am. I love American accents. I love the boldness. I love the confidence. I love the way American women own who they are.

Like this one. She's stunning, especially with those pouty red lips.

"That's what we call a chocolate croissant," I add.

"We?" she echoes. "That's what *we* call a croissant?" She arches a brow, but not in a haughty way. More like a "you don't say" way. She points at me playfully. "You don't really sound like you're part of that *we*. But I'll still give you a big old *merci beaucoup* for helping me."

When she smiles, it's like a sunbeam. A full-wattage grin.

"You're correct. *They* call it that. I simply partake of its deliciousness."

"You should partake of chocolate croissants. I hear the ones at this boulangerie are to die for." Then she winks at me and turns to Marie, who's watching our exchange with avid interest. The American woman orders properly this time, and Marie fetches the pastry for her.

I head out, but I dawdle. In fact, I'm pretty sure I'm on pace to set a record for sheer sluggishness. Just a few more seconds, and she should be exiting.

She strolls out the door, bringing the scent of chocolate with her, and for a fleeting moment I imagine she tastes like chocolate.

She stops in front of me. She takes a bite of the croissant wrapped in a waxy paper and chews. She hums her praise for the food. "This is a delicious chocolate croissant." Then she brings her fingers to her lips. "Oops. I meant *pain au chocolat*."

"Very good. And I apologize if it seemed out of line to correct you. I didn't want to see you commit a faux pas."

"*We* didn't mind," she teases.

"*We* are so glad to hear," I add.

She takes another bite and rolls her eyes, presumably in pleasure. When she finishes, she says, "So you're a Prince Charming rescuing damsels in distress from language faux pas?"

"Something like that."

"So gallant."

"I aspire to gallantry every day. Though sometimes it expresses itself in odd ways."

"Funnily enough, if you can ensure I'm getting access to one of the best chocolate croissants in all the city, then I'm good with those odd ways."

"Do you like . . .?" I pause, and her green eyes follow my gaze to the treat in her hands.

"I do. Very much." She points at me with the end of the croissant. Her eyes are inquisitive, studying me. "You're not French."

"You're not, either."

"But that's obvious."

"And it's obvious I'm not as well."

She smirks. "You're British."

I feign surprise. "What gave it away?"

"The accent might have been a tip-off."

"Damn." I snap my fingers, as if she's caught me. That makes her smirk a little more. "You're American," I toss back at her.

Her eyes widen, and she appears positively astonished, playing along. "However could you tell?"

She waits, tapping her toe, evidently expecting me to say her voice since that's what we've been chatting about.

"You want to know the giveaway?"

"I do."

I lean a touch closer to her. "Your smile."

That only makes her grin grow wider. She tries to contain it. She tries valiantly, it seems. But she has no luck. "They don't smile in France?"

"Not like that. Not like you do."

Yeah, I could flirt all day with her. That accent. Those eyes. Her hair. She's a welcome distraction. I almost don't mind my plans being massively derailed since it's given me this unexpected encounter, and I don't want this encounter with her to end. "What's your name?" But before she can answer, I shake my head, and hold up a hand. "Wait. Let me guess."

"Oh, by all means. Guess my name, Daniel."

I laugh. "Daniel?"

"Seems like a good English name. Was I wrong? Is it Harry? William? Clive? Oliver? Henry? Rupert? Alistair? Archibald?"

Laughing, I blurt out, "You can't possibly think I'm an Archibald?"

She waves dismissively. "Right, of course. My bad. You must be Archie."

"If I'm Archie, then how about you? Are you a Jennifer?"

She shakes her head.

"Amy?"

Another shake.

"Stacy, then?"

"Nope."

"You must be Katie?"

She rolls her eyes. "Try harder, Archibald."

"Taylor? Hannah? Madison? Chloe? Avery?" Every name yields a no. "I've got it." Her eyes widen. "Judy? You must be Judy."

She laughs loudly. "Judy? You think I'm a Judy? While it's quite a pretty name, let's be honest—when was the last time you met an American Judy who was under fifty?"

"When have you met an Archibald who wasn't bald and over seventy?"

She gives my dark hair a once-over. "True, you're not bald. But why would you think only an American would have those names? Jennifer. Amy. Stacy," she says, imitating me.

"Perhaps the same reason you picked Harry and William."

"I picked them because I like princes."

"Well, perhaps I like American-sounding names," I counter, and her green eyes sparkle as she laughs.

"They do seem quintessentially American, don't they?"

"They do."

"Does that mean you think I'm quintessentially American?" She brings her hand to her chest, and my eyes follow. Because ... breasts.

I allow myself a second to admire the potential of hers, then I refocus. "Quintessentially American is a fine thing to be."

I'm about to throw in the towel and ask her real name, when her phone brays. It's the loudest thing I've ever heard.

"So sorry, this is my . . ." But she trails off as she answers the phone. "*Bonjour*, Marisol."

Her brow furrows, and she listens intently to her call for ten seconds, twenty seconds.

And I've crossed the line.

I can't stand here and wait any longer. That would be rude. Her phone call is my cue to go.

I give her a tip of the hat. "Good-bye, Judy," I whisper.

For a moment, her brow furrows, almost as if she's surprised I'm taking off.

Then, she smiles brightly, waves her fingers at me, and mouths *good-bye, Archie.*

She turns the other way, her croissant in one hand, her phone to her ear in the other.

I let myself enjoy a few seconds of the view of her walking away.

Then reality swoops back in. I'm no longer flirting with a sexy American woman as if I don't have a care in the world. Instead, I'm left here holding a baguette and my helmet, wondering what I'll do next to earn the money to take the trip my brother wanted to take.

ALSO BY LAUREN BLAKELY

FULL PACKAGE, the #1 New York Times Bestselling romantic comedy!

BIG ROCK, the hit New York Times Bestselling standalone romantic comedy!

MISTER O, also a New York Times Bestselling standalone romantic comedy!

WELL HUNG, a New York Times Bestselling standalone romantic comedy!

JOY RIDE, a USA Today Bestselling standalone romantic comedy!

HARD WOOD, a USA Today Bestselling standalone romantic comedy!

THE SEXY ONE, a New York Times Bestselling bestselling standalone romance!

THE HOT ONE, a USA Today Bestselling bestselling standalone romance!

THE KNOCKED UP PLAN, a multi-week USA Today and Amazon Charts Bestselling bestselling standalone romance!

MOST VALUABLE PLAYBOY, a sexy multi-week USA Today Bestselling sports romance!

THE V CARD, a sinfully sexy romantic comedy!

The New York Times and USA Today Bestselling Seductive Nights series including *Night After Night*, *After This Night*, and *One More Night*

And the two standalone romance novels in the Joy Delivered Duet, *Nights With Him* and Forbidden Nights, both New York Times and USA Today Bestsellers!

Sweet Sinful Nights, Sinful Desire, Sinful Longing and Sinful Love, the complete New York Times Bestselling high-heat romantic suspense series that spins off from Seductive Nights!

Playing With Her Heart, a USA Today bestseller, and a sexy Seductive Nights spin-off standalone! (Davis and Jill's romance)

21 Stolen Kisses, the USA Today Bestselling forbidden new adult romance!

Caught Up In Us, a New York Times and USA Today Bestseller! (Kat and Bryan's romance!)

Pretending He's Mine, a Barnes & Noble and iBooks Bestseller! (Reeve & Sutton's romance)

Trophy Husband, a New York Times and USA Today Bestseller! (Chris & McKenna's romance)

Far Too Tempting, the USA Today Bestselling standalone romance! (Matthew and Jane's romance)

Stars in Their Eyes, an iBooks bestseller! (William and Jess' romance)

My USA Today bestselling No Regrets series that includes

The Thrill of It (Meet Harley and Trey)

and its sequel

Every Second With You

My New York Times and USA Today Bestselling Fighting Fire series that includes

Burn For Me (Smith and Jamie's romance!)

Melt for Him (Megan and Becker's romance!)

and *Consumed by You* (Travis and Cara's romance!)

The Sapphire Affair series...

The Sapphire Affair

The Sapphire Heist

Out of Bounds

A New York Times Bestselling sexy sports romance

The Only One

A second chance love story!

Stud Finder

A sexy, flirty romance!

ACKNOWLEDGMENTS

Thank you so much for everyone who helped shape this story including Jen, Dena, Kim and Lauren Clarke. Thank you to Helen Williams for the gorgeous cover, to Kelley for the daily grind and keeping track of so very much, and to KP for all her wisdom. Thank you to the talented bloggers, passionate readers, and outspoken advocates of books. Thank you to Candi and Keyanna for the day to day work that is so vital.

On the editorial side, thank you to Virginia, Tiffany, Karen, Lynn and Janice for their keen eyes.

Huge love to my family and my dogs! And forever hugs to my readers!

CONTACT

I love hearing from readers! You can find me on Twitter at LaurenBlakely3, Instagram at LaurenBlakelyBooks, Facebook at LaurenBlakelyBooks, or online at LaurenBlakely.com. You can also email me at laurenblakelybooks@gmail.com